The San Francisco Affair

The San Francisco Affair

A SPENCER MARLOWE ADVENTURE
ONE MAN, TWO CENTURIES

Kelvin White

This book is, as always dedicated to my wife Jenny. Her advice
and creative input have been invaluable.

CONTENTS

PREFACE

I'm supremely grateful to those readers who have followed Spencer Marlowe since the first in the series, *The Singapore Saga*, when Spencer was thrust back in time to 1942 and found himself on a mission to Japanese occupied Singapore.

Although each of the Spencer Marlowe novels are stand-alone stories, the reader may find it helpful to understand the background setting to the series for those who've not read the earlier novels.

Spencer goes to bed at night and awakes in the last century. Although he is gone from the present time for more than a year, time stands still at his home in Perth, Western Australia. On his return, family life resumes until he is once again sent on another adventure. The silver cornicello, a gift from reluctant soldier Bert Weadley in1942, is his constant companion. It's only when fortune teller Madame Zu, sees and touches the cornicello and is obviously distressed that he realises the amulet has mystical powers. His wife has difficulty in believing his story, as he hasn't left her side, but ultimately she accepts that if it's not real, it's very real for Spencer.

The third Spencer Marlowe book, The Manhattan Sting, introduces Special Agent Savannah Steele, who appears in all subsequent novels; LA Confrontation, The Chicago Story and now, The San Francisco Affair.

CHAPTER 1

THE SAN FRANCISCO AFFAIR

Strapped onto an Adirondack chair, the bloodied body of FBI Agent Ryan Tod slumped forward, as if lifeless. The worn linoleum floor beneath the chair was wet from the bodily waste that had emptied and seeped through the slats of the chair when he had lost control of his sphincter.

'Wakey wakey, Agent. Jimbo, throw some water into the sonofabitch's face. Jesus, what a stink.

Jimbo appeared to be a little too tall for his build. Were he a few inches shorter, he would have been considered well proportioned. As it was, he looked like he'd been stretched on a medieval rack. His thin face was largely obscured by a scruffy red beard that failed to conceal teenage acne scars. He smiled with a face devoid of warmth.

Filling a chipped ceramic jug from the faucet at a sink stacked with dirty dishes and take-out containers, Jimbo grimaced at the sight of the remains of fried rice and clumps of rancid vegetables. Pizza boxes from Magoo's littered the floor. Huge black and white photos of The Beatles covered one wall.

'Sure thing, BBQ.'

The man giving the orders was Big Ronny Delgado, aka BBQ. Big? Yes. And tall. Once a taut-bodied football player for the Dallas Cowboys, too much fast food had taken its toll. The hairy inner tube around his waist and the red veiny splotches across his flaccid face destroyed the image of what was once a strikingly handsome man.

Ryan Tod, the object of their displeasure, groaned and shook his head when Jimbo poured the water over him.

'C'mon, Brucey baby.' Ronny exhorted, 'time for us to continue our little chat. Only it's not Bruce, is it?'

'My name's Bruce Murray,' the man in the chair lied with a groan. These psychos were capable of anything, and the last thing he wanted was them going after his family.

BBQ's methods of coercion lacked originality, but they had always proved to be effective. Bruce, aka Ryan Tod, no longer possessed ten fingernails. His hands were a bloody mess. His laboured breathing came in short, wheezing gasps. Beside him sat a wooden trolley with a pair of everyday pliers and a bundle of bloody rags.

CHAPTER 2
HE'S BACK

Spencer Marlowe slept on a camp stretcher, long legs dangling over one end.

'Wake up, sleepyhead,' a brusque female voice disturbed his dream.

'Michiyo, please, it's Sunday. Can't a man sleep? C'mon, please, sweetheart.'

'It's not wifey and it's not Sunday, Spencer. It's Savannah. Now wake up. Things are happening.'

Spencer cracked an eye open and glanced at his watch. 'What?'

The Bulova watch told him it was 7.04. Bulova…. oh shit. The Rolex. Gone. He knew. He was back in the past. He felt no panic. This was his fate. His wife, Michiyo, slept, blissfully unaware in the next century. She would awake the next morning with Spencer by her side. In the intervening hours, Spencer would be with Savannah Steele. When he woke up, he may have spent a year or more in the past century. But now he would resume his other life, once again with Special Agent Savannah Steele. *Well at least it's not boring.*

Was it real? Maybe he was mad. Spencer had given up asking the question.

'Good morning, Savannah, nice to see you.'

The owner of the voice grinned, handing him a styrene cup of coffee. 'Sorry, princess, not your preferred drop of heart starter.'

Spencer sat up, relieved to see he was fully dressed. He had on worn Levi's, a tie-dyed T-shirt and hip, tooled cowboy boots. He took a sip and spluttered.

'Stone the bloody crows. Instant?'

'Yeah, yeah, it's instant. Like I said, things are happening. How the hell can you sleep, boots and all? Must be an Australian thing.'

It was more of a time traveller thing.

Spencer's lips curled as he took another sip. 'Sorry, Savannah, but where exactly are we?'

'Kiss my go to hell. Don't do this to me.'

Spencer sat up and gazed around a spartan room. Savannah Steele peered out of the window, a pair of binoculars glued to her face.

'I'm not happy. Ryan hasn't called in as he was supposed to and I think he's in trouble. We're going in.'

Confused but alert, Spencer reached in his pocket for the cornicello. *Thank God.*

'Savannah I'm sorry, but you know I have memory lapses and…'

'I don't have time for this. We have to move.'

Savannah stepped back from the window, pulling a small automatic pistol out of her shoulder holster.

'I think the 0.22 with a suppressor is what the doctor ordered.'

'Nice outfit,' Spencer said.

Savannah wore a pair of tatty, low-slung flared jeans and a bold T-shirt with a picture of the British rock group, the Who, pictured on the front. She shrugged on a grimy army-style canvas jacket, hiding the shoulder holster.

'Love the headband. It's very cool.' Spencer grinned.

'This is San Francisco, dear. Peace, love and all that bullshit. Now please get a wriggle on. Grab this damn coat, and this goddam hat, and get ready.'

Savannah handed him an unfashionable gabardine raincoat and a plaid golf hat. Spencer climbed off the stretcher and pulled on the coat, jamming the hat on his head.

'OK, what's going down?'

He got a fury-filled rundown of the situation that he'd apparently been over before: they were looking at 4 Haight Street, San Francisco. Yes, San Francisco, not Sydney bloody Australia.

'Hell in a handbasket, now of all times,' Savannah muttered.

Here it was: the bad guys (Ronny "BBQ" Delgado and most likely Jimbo Cline) and their undercover guy (Ryan Tod) were in an apartment above the record shop at 4 Haight Street. The problem was they had another one of their merry men standing watch downstairs, a big mother who was definitely carrying. Savannah wanted him to do as discussed: immobilise the fella downstairs, quietly, efficiently, in his inimitable style. If he could remember how to do that. After that they'd toddle upstairs and have a love-in with Ronny-of-the-ridiculous-nickname, and Jimbo.

'Ok, I get it,' Spencer replied, 'I think. We then go upstairs and you shoot someone?'

'Don't start with the bolshie stuff, Spencer. Yes, very probably. But only as a last resort.'

Spencer roared with laughter. 'Last resort. Yeah, right.'

'Are you coming?' Savannah was already at the door.

Spencer followed meekly, glancing quickly at a big mirror on the living room wall. Yep, he looked the same. He rubbed the stubble on his chin. *Could do with a shave.*

Early morning San Francisco was buzzing with bearded men, flower power gals, but sadly no flowers in their hair, Spencer noticed. Big finned old Chevies and Volkswagen Kombis in psychedelic colours rattling up the packed streets. The guys all had long hair, the girls in miniskirts or long cotton dresses, the musky odour of patchouli oil mingling pleasantly with the heady aroma of marijuana.

Savannah pointed across the street at The Beat Box record store.

'Do you see what I see?'

'You bet. The sign in the window says Jefferson Airplane are playing the Winterland Ballroom in March. I'd love to hear Grace Slick live. Bloody hell.' He shivered. 'It's Baltic out here.'

'Poor Diddums. Anyway, I'd sooner Tony Bennett.' Savannah sneered. 'Stop fooling. Look at the entrance to the upstairs rooms next to the record store.'

They stared at a big guy lolling by the doorway. *About 6 foot 2*, Spencer thought, *a long chin, prominent teeth, flared jeans, Cuban heels, aviator shades and a fleecy jacket almost hiding the bulky shape of a shoulder holster.* Most of all, Spencer saw confidence and instinctively recognised a street fighter. Nothing showy, but this guy knew his stuff.

'Jesus, he's a big sucker. Can you take him, Spencer?' Savannah whispered. 'We can't have prolonged fisticuffs. It has to be quick, and quiet.'

Spencer noticed an overflowing trash can and an empty bottle of Jim Beam Bourbon. He grabbed the bottle and carefully wiped the rim. The lights changed. Spencer tottered across the street, swigging from the empty bottle. He thought the gabardine coat and the stupid hat were great props. He staggered up to the man, a silly grin on his face. Savannah followed surreptitiously behind, gazing with feigned interest into the Beat Box window. An SFPD helicopter clattered overhead.

'Shay, buddy, can you shpare a quarter?'

The muscle gave him a disdainful sneer. 'Fuck off, you old drunk.'

Spencer grinned and glanced skywards.

'Check out the chopper, buddy. I reckon it's gonna…'

Irresistible. Spencer knew no one could refrain from a quick look. In the second the eyes went skywards Spencer drove fingers made of steel into the outstretched throat. The lightning thrust was silent and calculated to incapacitate. He stopped just short of killing force. The thug collapsed in a heap, his hands clasped around his neck, eyes bulging.

Savannah sprang into action, opening the stair well door. Spencer grabbed the man by the shoulders and began dragging him inside. A concerned old lady put a hand on Spencer's arm.

'Oh dear, is he OK?'

Savannah gave the old girl a winning smile. 'We're paramedics, dear. Sadly, Reverend Irving here has regular seizures.'

'Oh my gosh,' the lady exclaimed, 'a man of God. This is terrible. Should I call an ambulance?'

'Don't bother. Truly. He'll be OK. The Lord will look after him,' Savannah added piously.

Spencer dragged the semi-conscious guard into a narrow foyer, while Savannah gave the old lady another reassuring smile before slamming the solid timber door shut.

'Hey, what the fuck's going on down there?' A strident male voice rang out from the top floor of the three-story building.

'We've been sprung.' Spencer glanced upstairs in time to see a tall, red-bearded man disappear. They heard the thunk of a door slamming. The man on the floor groaned and tried to climb to his feet. A strangled gasp was all the sound he could make.

'I don't think so, petal.' Savannah grabbed his arm, dragging it roughly upwards and handcuffing it to the steel support of the post box holders. She and Spencer bounded up the stairs two at a time.

'Did you see which door?' Savannah panted.

'First on the right.'

At the top of the stairs, Savannah leant against the balustrade, breathing hard.

'I'm not as young as I once was.' She grabbed her automatic, yelling, 'FBI! Open the door.'

She nodded at Spencer, who winked and slammed his booted foot into the worn timber. The cold March wind swept through the open window leading to the fire escape. Worn curtains fluttered in the breeze.

'Don't even think about it, Jimbo!' Savannah shouted. The red-bearded man looked wildly around, grabbing at a black snub-nosed 0.38 on the sink.

Spencer rolled his eyes.

'Not again,' he murmured.

Phut phut. Two rounds from the Hi-Power 0.22 smashed into Jimbo's face and chest. He dropped like a stone. A short exhalation of air and a moan, and it was the end of life.

Savannah climbed through the open window onto the rusty steel landing, in time to see the hurriedly retreating form of Ronny "BBQ" Delgado jumping off the fire escape and legging it down the alleyway.

'God dammit.'

Spencer untied the bonds of the unconscious and brutalized Ryan Tod.

CHAPTER 3

SPENCER'S LEARNING CURVE

'I don't even know if we have enough to arrest BBQ,' Savannah complained, pushing a taco salad around her plate.

She and Spencer had been waved to a table in the corner of the homely Balboa Café by a friendly waiter who recognised Savannah.

'How y'all doin?' the cheerful waiter asked, dragging out a chair for Savannah. The landmark Café on Fillmore was quiet, the lunch trade yet to arrive. Spencer gazed approvingly at the cosy old establishment, with its long walnut bar and smiling white-coated wait staff. His mouth watered in anticipation as the enticing aromas of fresh coffee and hamburgers on the griddle wafted across the room. Spencer watched, fascinated at the speed of the short order cooks, every motion precise, the result of intense repetition. Their meals appeared with dazzling speed.

'Here you are, folks, enjoy.' The waiter placed the tempting fare in front of them.

'Hey, this looks great.' Spencer munched on a burger and took a gulp of his beer. 'You've been here before?'

'What on earth is happening? 'Savannah mumbled.

'What are you talking about?' Spencer greedily stuffed a French fry into his gob.

'I'll tell you what I'm talking about. You and I have been here at least…I don't know, five times, ten times. A lot. You always have the same burger. C'mon, Spencer. What's the story? You don't remember? I don't get it.'

'Oh shit. I do have a confession to make.'

'I have a bad feeling. C'mon. Out with it.'

'It's my memory.'

'For Chrissake, Spencer, this is becoming just a tad annoying. What do you remember, and what don't you?'

Spencer never liked admitting he had memory problems. He'd tried confessing about the time travel before and was met with total disbelief. But he and Savannah had been through enough that he gave it to her plain: she'd rescued him from the clutches of Officer Doolan in the hospital in Chicago, all those years ago.

'How could I forget? What a klutz that man was.'

'As you may recall, I had no memory of anything.' She would be pleased to know his memory had completely returned. Well, almost. He remembered meeting in New York in 1955, and running the diner together. He recalled her taking down two of New York's notorious mobsters with her hand cannon, Isaac the Jew and his pal Dutch Ambroos.

'I remember all of that. And the lawyer. It's a long list.'

'Goody goody. I'm delighted. What about LA? Mexico? You killing that Federale?'

He remembered the whole insane adventure through rural Mexico, meeting with the Sinaloa Cartel boss, the kilo of cocaine and the arsenal Savannah had smuggled across the border and the firefight she had instigated that put them on the run. He recalled the shot that had taken the crooked cop in the neck. He also figured Savannah had taken out the monster of a movie producer, Zacharia Colchester.

'Stand up for a minute,' Savannah hissed.

'What are you talking about?'

'Indulge me.'

Spencer climbed to his feet. Savannah carefully ran her hands along his chest.

'Let's just have a peek under that shirt.'

'Savannah, people are staring.'

Spencer waved at the barman, mouthing *It's OK*.

'You're clean.'

'Seriously, you didn't think I was wearing a wire, surely?'

'It had all the hallmarks of a sting. A set up. What's with all this trips down memory lane? Anyway, I'm not admitting to Charlie and the lovable Colchester.' Savannah gave him an affable grin. 'Would I do such a thing?'

Spencer shrugged. 'Who cares? They're dead and that's a good outcome. But here's the thing. I remember everything after the hospital in Chicago. I remember Sturgis, that fabulous chopper, you as the tattooed biker chick. The shootout in Warbonnet. Oh, and Miami. That was bloody scary.'

'But?'

'I remember everything. Ramirez and the outcome in Miami late last year.'

'Great. So, what's the problem?'

'I might add I also know everything that happened in Miami wasn't sanctioned by Dale Fletcher. And the fact is, what we did was completely illegal.'

'I thought we'd sorted all that.'

'We have. But the only small problem is, my memory stalls right there.'

'What do you mean? That's everything, isn't it?'

'Not quite. I remember everything up until we went back to our hotel in Miami.'

Savannah gave up on her taco salad and took a swig from her Budweiser.

'So, what gives?'

'My memory stops, there. Late 1965 in Miami. It's now March 1966 and I have a gap of about three months.'

'It could be worse, I guess. I'm going to have another beer. You?'

'OK.'

Savannah motioned to the waiter, holding up her bottle of Bud and two fingers.

'This seems slightly ridiculous, but here goes. You and I went back to LA. Inez was safely back in our home in Marina Del Rey. Dale Fletcher was as happy as a clam. You and I went to New Orleans in February for the Mardi Gras weekend, undercover of course.'

'What was going down in the Big Easy?'

'You seriously don't remember? I mean it's just a couple of months ago?'

'Savannah!'

'All right already. It was a counterfeit racket. Nasty brute. Jorge Simonson. A little guy, but pure evil. Everyone feared the bastard.'

'What happened? Oh, let me guess. You shot him?'

She placed a hand innocently on her chest, as if to say *she would never!* 'It was a righteous kill. I was cleared. Jesus, Spencer, he had a gun pointed at you.'

'Bloody hell. A white Jaguar.'

'Come again?'

'Jorge Simenson. He drove a Jag. Nice. White duco, red leather trim. Maple dash.'

'That's right. You do remember?'

'Thank God. Yeah. Bourbon Street. The music, the food it was great. It's all coming back. Christ, I thought I was dead, until...'

'Yeah, until I shot the creep.'

'So you did. And thank you, Savannah. But here's the thing. I remember all of that. Standing in Frenchman Street, listening to a black guy play the harp and singing the House of The Rising Sun. Simenson driving like a lunatic. And then the warehouse and you appeared like magic.'

And that was all he remembered. The next thing he remembered was waking up just before this little skirmish. If you counted one more dead bad guy as a little skirmish.

She took another swig of beer before answering. 'Not much more to it really. We flew back to LA after Simenson. We had a meet with Dale to debrief us, and he sent us off to the Golden Gate City, and here we are.'

Savannah smiled, but Spencer's heart sank, because that was where his memory cut off.

'I don't want to be difficult, but I have absolutely no idea what's happening right now. I have no idea what the job is. I remember waking up yesterday on that stretcher and wham, we're into it. Who exactly are the bad guys? I mean BBQ. Seriously, he cooks folk and eats them?'

'Ronny Delgado, aka BBQ. Dear Ronny is an ex-football star. The Broncos. No sorry, the Cowboys, I think it was from memory. He was a real pin-up boy. The BBQ stands for Big Beautiful Quarterback.'

'But he's a bad guy?' He checked himself as soon as he'd said the words. He'd untied Agent Tod and seen exactly how bad BBQ and the dead guy were by all the bruises, scars, and missing fingernails.

'You betcha,' Savannah answered.

'So aside from the kidnapping and torture of an FBI agent… what are they doing?'

Savannah didn't know.

'Oh, isn't that simply topping? You don't know. Really?'

'I would consider kidnapping and torture enough,' she shot back, lamely. If they didn't know what BBQ's crimes really were, this operation wasn't going to get anywhere.

'I don't want to be difficult but all you saw was a big guy jumping off a fire escape and hot footing it down the alley. And I might add, in your inimitable fashion, you shot his partner in crime.'

Savannah grabbed a sugar cube from the stainless-steel container and threw it hard at Spencer.

'Hey!' Spencer yelped. 'That bloody well hurt.'

'Good. He was going to shoot us.'

'Well. As I recall, in the movies the Cisco Kid used to shoot the six gun out of the bad guy's hand, didn't he?'

'Oh, I see. Silly me. Just like the movies I shoot the gun out of his hand. Australia must be such a wonderful place,' Savannah said sotto voce.

'Well, why not? Your shooting skills are Olympic standard.'

Savannah stabbed a finger at him.

'This is it. For the last time. When I shoot, I shoot to kill. Our training teaches us: *Centre mass. Centre mass.* Got it?'

Spencer turned, smiling at the other diners who appeared to be hanging on every word.

'It's OK, folks. We're rehearsing for a TV show.'

'Now that we've covered the lefty peace, love and all that crap, did you also forget Dale Fletcher was meeting us here? And speak of...'

Spencer peered out of the window to see a tan Pontiac Catalina sedan swerve into a parking space.

CHAPTER 4
HELLO DALE

Spencer smiled as he waved at Mr Ordinary. 'He doesn't change much, does he?' he remarked to Savannah.

Spencer remembered when he first met Dale Fletcher at Antonio's in New York, in 1955, immediately after Spencer had disabled two of Tony Romano's goons. He had thought Dale looked like a recruiter for a Southern Baptist Bible College. Was it the pork pie hat, or the daggy basket weave loafers or even the Argyle socks? Probably it was his earnest manner. Spencer remembered he could have been knocked down with a feather when Dale identified himself as FBI. He wondered how long it had taken Dale to realise country bumpkin FBI Special Agent Savannah Steele was every bit as ruthless as the criminals that were being pursued. Savannah had a longer list of kills than a deer hunter in a busy season.

'Spencer, Savannah, good to see you.'

The meet and greet waiter scurried over to the table.

'Coffee please, buddy.' Dale fished through his pockets, grabbing his trusty Zippo and a crumpled packet of Luckies.

'I thought you'd quit?' Savannah said with a grin.

'Well, I have, mostly. The little woman, you know.'

Rather patronising, but it is 1966. Spencer gave Dale a wide, friendly grin and scooted into the booth to make room.

'Anyhow, I don't have a lot of time. Shame about Jimbo Kline.'

'Hang on, Dale, it was…'

'I know, I know, Special Agent Steele,' he added hastily, 'but unfortunately we don't now have a witness.'

'What about poor Ryan Tod?' Spencer threw in.

'Ryan mumbled something. He said something along the lines of…' Dale yanked a notebook out of the top pocket of his plaid shirt. 'Let me see… *You gotta stop them, this is huge.*'

'Yeah, huge. And then?' Savannah leaned forward.

'He had to be sedated and he's, he's sort of not with us.'

'Christ almighty. He's not dead. Can't be.' Savannah flashed a worried glance at Spencer.

'The doctor said he's in a catatonic state and he's, well, he just stares at the wall. Nothing. Zip. Nada.' Spencer's heart went out to the poor guy. He slowly pushed his plate away, his appetite having taken a hiatus. With luck, Agent Tod would recover.

'Surely, we have enough to go after BBQ. Arrest him. Bring him in?' Spencer urged.

'I've had a word with our legal eagles and we don't have much.'

'I saw him jumping off the fire escape, surely…'

'Savannah, Ronny Delgado's lawyers will argue you didn't make a positive ID. We don't have prints. His partner in crime is dead. Ryan can't help. We just don't have enough.'

The fury of a woman scorned came over Savannah's face. 'We can at least talk to him.'

'He'll just get lawyered up. He'll take the fifth. We need more.' Dale stubbed out his cigarette before fishing out another from the pack.

'Any idea where he hangs out?' Spencer asked.

'I have a pretty good idea. And that's what I want to talk to you both about.'

Savannah sighed. 'Let's have it.'

'We reckon he's headed back to his commune in the Diablo Mountains.'

'A commune? Really? Wow, this is getting deep.' Spencer glanced at Savannah and Dale.

'Spencer,' Dale said sharply. 'We've discussed Ronny's commune.'

Savannah put her head in her hands. 'Dale, Spencer has had one of his memory lapses.'

'Great, that's all I need.' Dale stared hard at Spencer.

'Dale, it's OK. Just a temporary lapse. I'm OK. Honestly, I'm fine.'

Dale ran through it again, since Ryan Tod was no longer part of the operation and these two were all he had.

Ronny Delgado was the head of a commune, a cult. A collection of misfits, nationalists, commies, God knew what exactly. They were known as The American Family. They hadn't broken any laws, but Dale believed they were up to no good. First of all, they were armed. They played war games. They were secretive. Also, a number of former criminals had been seen coming and going. Essentially, they believed the government was evil and Armageddon was imminent. All the usual rubbish. Nothing that was terribly original. They handed out pamphlets on street corners.

'You must have seen them, surely? Oh yeah, of course, memory lapse. And let me guess. *It's a long story.* You're still a goddam mystery man.' When Spencer shrugged, he continued, 'Anyway, Agent Steele can tell you more later.' He fished in his cigarette pack for another, but came up empty. He sighed. 'Moving right along. As far as we know, Ronny and his cohorts don't know you or Agent Steele. Delgado didn't see you, did he, Savannah?'

'No, as I said, I caught a glimpse of him as he made his escape, but he didn't actually see me or Spencer.'

'I want you two to do what you do best.'

'Without wanting to dwell upon the obvious, what might that be, Dale?'

Spencer didn't have a clue.

'C'mon, Spencer. Hey, I know what they say in your country—*you have a few roos loose in your top paddock.*' Dale laughed at his own witticism, then coughed uncontrollably.

'Dale, I'm not sure what you're suggesting either,' Savannah said.

'Must be all the Mary Jane in the air. I want you two to infiltrate. Become believers. Join the commune.'

***

'Don't you just love it?' Savannah strode around the spartan living room in their temporary apartment in Haight Street. Spencer had explored their domain after their meeting with Dale. It had two spacious bedrooms, a bathroom with an old-fashioned claw-foot bath, a pink porcelain basin that clashed with the vintage pea-green wall tiles, and a large sash window unencumbered by any sort of curtain. The ceilings seemed impossibly high. The oak floor was well worn. Their booted feet clunked and echoed noisily, adding to the harsh warehouse feel of what could have been a renovator's delight. The living room was as big as an aircraft carrier flight deck.

'I could really do something with this place.' Spencer's lip curled at the sight of the cracked plaster walls and the sagging ceiling. 'But it really is pretty bloody damned rough. I will say though, it's not cold in here.'

'Coal-fired furnace in the basement.' Savannah's gaze remained focussed on the apartment across the street. 'As I was saying, don't you just love the way Dale throws us in the deep end? Are you listening?'

'Yep, of course. Deep end.'

Spencer watched the black and white television. His bare feet rested on the coffee table while he reclined on a worn, cracked, brown leather chesterfield, as old as the 1920s apartment.

'What in hell is that rubbish you're watching?' Savannah scowled.

'This is great. Bewitched. It's about a lady who's an everyday housewife but is actually a witch.'

'Give me strength,' Savannah mumbled. 'If you can tear yourself away, we need to talk about what's going to happen. We have to infiltrate this mob of goddam hippies and you're watching a mindless TV show.'

'Dammit, just when Samantha's mother, a vindictive witch, is about to turn her husband into a frog or something.'

'Whose husband? Hers or her daughter's?'

'See what I mean? You're interested; I can tell.'

Savannah strode over to the Kreisler 18 inch and pressed the off button. 'Enough already. Focus, damn you.'

'Goodbye, Samantha. See you again soon, I hope.'

'How should we tackle this? Any ideas?' Savannah sprawled on a 1940s club chair upholstered in threadbare red velvet.

'Well,' Spencer drawled. 'Piece of cake, really.'

'Explain please?'

'Honestly, I don't see a problem. This outfit is looking for recruits. It's not like they're going to check with law enforcement to see if we have outstanding warrants. They're not going to want see references or employment history. What's the problem? Dale needs to supply us with a suitable vehicle.'

'No more goddam Harley Davidsons, thank you very much.'

'I must admit that would be cool. However, what I would suggest would be a battered V Dub Kombi, preferably with some sort of bedding and maybe some cooking gear in case we find ourselves not able to get into the commune immediately. So, like I said. Piece of cake.'

She levelled a disbelieving look at him. 'So, we get the address of the commune, rock up and say, 'here we are, our names are Spencer and Savannah, can we please move in?'

'I can see you're still a sceptic. No, but almost. I reckon they'd have some of their people up at Golden Gate Park. We wander up there, mooch around like lost souls, strike up a conversation. See where it goes.'

'I guess that's a plan of sorts,' Savannah said moodily.

'The other thing is the music.'

'What about the music?'

'Did you notice those huge posters of the Beatles on the wall where Ronny and Jimbo were performing their manicure on poor Ryan?'

'Yeah, so they like the Beatles. Goddam blaspheming, long-haired, mummy's boys, if you ask me.'

'Nobody's asking you, Savannah. Believe me, the world's moved on from Bing Crosby and Lawrence Welk.'

She turned from the window looking out on 4 Haight Street and regarded Spencer. 'Now that was music. Bing singing White Christmas. Oh boy. I remember back in South Dakota…'

'You're showing your age, Savannah. Believe me, this isn't Bing Crosby, Sinatra or Perry Como territory. Do you remember the sign at the Beat Box record store?'

'What in hell…'

'I'll take that as a no. Jefferson Airplane, featuring none other than Grace Slick on vocals, are going to be live at the Winterland Ballroom. I'll bet you some of the American Family will be there'.

CHAPTER 5

THE AMERICAN FAMILY

S tanford Delaware was not happy.

'Ronny, Ronny, you have failed me. Oh dear, what's to be done, eh?'

Ronny Delgado, aka BBQ, was afraid of no man, was what he would have said before meeting The Prophet. Stanford Delaware unnerved him. Whether it was the eyes, hairless head, or the sheer presence of the man, BBQ couldn't say, but The Prophet got under his skin like nobody else on the planet.

The Prophet leaned back in his comfortable timbered executive chair. The ergonomic chair had wheels that could rotate in all directions. Stanford enjoyed swivelling in the high-backed recliner to periodically turn his gaze on the commune from his wide picture window. Below him he could view his subjects toiling in the fields of his very own piece of paradise in a cosy valley high in the Diablo mountains.

His home had been lovingly constructed by the builders and artisans now faithful members of The American Family. The building had magnificent architectural lines and dynamics but still held that cabin aesthetic with the wood, stones, and all the windows which made you feel like you were in the woods.

Stanford had been rifling through a stack of documents and singing along to a record when Ronny knocked. Stanford was wearing his usual kaftan, an undeniably gorgeous garment. Made of eye-catching colourful silk, it was almost feminine. Stanford himself, at first glance was unprepossessing. Average height and with the condition known as alopecia universalis, which literally means 'no hair', he should have been considered ordinary. He had a bald head as bright as a Christmas ornament, a pleasing if rather bland face, but the eyes. Hitler had them, Rasputin had them. Pale blue, they were mesmerising. Women found him irresistible. There were more than 500 members of The American Family living in mostly comfortable if basic log cabins on the sprawling acreage that was the home of Stanford's compound.

The normally confident and articulate Ronny Delgado stuttered and felt like a schoolgirl when he had to face Stanford.

'I, I'm sorry, Stanford. There was nothing I could do. I'm sure they were Feds.'

Ronny hated the effect that Stanford always had on him. 'Nowhere Man' by the Beatles played on a Garrard turntable.

'Sit down, Ronny. I'll just turn the music down. Just listen to that. Three-part harmony, Lennon, McCartney and Harrison. Brilliant, eh?'

'Yeah, great, Stanford. One of their best.'

Ronny went to sit on the bentwood chair opposite Stanford's impressive, recycled wood desk. Resting upon sturdy iron legs, the sea worn planks had been polished to a high lustre.

'No, no, Ronny. BBQ. I just love the acronym. It makes one think of… Anyway, enough of that. Sit. Over there. On the lounge. My happy place.'

It was a wide fabric sofa in pastel colours with scatter cushions. Ronny perched awkwardly. Stanford sidled over and with a sigh, he breathed, 'That's better, I think.' He briefly placed a hand on Ronny's leg. BBQ shivered. He'd always considered himself heterosexual.

'Now I'm in my happy place. How about the happy juice? What do you think?'

'Sure,' Ronny croaked.

'I'll get it.'

Stanford padded over to a small refrigerator and drew out a glass pitcher and two glasses. He carefully poured two measures of the bright orange liquid.

'We don't want to overdo it, now do we, Ronny?'

Ronny gratefully accepted the refreshment and took a sip. Immediately a wave of contentment washed over him.

'Aah, that feels better, doesn't it?' Stanford took a healthy swig. 'However, we still need to discuss some business. We need to find some new insurance companies. I think perhaps interstate. I'd like you to start looking further afield Ronny, maybe Oregon.'

Ronny struggled to focus; everything was so serene.

'Are there problems, Stanford?'

'No, Ronny dear. But one shouldn't get too lax. After all, there are hundreds of companies and I'm sure they would welcome new business. Now about the other thing. The Candlestick Park event is still going ahead?'

'Oh yeah. It's going to be huge.'

'You know where they'll be staying?'

'It hasn't been absolutely confirmed but I believe it'll be the Hilton.'

'Good, good. Keep me posted.'

CHAPTER 6
A REAL BLAST

The night sky was aglow with bright city lights when Savannah and Spencer left the apartment. At times like these, Spencer loved the purity, the naivete of the past.

'Where are we going again, Spencer?'

'Winterland Ballroom. Jefferson Airplane are on.'

'An Airplane, seriously.'

'Really, Savannah?' Spencer rolled his eyes.

'OK, OK, I get it; another goddam noisy pop group. Just what I need. And there you go racing down the street. Do you even know where the Winterland Ballroom is?'

Spencer scowled. 'Um no, I guess not.'

'Well dear, as it happens, I have a car. And what a car, I might add. Not that you care,' Savannah, stopped mid-stride. 'OK, this is it.'

'This is what?' Spencer asked.

'My current new wheels, Superman.'

Before them, in all its glory, was a brand-new gleaming white Chevrolet Impala, just slightly smaller than the Titanic. Savannah opened the driver's door and climbed in, leaning over to unlock the passenger door.

'Whoa. Nice.'

Spencer opened the passenger door and slid in, admiring the red trim and black carpet. Savannah grinned. The big V8 rumbled into life.

'Yours?'

'Well, sort of. Government issue.'

'What is it?'

'It's the latest Chevrolet. Like it?'

'You do love your cars, don't you?'

Savannah laughed as she accelerated. Spencer gazed out of the window, observing the colourful San Francisco Street denizens. Focussing on where they were going, he thought Savannah seemed to be heading towards a more permanent precinct dominated by stone buildings which the city had erected when it rebuilt after the great fire.

'Check out those baroque domes, Spencer. Pretty impressive, huh?'

'Awesome.'

'Yep, that's City Hall. Just about the most distinctive edifice in San Francisco. It takes up two city blocks.'

Spencer stared at the graceful old pile, currently bathed in multi-coloured lights. The death of Jimbo was beginning to retreat from his mind. He was with Savannah, and they were out on the town.

'Almost there.'

The Chev turned into Post Street and then Steiner, where it swerved effortlessly into a parking space. The power steering whined as Savannah threw it onto full lock and adroitly manoeuvred the sedan into the vacant spot.

They were barely inside the doors of the vast Winterland complex before they noticed an assortment of what might have been San Francisco's upper crust, judging by the array of gold and precious stones being flashed around by the women. Spencer thought he recognized Janis Joplin from the pictures he'd seen in the press. As for the rest, he *imagined* he'd seen them somewhere. Wasn't that Clint Eastwood, the tall guy in the corner with the beautiful woman on his arm? Over by the ticket office, a stunning dark-haired woman with soulful eyes. Natalie Wood perhaps?

'All right, Special Agent Savannah Steele, tonight you'll hear some real music. Let's go check out the Airplane.'

They walked out past the lobby and the maybe-celebs, past the doorman, who gave them an elaborate salute, and into the main hall, a converted ice-rink. The strobe lights made the whole place look like a war zone. Out front was the biggest bank of speakers Spencer had ever seen. Rows of seats around the perimeter were filling fast. Taped music was pumping hard. Out in the middle, the fans milled around, drinking and laughing and popping pills.

'Oh boy, Savannah! This is going to be great!'

Savannah rolled her eyes, but she began to move, swaying to the irresistible beat. Spencer swayed with her, abandoning any pretence of cool. For a moment they were a happy little pair of hedonists, pursuing pleasure for pleasure's sake. The moment was shattered by an unearthly scream from the speakers, then a loud chord and a disembodied voice.

'Ladies and gentle, people. The Wintergarden per-oudly presents Grace Slick and the Jefferson Airplane.

The surge of excitement was irresistible. Spencer felt himself being driven forward by the crush of fans, towards the speakers and despite the pain in his ears, the opening number was pure rock and roll heaven. By the time the second song began, Savannah was grooving like a true 1960s flower-power girl. Spencer could hear her quietly singing the words, which came to him in snatches, garbled phrases and images mixed with the thumping bass and a screaming Les Paul Gibson. He wondered how Savannah knew the words to *Someone to Love*.

Spencer moved closer to hear better. A gorgeous African American girl with glassy eyes threw her arms around Spencer and shouted. 'Are you one of the Family?'

Spencer shook his head. She thrust a glossy pamphlet at him.

'Come. You will find what you seek.'

She smiled and briefly stroked his cheek. Before he could answer Savannah glared at the lady, turned around and wagged her finger at him. 'Enough!' she said. But she was still smiling.

Spencer folded the paper and thrust it into his hip pocket. The rest of the night passed in a blur. The Airplane continued to play an endless repertoire of good ole new songs, and as Spencer downed one Bud after another and moved his feet to the rhythm, he let the words of the song come back to him. "When the truth…" *Be careful*, the words seemed to say. *You are in deeper than you think.*

***

Savannah made an angry racket in the kitchen the next morning, huffing and stomping and banging. He was surprised and amused when the result was mere coffee.

'Well, that was a goddam waste of time. Here you go, mystery man, I've made your coffee. Again! You can make breakfast.'

Spencer grabbed the steaming brew and yawned. His head was pounding. He didn't know if it was the numerous bottles of Bud or the marijuana fumes that had drifted through the ballroom like a San Francisco fog. They sat down to a mess of bacon and eggs and sourdough toast slathered in butter.

'Hey, Spencer, you're not a bad little chef, are you?'

Savannah crunched on a thick slice and a mouthful of bacon.

'Like I said, last night was a total waste of time. I think you just wanted to hear that goddam noise.'

'I have something.'

Spencer handed Savannah the crushed pamphlet.

'And anyway, I could tell you were loving it. It sure as hell wasn't Pat Boone, was it?'

She glowered, without any real menace. 'Yeah, yeah, I have to admit. It was a blast. But that aside, where did you get this?'

'That charming lady you dragged me away from.'

'You're a married man. I was saving you from yourself. But, interesting. Have you read it?'

'Of course. The Family are putting on a free cookout at Golden Gate Park.'

'There's no such thing as a free lunch.'

'Agreed. The Family are looking for recruits, I'll just betcha.'

'Hey, the phone. It's probably Inez. Who the hell would be ringing you? Your ever-loving wife? If she damn well exists." She picked it up. "Dale, how nice. What now? You have a surprise? I can hardly wait. Where? OK. An hour, give or take.' Savannah hung up the handpiece. 'I just love Dale's surprises. OK, Spencer we're on the move.'

***

The Impala cruised up Haight, turning into Ashbury.

'So, what's going down, Savannah?'

'We're off to the basement of the Federal building on Golden Gate Avenue. Dale will be waiting with our surprise.'

'You don't look happy.'

'He's a sly one, is Dale,' Savannah grunted.

The big Chevrolet glided down the ramp into the sprawling underground car garage. A guard held up an imperious hand as Savannah stopped at the steel barrier.

'Special Agent Steele?' the guard enquired.

Savannah proffered her ID. The officer studied it carefully. With a nod he indicated a vacant slot in between a green Ford LTD and a battered old Volkswagen Kombi.

'Park your car over there, Ma'am.'

'Is Agent Fletcher meeting us here?' Savannah asked.

'Don't know for sure, Ma'am. I believe you're just exchanging ve-hicles.' His southern accent drew out the vowels.

'What now?' Spencer asked as they scanned the parking lot. They heard a hiss and whirr as an elevator door slid open. A harassed-looking Dale Fletcher tore out waving a set of keys.

'Well, it's all go, isn't it? You're gonna love what we've managed to dig up for you. It's groovy.'

Savannah glanced sideways at Spencer.

'Tell me I'm hearing things? Groovy?'

'Follow me, troops.' Dale marched over to the Kombi. 'How about that, Agent Steele?'

'Dale, you gotta be kidding. My Impala has aircon, power windows, and power steering,' she wailed.

'Sorry, kiddo, you both have to look the part. Look, see, it's even got a ban the bomb sign on the spare. And, hey, it's got a radio. What more could you want?'

Dale jerked open the Volkswagen side door and pointed out the features with all the sincerity of a Las Vegas car salesman.

'Look, it has fold down bunks and check out this dinky little stove. A home away from home.' Dale beamed proudly as he held out the keys.

***

Savannah fumed as the Volkswagen rattled its way to the Golden Gate Park.

'Blasted heap of junk. If you crunch the goddam gears one more time…'

'Stick shifts aren't really my speciality. Anyway, I'm getting the hang of it.'

The Kombi stalled as it took off from the lights at Castro.

'Oh yeah. Perfect. Brother Spencer, do you seriously think anyone's going to believe we're related?'

'My foot slipped, the clutch pedal, it's, you know…? And yes, why not? Same mother, different father, or vice versa.'

'Oh yeah, and I'd have a brother who can't drive and is a lousy shot. What was that quote? I know. "It's a poor workman…" You know the rest, I'm sure.'

'Enough. Here we are on Fulton. This is somewhere near where the Family's little shindig is going down. Look, over there.' Spencer pointed to a boldly coloured marquee and a timbered platform.

'Wow, this is quite an event. And there's a band playing. And just look at all those goddam people. Hippies, Christ Almighty. My God, Spencer there must be at least a thousand people here. And look, hot dog stands, pizza, hamburgers and apparently, it's all free. Someone has deep pockets.'

Spencer levered the Kombi into a space between a battered Citroen 2CV and a gleaming T-bucket hot rod.

They wended their way through a sea of people, resolutely striding towards the hypnotic beat of the psychedelic San Francisco sound. A sullen group of Hells Angels lounged on their Harley Davidson choppers, their black leather and violent ink contrasting with the peace, love and understanding vibe of the day. 'Hey man. You want some graaas?', a bearded giant with long greasy locks and a Harley Davidson T-shirt growled.

'No mate. We're cool,' Spencer told the guy cheerfully.

As they neared the platform, the crowd went wild as The Sons of Champlin bounded onto the stage, blasting the Bay area with their strident horns, thumping Fender Precision Bass and soaring chords from the Hammond organ.

'Wow, this is awesome.'

Spencer sang along with a classic delta blues number powering its message through a howling Marshall amplifier.

'It's loud. I'll give you that. I don't suppose there's any chance they might play something by Johnny Ray?'

As they climbed out of the Kombi the band finished its set, a hirsute man with a tie-dyed T-shirt bounded on to the stage.

'How about a big hand for the faaa-bulous Sons of Champlin!'

The crowd roared. As the applause died down the tie-dyed guy yelled into his mic.

'And who do we have to thank?

He held a hand to his ear. The crowd obliged, yelling in a ragged discordant unity, 'The Family!' they bellowed.

As Spencer and Savannah pushed through the throng, the compere motioned for silence.

'And as a special treat we have our wonderful benefactor, here to have a few quick words.'

'Spencer, look, see that trailer next to the stage? See that big guy standing there?'

'Yep, big guy with the flat stomach.'

'Flat stomach. Are we looking at the same fella?'

'My little joke. The "L" is silent.'

Savannah rolled her eyes.

'OK, I get it. That's the lovable BBQ Delgado.'

'Let's get closer to the trailer.'

As they drew alongside, the trailer door flew open and a totally bald man with piercing blue eyes and a shimmering multi-coloured kaftan stepped out. A hush fell over the crowd as they parted to allow him to make his way to the stage. Spencer was close enough to touch him when a hoarse voice screamed.

'You bloody murderer! You killed my son.'

A thin, worn old man in dirty blue coveralls held a small automatic pistol in both hands, pointed directly at the man in the kaftan. Spencer sprang into action, launching himself through the air like a bird in flight. He kicked the man's gun hand. The pistol flew into the air. Ronny Delgado and two other solid men piled on top of the man, kicking and punching.

'Hey, enough!' Spencer yelled. 'He's not a threat anymore.'

The bald man stepped forward.

'Ronny. Stop. Let the police handle this.'

Delgado dragged the man to his feet.

'Yeah sure, Stanford.'

The bald man gathered his kaftan around him and held a hand out to Spencer.

'Thank you, friend. My name is Stanford Delaware.'

Spencer shook the proffered hand.

'Nice to meet you, Stanford. My name's Spencer Marlowe, and this is my…sister, Savannah Steele.'

'Please step into my trailer, it's so noisy out here. But you can almost feel the love, can't you?'

Spencer glanced at the old man now handcuffed and being hustled away by San Francisco's finest, and wondered was Delaware a master of irony. *And what about those cops? They were pretty darn quick.*

'Stanford, the people are waiting for you to speak.'

'Let 'em wait, Ronny. I have to thank these two lovely people.'

Savannah and Spencer were ushered into the luxurious trailer, adorned with photos of Stanford apparently preaching to legions of devoted fans.

'Have a seat. Spencer and…Savannah, is that right, my dear?'

Savannah nodded. Stanford pointed to a sofa. Like everything else in the room, the couch, in a soothing aqua velvet, made a statement, a testimony to the taste and whims of the owner. The trailer and everything in it reeked of wealth and class with a warm inviting atmosphere. Even the air made you feel warm and clean. Taking up one end of the trailer Spencer admired a bright and airy kitchen with its tan laminate bench tops with bold nut-brown tile splash backs, bathed in natural light from a discreet skylight.

A stack of long-playing records sat in a rack on the shelf, next to it an autographed black and white photo of a smiling John Lennon. Spencer could just see into a cosy bedroom. A window that Spencer suspected had one way glass, overlooked the concert area, the soundproofing so efficient it looked like they were viewing a movie of a rock concert with the sound switched off.

'Where are my manners? How about a refreshing libation? Non-alcoholic, of course.'

Without waiting for a response, Stanford glided noiselessly across the deep blue plush pile carpet, his long kaftan making him appear footless. He produced a pitcher of an orange-coloured liquid from the refrigerator. Ice cubes clinked as he carefully poured the drink into three crystal tumblers.

He raised his glass. 'Good health.'

Savannah cast a worried glance at Spencer as she took a tentative sip. Spencer waited until he saw Stanford raise his glass to his lips before having a swig. He winked at Savannah. He thought it the most delicious and invigorating non-alcoholic beverage he'd ever tasted. Almost immediately any misgivings about Stanford Delaware evaporated. *I think Dale and Savannah must have it all wrong.*

Stanford started to explain the doctrine of the Family. Spencer glanced sideways at Savannah who looked like a contented pussy cat. She appeared to be hanging on Delaware's every word. Stanford sat behind a handsome teak desk; his hands clasped as if in prayer.

'It was most unfortunate. That poor fellow. His only son, Travis, a troubled and lonely young guy, had joined our commune. I tell you, the transformation in him was truly wondrous. He toiled happily in our garden. We grow everything. We really are quite self-sufficient you know.'

Spencer nodded. 'And something happened?'

Is that a tear in Stanford's eye?

'A rattler. A black-tailed rattlesnake bit the poor boy. There was nothing we could do. There was no anti-venom within miles, and sadly…Well. Of course we did what we could. The authorities were notified. We told his father, but for some odd reason the old gentleman got it into his head that it was foul play. Anyway, these things do happen. But please tell me about yourselves. I was amazed at how effortlessly you disarmed him, Spencer. Are you ex-military? Law enforcement, perhaps?' Stanford fixed Spencer with a shrewd stare.

'Good Lord, no. I studied martial arts as a kid. I've forgotten most of what I'd learned. But I guess reflexes just kicked in.'

'I see. And you are brother and sister? Your accents are quite different. Savannah is obviously American. But you…British perhaps? I don't wish to pry, but please, I'm interested in people.'

Spencer glanced sideways at Savannah. He was feeling uncomfortable about spinning the story they'd concocted. Savannah sipped her drink.

'Yes, Mr Delaware…'

'Stanford. Please.'

'Yes, of course. Stanford. Spencer and I have the same father but embarrassingly different mothers. Our father, Dale, had a wartime relationship with Spencer's mother in the 1940s in Perth, Western Australia. Sadly, that union didn't last. The war. It was difficult times. Spencer's mother didn't want to relocate to the States and well…' Savannah shrugged.

'I understand. A common story I imagine.' Stanford smiled sympathetically.

'Savannah and I only recently connected. I decided to come to America and meet my American family.'

'I see. And you've both been travelling around our great country. What about you, Savannah? Please, where do you hail from?'

'I'm from South Dakota. Pierre, in fact. My father, Dale, owned a hardware store until he passed away a few years ago. Lung cancer. The doctors said it was caused by smoking.'

Spencer stifled a laugh at the smoking comment.

'Sadly, my mother passed away a year later. So, Spencer and I have been travelling in our VW Kombi.'

Stanford's eyes seemed as if they were trained on some invisible spectre, his heavy eyelids a fraction too slow to blink. Then after a long pause he spoke, his voice slow, sonorous, sensual even.

'I believe you are both seeking enlightenment. A better way.'

Spencer found himself nodding. It seemed the universe had shrunk. All that existed was Stanford, Spencer and Savannah.

'You must visit our little commune in the Diablo Mountains.'

CHAPTER 7
SECOND THOUGHTS

Gears were never Spencer's thing, but he thought he was getting the hang of the four-speed manual transmission.

'Spencer, that's the third time you've crunched those darn cogs. Where on earth did you learn to drive?'

Spencer shrugged.

He changed the subject. 'What is happiness?' He pushed harder on the accelerator as the Volkswagen laboured up Bradford Street.

'Come again?' Savannah said dreamily.

'I guess it was sort of a rhetorical question. What is happiness?'

Savannah giggled. 'Happiness is a warm gun.'

'Trust you. That sounds like a song title. No. I was just thinking. I mean, how would you describe happiness?'

'God, I don't know. No idea really. It sounds like you've been doing some serious navel gazing. Tell me, oh wise one?'

'It just occurred to me. Happiness is an absence of all negative emotions.'

'It's funny you should say that. You know, I feel absolutely at peace with the world.'

'Dale wants us to infiltrate Stanford's commune. You still OK with that?'

'Of course, but I'm sort of having second thoughts about Dale's take on Stanford. He's just…so…Spencer, what's the word I'm looking for?'

'Don't know. But he just, he just sort of radiates "goodness". That sounds corny, but I just can't imagine this guy being bad. I just can't.'

'But what about Delgado? We know for sure he's an evil bastard.'

'That's a given.' She tapped her chin in thought and gave a hefty yawn. 'Let's just sleep on it.'

***

'What's this meant to be?' Savannah eyed the strange mass on her plate, cheesy with some dark leafy greens.

'Well. It sort of started out as an omelette, but I think now it might be scrambled eggs, with whatever that green stuff is. It'll taste OK. And here's your coffee.'

Reaching into his pocket Spencer grabbed the cornicello. It was his one tangible link with his other life. He wondered if the faint vibration he felt was real or imagination.

'Spencer, what the hell is that thing? I remember you had it when we first met. You said it was a lucky charm. What's the story behind it? May I have a look?'

Spencer placed the cornicello in her palm.

'Oh my…' Savannah's face was white.

'What is it, Savannah?'

'How in hell did you do that?'

'Do what?'

'Look, I don't believe in goddam mumbo jumbo or party tricks.'

'I'm sorry. I have no idea what you're talking about.'

Savannah handed the trinket back.

'This is seriously weird. It felt like static electricity and then I had, like a vision, it was just a flash.'

'A vision of what?'

'Your mysterious wife that nobody's ever seen. She's Japanese, right? '

'Of course. But you know that. But what made you think it was Michiyo?'

'This is crazy. I just knew. This, call it a vision, even though it was momentary, it was real. I felt like I could have spoken to her. Does she have long black hair parted in the middle?'

'Yes, but so do a lot of Asian women.'

'Tell me she doesn't have a small mole, a beauty mark, on her neck. Just tell me that.'

Stunned, Spencer stared at Savannah. He felt a twinge of jealousy. The one and only constant in his life, and he thought it was exclusively his.

'No, she doesn't have a mole,' he lied.

Spencer and Savannah had slept late in the Kombi. It was now mid-morning, and a glorious one at that.

'Now we've had a snooze, what's your take on yesterday? Stanford Delaware. The old guy who wanted to fill him full of holes? The prompt arrival of the cops?'

Savannah groaned.

'Hey, whatever this is, it tastes all right. Look, frankly, I'm a little confused. In the cold, hard light of day Stanford Delaware still looks a bit suspicious. But, I don't want to sound like I'm, you, know, wishy washy, but it's almost like he cast a spell yesterday. Hell, if the sonofabitch was selling Edsels I would have bought one.'

'I'm with you. He was as smooth as. Let's stick to the plan. We'll call Dale and tell him we're going to head off to the mountains and join the love-in.'

CHAPTER 8
THE BANK HEIST

R onny Delgado checked the magazine on the M1 carbine. The dark blue Pontiac GTO graced the small parking lot in Noriega Street; dark tinted windows made it difficult to see inside the flashy car. He could feel the adrenaline building.

Ronny and Xavier sat quietly, scanning the street from the vehicle they'd stolen a day ago. Sure, the car was a head turner, but with the 389 V8 it was the fastest car on the road and, you never know, there might be a chase. They'd been parked for an hour in the parking lot tracking everyone who had gone in and out of the building.

Xavier hadn't always been so careful. After serving time for involuntary manslaughter in San Quentin he'd vowed to go straight, but under the spell of Stanford Delaware, he'd done whatever the Prophet demanded. The Family would rule America and he, Xavier Martinez, would be an *el jefe*, a boss, a leader. Turning to his swarthy partner, Ronny grinned as he slipped a red patterned bandana over his face.

'You ready, Xavier?'

Both men scoped the street for the last time, focussing their attention on the Sunset District branch of the Hibernia Bank. Xavier grabbed the 12-gauge sawn off from the back seat.

'Si, amigo, we scare the shit outta them mothers, eh?'

In unison they strode across the street, firearms hanging loosely at their sides.

Ronny and Xavier each grabbed one of the handles of the double brass doors and ran into the bank, screaming.

'On the floor, motherfuckers. This is a robbery. Do as you're told and you won't get hurt.'

The old gray-haired security guard stared. open mouthed, fumbling for his holstered 0.38 pistol.

Without hesitating, Xavier blasted the rent-a-cop in the chest. He collapsed, dead before he hit the floor, his shredded pullover a mass of red. Pumping another round into the shotgun, Xavier fired into the ceiling just for the hell of it.

The bank wasn't large, with only a half a dozen customers. Facing them were the tellers' cages, four occupied by women in the sky-blue uniform of the Hibernia Bank. Each with a cash drawer stuffed with bank notes. Screaming like a banshee, Xavier leapt onto the counter brandishing his shotgun.

'Put the money into the teller bags. Fucking move it.'

Two of the tellers cried, the other two steadfastly filled the cotton bags with notes. A long-haired guy in blue jeans and a denim jacket entered the bank and swore, as he turned and ran for the street. Xavier grabbed the four bulging teller bags, yelling at Ronny.

'Time to go, amigo!'

Four customers lay on the floor, spreadeagled. The other two were curled up in the foetal position. Someone had wet themselves. The stench of urine mixed with the metallic smell of blood and gunpowder.

Without a second glance, Ronny and Xavier stepped over the slain security guard. They trotted across the road to the parking lot.

The big V8 coughed, then roared into life as Ronny put his foot down. Fishtailing wildly, the Pontiac howled as it tore along Noriega Street weaving in and out of traffic.

CHAPTER 9

WELCOME TO THE FAMILY

The Kombi chugged over the mountains. Savannah and Spencer gazed at the scenery punctuated with creeks, ravines, ancient oak and the plentiful California poppies. Stretching onward, the road hugged canyon walls, taking each turn in an easy sweep. Spencer turned up the heater as the temperature dropped. He was grateful for his fleece-lined leather number. Savannah wore a goose down, hooded long-line jacket.

'This really is something,' Savannah enthused.

'The original home of the *Ohlone and Yokuts*,' Spencer announced proudly.

'Who? What?'

'The Native American tribes living here before the settlers.'

'Oh, clever Dick. How would an Australian know that, might I ask?'

'Actually, I read it in one of those National Geographics lying around the apartment.'

The Kombi had just breasted a steep incline and was motoring into a lush valley. Spencer crunched the gears into third, using the engine as a brake. The little motor huffed and puffed and backfired.

'Hey, look. Over there.'

A mile in front, nestled against a steep canyon wall, the commune came into view, a collection of rustic cedar cabins and outbuildings. A grove of fruit trees and precise rows of some sort of green vegetable stretched up to the rocky base of the canyon. Set back on a small hill an impressive timber and glass residence of sizeable proportions dominated the landscape.

Spencer pointed. 'That'd have to be Stanford's little pile, I reckon.'

***

A stocky man in tattered jeans, flip flops and a battered top hat held up a hand. Behind him there was a steel barrier and what looked like a military guard post, a small timber structure which reminded Spencer of an Australian outdoor dunny.

Spencer glanced sideways at Savannah.

'Well, at least he doesn't appear to have a gun.'

'Good day, folks, peace be with you. And you would be?'

The guard spoke in a monotone like a scripted mechanical dummy.

'We're sort of expected, I guess. Spencer Marlowe and Savannah Steele. Stanford invited us to come and see him.' Spencer flashed his widest smile.

'Please wait.'

The guard slouched into his hut. Through the four-paned window they watched as he picked up a phone, then began nodding his head vigorously, before hanging up and strolling to the barrier comprising of a length of steel pipe with a simple square red and white sign saying "stop". He grabbed the far end of the pipe and swung it wide.

'OK, folks, the Prophet will see you.' He pointed to the big house on the hill.

The Kombi rumbled along a well-kept earthen road bordered by vibrant Purple Warrior's Plume flowers. Orderly rows of what Spencer thought looked like cabbage or collards crowded the rich dirt. The musty earthy aroma of freshly turned soil was pleasant and strangely reassuring.

'They sure take their horticulture seriously, Spencer. Do you like flowers?'

'Yeah, I guess. I mean, sooner or later they grow on you,' he said, with a grin.

Savannah rolled her eyes.

'I think I'm finally getting a handle on your Aussie humour.'

'About time. Meanwhile just check out those four nearly completed houses next to Stanford's mansion. There must be about thirty tradesmen beavering away. Very impressive. They're not going to be for the proletariat, that's for sure.'

Each individual house, born of an architect's plan, lived and breathed as a perfect accompaniment to the nearby mansion. The impressive dwellings were a combination of timber and concrete with tall glass windows giving a view of the mountains. Spencer could imagine taking in the changing of the seasons from the comfort of an easy chair.

'One thing's for sure, they cost a lot. Where does the money come from?' Savannah snorted.

'That's one of the things we're going to find out.'

Spencer was fast getting the impression Stanford Delaware's laid-back commune was rather more than another eccentric hippie movement. He wondered if he and Savannah hadn't bitten off more than they could chew. He imagined unseen eyes watching as they turned into the semicircular drive.

Before them, impressive wide timbered steps led up to the oak and glass doors and a broad veranda scattered with an array of cane furniture. Spencer could picture being draped on the chaise longue, martini in hand, watching as the workers toiled in the fields below, just as they were doing now, in the weak winter sunlight.

'My God, there must be at least fifty of 'em.'

'I have a feeling that's what our role is going to be.' Savannah grunted.

A stunning white Silver Cloud Rolls Royce parked in front of the house completed the scene. Savannah and Spencer trotted up the five broad timbered steps and made their way to the front door.

'Well, here goes.' Spencer rang the doorbell; it had a loud cheery sound as if each visitor was reason for celebration. A dozen or so of the closest workers stopped and stared. Spencer waved. No acknowledgement, no smile or wave in return. Savannah shivered.

'You'd never guess what that reminds me of?'

'What?'

'It's sorta like being back in South Dakota and I'm looking at a bunch of cattle and they just stare blankly and then go back to chewing their cud.'

'Yeah, I thought the same, only sheep in Australia.'

'I think we're looking for something suspicious, when, I mean seriously, what do you expect farm labourers to do? Cartwheels and throw their hats into the air?' Savannah grinned.

'Just look over there.' Spencer pointed.

Two men, wearing bib and brace coveralls had rolled a wooden trolley laden with a large steel tub. The workers gathered around as a beverage was poured into mugs and handed around.

'Well, they're certainly being looked after,' Savannah said, approvingly.

'Savannah, Spencer,' the voice of Stanford rang out from the open doorway. 'Come in, come in. So nice to see you both.'

Stanford held the door open and ushered them inside to a small lobby. The floor was made of gray slate, separated from the lounge area by a frosted glass partition.

'Let me take your coats.'

Stanford hung the jackets on a timber rack with a dozen steel coat hooks and then opened the door revealing an expansive living room. *Shock and awe,* Spencer thought, admiring the soaring ceilings and flooring of sanded and stained red oak planks. One wall was dominated by a fireplace radiating warmth and cosiness as burning logs crackled.

The massive picture window overlooked the valley, the mountains, the workers, their cabins and a collection of timber sheds. At the far reach of the commune, they observed a medium-sized rectangular red brick building. A tall chimney pumped thick smoke into the pristine mountain air.

'Come in, come in. Take the load off.' Stanford pointed at a large cream leather divan. Rock music blared from the hi-fi system.

'Hang on a minute. I'll turn this off.'

A Dual turntable, with a bank of speakers belted out a "Hard Day's Night," by the Beatles. Poised dramatically on a white rug, sat an ebony Steinway grand piano. Stanford clicked the off switch and watched as the stylus lifted. Carefully picking up the album, he softly blew off imaginary dust and lovingly slipped the record into its sleeve. He proudly held the cover up, highlighting the twenty black and white photos of the Fab Four.

'What a band, eh? '

'We're both fans, aren't we, Savannah?'

Savannah glared at Spencer for the briefest of moments. Turning to Stanford, she gushed, 'Absolutely. Love 'em to bits.'

'Right you are.' Stanford rubbed his hands together. 'Now, how about a refreshing drink. You both must be gasping?'

Seated on the cream leather lounge, Savannah and Spencer each accepted a tumbler of the same refreshment they'd received in Delaware's trailer.

'I must say, Stanford, this really is a delightful concoction. What is it exactly?' Spencer sipped his drink.

'Ah, now, that really is a secret. I could tell you but then…'

'You'd have to kill us, right?' Savannah laughed.

Over the next hour Stanford explained in detail how the commune worked. Spencer peered at their host, who appeared to have an aura. He glanced at Savannah who hung on Stanford's every word. Stanford spoke affectionately about different commune members and how their lives had been transformed since joining the American Family.

'Sadly, although lives and attitudes have been changed by the flower power revolution and the words of Dylan, Baez, the Stones and the Beatles.' Stanford paused, then picked up the Hard Day's Night record cover.

'Where was I? Oh yes, even though these geniuses, these soothsayers are changing the way people think, unfortunately the scourge of drugs, introduced by the capitalists to enslave our youth, are wreaking havoc. But the American Family will bring about change. Oh yes, there will be not only a new America, but a new world.'

Spencer found himself nodding in agreement. It all seemed to make perfect sense.

'Let me refill your glasses.' Stanford leaned forward, topping up their drinks.

'We noticed what appears to be four very grand houses under construction.' Savannah spoke.

'Magnificent, aren't they?' Stanford said with pride. 'There is a story behind them. As our message of hope spreads, we are attracting more and more wonderful people. Those homes are being purpose built for some, how shall I put it? Just let me say, very influential people who will win over the hearts and minds of the cynics. More and more people of influence and power are becoming a part of the Family'. I tell you, Spencer, Savannah, we are changing the world.'

Savannah and Spencer nodded in agreement.

Finally, the message drew to a close.

'Well, enough of the commercial.' Stanford rubbed his hands together 'So, of course we're delighted to have you both. There is some paperwork in your cabin, some forms we need you to sign. Honestly, government nowadays. Just the usual stuff, names place of birth, social security number. You may stay as long as you like. All we ask is that you become willing workers in our little slice of paradise. We have concerts, poetry readings. There are some very artistic people here. Anyway, again, enough of the sales pitch.'

More than anything Spencer wanted to be a part of this Nirvana. He now questioned whether any of his past life had any meaning. Stanford grasped a small brass bell from the coffee table. At the sound of the bell pealing, a tall gaunt man in a multi-coloured robe and sandals appeared.

'Ah, Roberto, show our guests to their cabin. And Savannah, Spencer, breakfast is at seven in the great hall.' He pointed to an impressive two-storey brick building with a gabled roof, and wide veranda overlooking a well-tended green canvas of lawn.

'You have luggage?' Roberto asked as they stepped outside.

'Yes, in our van,' Savannah replied.

'Give me the keys. Later I will park it somewhere secure. Grab your luggage and follow me.'

Without hesitation, Spencer handed over the keys, then counted a row of ten cabins immediately to their right. Bags in hand, they followed Roberto who said nothing. At the third hut, Roberto pointed.

'Here is your new home.' The cabin was made of oak logs, the timber's natural beauty radiating a warmth as if it had been waiting to welcome them. A small veranda with two steamer chairs overlooked a neat patch of lawn. In the distance, a solitary deer picked its way delicately across a meadow of clover and grass.

CHAPTER 10

THE END OF THE LINE

The man knew his life was about to end.

'Ronny, what the fuck have I done?'

Ronny Delgado leaned on his shovel, wiping his brow.

'What you have done, Marty, is created a lot of work for us. Isn't that right, Perez?'

Perez threw another load of coal into the combustion chamber. The cast iron doors of the oven were open, revealing the lining of heat-resistant refractory bricks. The cremator was an industrial furnace able to generate temperatures of 980 degrees Celsius.

Sweat ran in rivulets down Ronny and Perez's faces. Perez now paused, wiping his face with a dirty black and white bandana.

'Reckon she hot enough, Ronny.'

It was a fair-sized storeroom, originally a granary. Brushed concrete flooring with red brick walls stretching upwards, it was a building of function. Meagre furnishings included an old wrought iron bed with a stained mattress and an old tanker desk, with a flat surface and three drawers on either side. The unfortunate Marty sat on the floor, naked, hands and feet both cuffed.

'Ronny, please. Just tell me what I have done?'

Ronny pulled up a bentwood chair and sat behind the desk. He rifled through the top draw and pulled out some papers.

'Right, here we are. Martin Farrell, born sixth of June in, wow, Hong Kong. How interesting. And we have your social security number, good. Marty, tell me, Hong Kong?'

'It was wartime, my father was a British sailor. It's a long story.'

'I'm sure it is. Actually, I don't really give a fuck.' Ronny glanced at his watch.

'Ronny, I beg you. What have I done? Please?' Marty sobbed.

'For fuck's sake, shut up. You're giving me a headache. Marty, it's simple, you were going to leave. You made the mistake of telling your roommate you were thinking of talking to the press. And as it happens, you're worth more dead than alive.'

Ronny opened another drawer and grabbed a Walther PPK pistol with an attached silencer. *Pfft.* A small hole appeared in Marty's forehead.

CHAPTER 11

HI HO, HI HO, IT'S OFF TO WORK WE GO

It was one of those baby-blue skies, not the psychedelic candy-blue nor the laundered grey so characteristic of wintry mornings. The only blemish on the landscape was the thick plume of smoke billowing from the old granary.

Savannah sang as she harvested cabbages, cutting through the tough stem with a sharp knife and throwing the leafy vegetable into a funnel-shaped wooden hopper. She paused, wiping her brow with an old red bandanna she'd found in their cabin.

'Hey, Spencer, how's it hanging?'

Spencer wielded a garden fork to dig up carrots.

'Great, never better.'

The month they'd spent sweating in the fields had toughened them. Spencer's six pack had become an eight. Around them at least fifty workers toiled happily, singing, cracking jokes and laughing. A lot of laughter.

'Here comes the drinks.'

'Hey Perez, over here man, I'm parched.' A bearded man with long blonde hair yelled.

'Ok, compadres. Have a break!' Perez yelled in return. He was a hard muscled man, short and squat, his long black hair in a ponytail. He poured the orange drink into tin mugs; workers downed tools and drank their fill.

As the day drew to a close, Spencer actually relished the ache of his back from kneeling over the harvest of fresh carrots; he enjoyed the smell of the earthy loam. He was content.

'You're an Aussie?'

Spencer straightened up, rubbing his aching back. He grinned at the speaker, a lean raw-boned lanky man in tattered jeans, a blue polo-necked sweater and a large brass 'ban the bomb' pendant dangling on a metal chain around his neck.

'Peace, brother. Randy, from Ohio.' He held out a grubby hand and offered Spencer a cigarette.

'No thanks, Randy. I don't smoke. Spencer, and yes, I'm an Australian, and over there.' Spencer pointed at Savannah. 'My sister, Savannah is from South Dakota.'

'South Dakota? Australia?' Randy lit a cigarette, scratching his head.

'Well, it's a long story.' Spencer laughed.

'It seems the Prophet has attracted people from everywhere. I came here with my buddy, Marty; he was born in Hong Kong. Do you know him? Short fella, always wore one of those goddam ponchos.'

Spencer vaguely remembered a quiet, serious man he'd noticed in the recreation hall playing chess and loudly discussing politics.

'Yeah, I'm a bit worried. Marty is one of these guys that wanted to right wrongs. The rich are getting richer, the poor are getting poorer, that sort of thing. He was one of the few here who had any complaints.'

'You said "was" past tense? Did something happen to him?'

'Dunno. We share, or I should say, shared a cabin. I woke up yesterday, he wasn't there. I went to work picking radishes and when I got back to the cabin that night, he was gone.'

'Weird. Have you asked anyone?

'I spoke to Perez. He's the only guy here I don't like. I don't know what his story is, but…' Randy looked nervously over his shoulder. 'He's not like everyone else. Never smiles. Know what I mean?'

Spencer said nothing.

'Yeah, Marty and me and another fellow, Joshua, he was from New York, Yonkers. We all came here from a commune in Missouri.'

'Did you ask this guy, Joshua, about Marty?'

'No. Here's the thing. Joshua just up and left about two weeks ago. Never said diddly.'

'Was there any sort of problem? Complaints, that sort of thing?'

Once again, the nervous glance.

'Joshua and Marty were peas in a pod. Political. Know what I mean?'

'You mean like conspiracy theories?' Spencer asked.

'I guess. Joshua said he was gonna have things out with the Prophet. Dunno exactly what. All this produce? We work it. We harvest it. We don't get nothin' 'ceptin' our keep. He reckoned he was going to the press. Then pshht, he's gone.'

The drinks trolley rolled up silently behind them, an unsmiling Perez whispered.

'You spreading your bullshit again, Randy? Joshua up and left, just like that other *hijo de puta*. How about more work less talk.'

Randy spun around.

'You don't scare me, Perez, I'm not being paid. If I want to have a powwow I can. Who are you, anyway, the goddam drinks waiter?' Randy grabbed a mug from the trolley. 'Hey boy, fill 'er up, and be quick about it.' Randy turned and winked at Spencer.

'You son of a bitch.' Perez grabbed Randy by the throat, wielding a large Bowie knife.

Spencer was alarmed. 'Hey Perez, drop the blade. Randy was just talking.'

'Shut your trap. I might just slit his throat. Stay out of it, or you're next. *Comprende?*'

With one deft blow Spencer karate chopped Perez's forearm. Perez screamed as he dropped the knife. Bellowing obscenities, he knelt, grabbing the weapon in his other hand, lunging at Spencer. Randy gasped as he watched Spencer's response. A solid kick crunched into Perez's groin. His eyes bulged. Dropping the knife, he fell to his knees struggling for breath.

Spencer waited until Perez appeared to have recovered and tried helping him to his feet.

'I'm sorry, Perez, but you can't just pull knives on people. Randy didn't mean any harm. Did you, Randy?'

As Spencer spoke Perez launched himself, trying to wrap Spencer in a bear hug.

'Perez, come on man.' Spencer grabbed his right arm, twisting it behind his back. Perez howled. Spencer threw him bodily into the drinks cart. As the urn fell into the dirt and bright orange liquid gushed into the soil, tin mugs scattered amongst the row of vegetables. Perez rolled onto his back screaming at Spencer in Spanish. Across the field, stunned workers gaped at the sight of the feared Perez covered in liquid and lying in a pile of horse manure. From the veranda the Prophet watched the proceedings with interest.

CHAPTER 12

COMMUNE NIGHTS

Savannah and returned to their cabin, both a little bemused at the latest turn of events.

Savannah grinned at him. 'What a day. I turn my back and you're at it again.'

'Watch it or you'll be next. Now go to the fridge and get me some of that delightful cordial. And be quick about it.'

'Yes, master.'

'Actually, I must admit, I reckon I'm suffering withdrawal symptoms. I'd really like to know just what's in that concoction. It really puts a rosy glow on the day.'

Spencer gazed through the window of their cabin at the now deserted fields. Savannah mooched over to the fridge, returning with a pitcher of the beverage. She held a tray with two glasses and the plastic container, filled to the brim. Spencer was plonked on the settee his bare feet resting on the coffee table.

'Dammit.' Savannah tripped on the spotless red rug.

'Oh shit. Now you've done it,' Spencer remarked, staring in dismay at the orange stain. 'Hell, we'd better clean it.'

After washing the rug, they hung it over the balcony to dry. Yanking on his boots, Spencer said, 'Well, time to go to the mess hall for dinner.'

The lights of the dining room beckoned as they strolled in the twilight along the bitumen pathway.

'How are you feeling, Savannah?'

'What do you mean? I'm a bit sore. Being a field hand is hard work.'

'That's not exactly what I meant. Stop me if I'm sounding foolish. But usually, we have some of that blasted cordial three or four times a day. Because of that nonsense with Perez, we didn't have a drink this afternoon, then you tripped, we had none, this evening. And I know this sounds silly but all of a sudden, I'm feeling…I don't know how to describe it. Anxious, I guess.'

Savannah's brows knitted. 'Darn, you're right. I thought it was just me. You don't really think…?'

'When Perez pulled that Bowie knife, at the time, I just thought… well, I'm not sure exactly what I thought. But I reckon he really would have cut that fellow Randy's throat. I think Perez is one evil bastard.'

'I think you've nailed it. What the hell's happened to us? Ronny Delgado is one of Stanford's men. We know he's one very bad dude. And remember when we met Stanford, and we first drunk this stuff, we walked out all starry-eyed like goddam teenagers in love with Sinatra.'

'I'm not sure teenagers still love Sinatra. Paul McCartney perhaps.'

'Whatever,' Savannah snapped.

Spencer swung open the double door to the mess hall. The room went quiet as every eye honed in on them. Long wooden trestle tables stood side by side. Impossibly high vaulted ceilings crisscrossed with sturdy timber beams added to the ambience. Picture windows with a view stretching to distant mountains created an image of permanence and order. Waiters scurried to and fro, out of the industrial-sized kitchen, wheeling trolleys of food. Hordes of chefs, kitchen hands and dishwashers toiled in the steaming kitchen.

At the far end of the hall a raised bandstand with a collection of musical instruments and a bank of speakers sat waiting. A large black and white picture of the Beatles playing a live gig somewhere, served as a backdrop.

'Check out the stage, Savannah. It looks like we may be having some entertainment. Maybe Stanford has enough clout to get the Beatles themselves up there belting out a tune.'

'Let's hope not. I hate loud music. Especially rock and roll. Let's eat, and if a noisy band comes on, we can quietly up and leave.'

A burly waiter with a multi-coloured mohawk held out a tray of drinks. Savannah glanced sideways at Spencer and shook her head. Spencer grabbed two of the mugs.

'Thanks buddy. Nice haircut.'

The big guy mumbled a response.

They threaded through the packed dining room, now alive with chatter, and took a seat at a long trestle table. Savannah whispered.

'Why did you take the drinks?'

'Don't touch the stuff. When no one's looking just, I don't know, pour it on the floor, throw it out the window. Use your imagination. I could be wrong but I'm beginning to think it's mandatory. Everyone seems to be swilling the stuff.'

Mountains of food started to arrive from the kitchen on wooden trolleys pushed by a motley collection of men and women in the uniform of the day, bell bottom jeans and tie-dyed t-shirts.

'What is it with that goddam rock and roll band?' Savannah pointed at the walls of the dining room. Large black and white photos of the fab four adorned the walls. Beatles song "We Can Work It Out" blared from a juke box.

'Hey, they are the greatest music phenomenon of all time. I love this song. Did you see their movie?'

'They made a movie? Well fancy that. Academy Award winner, was it? Jesus, give me a break. Would you please stop singing along with that stupid song and pass me one of those rolls, Spencer dear?'

'Excuse me, mate.' Spencer smiled at the vacant face of a round-faced bespectacled guy next to him, as he reached for a wicker tray of bread rolls.

'Yeah, man. Say this's a groove isn't it?' He had a dreamy smile and slurred his words.

Spencer noticed a lean sharp eyed Hispanic guy sitting opposite, his stare as uncomfortable as a chorus girl's corset.

'Buenas noches, I haven't seen you two before. Why are you here?'

'The Prophet has asked us to be here,' Savannah said quietly, 'and you?'

'And me, what?' the man's eyes narrowed.

'My sister just wants to know why you're here, my friend. I mean, it's a great little commune, isn't it? My name's Spencer. This is my sister, Savannah.' Spencer held out his hand. The man grasped it fleetingly.

'My name's Xavier.'

'Cool. And what do you do here, Xavier?'

'What I don't do, señor, is ask questions.'

'Look, Spencer, big bowls of chilli. Wow! I love Mexican food. Nice to meet you, Xavier.'

Xavier grunted and ladled food into his bowl.

Spencer winked at Savannah who shrugged. Xavier certainly didn't fit the bill of *peace, love and understanding.*

CHAPTER 13

A ROCKIN' GOOD NIGHT

Dessert was a New York cheesecake with all the pizzazz of Hollywood; a total East Coast-West Coast mash up, pitch perfect; a superb creamy confection.

'I thought Inez was a great cook. She is a great cook, but the food here is something else. I reckon I'm going to be putting on a few pounds if we're here for too long.'

Savannah licked her spoon. Spencer swallowed his last morsel.

'That was so good. Hey, look the lights are dimming.'

A round of applause erupted from the diners as four long-haired guys strode confidently on to the stage, three picked up their guitars. The drummer sat at his Ludwig kit and adjusted his high-hat cymbals. The bass player tapped his mike and nodded at his fellow musicians. The heavy back beat and uncomplicated lyrics of *She Loves You,* one of the earliest Beatle songs, blasted the room. Erupting into applause, the audience shouted their approval.

'Hey, these blokes are great.' Spencer's feet were tapping.

'Give me a break.' Savannah held her hands over her ears. 'I don't think I can stand too much of this.'

'Apart from the fact I love the music, I really think we have to stick around and see what's happening. I could be wrong, but I reckon these guys are a warm-up act for something or someone. But not only are they just about as good as the Beatles, they even look like the Beatles. Hell, look at the guy playing the Rickenbacker Guitar, he's the spitting image of John Lennon. In fact, they all look just like them, it's amazing.'

'Wonderful, but seriously, who cares?' Savannah yelled.

Segueing into a medley of Beatle hits, the band kept the house rocking. Couples began dancing in the aisles, singing along with the band and laughing. The group kept pumping. The volume blasted. After a half an hour the guys put down their instruments, the bass player paused for effect, then announcing:

'And now, groovers, the moment you have all waited for.'

The house lights dimmed. A single spotlight burst into life and from the wings strode Stanford Delaware, the Prophet, wearing a voluminous pure white robe. Erupting into applause, everyone jumped to their feet. Savannah whispered to Spencer.

'You're kidding me. I'm not going to stand.'

'We're converts, remember?' Spencer hauled her up roughly.

Basking in the glory, Stanford stood motionless a half smile on his face. It reminded Spencer of black and white footage he'd seen of Nazi Party rallies in the 1930s.

'How about a round of applause for the band.'

Stanford clapped; the crowd joined in.

'Excellent job, boys.' Stanford turned, smiling at the four musicians.' Yep. Our band did a great job as always. In a few months' time, however, the actual Beatles, John, Paul, George and Ringo will be invited to perform right here.'

Savannah nudged Spencer.

'He's nuts. That'll never happen.'

It was almost as if the Prophet had heard, when he announced, 'Why would the Beatles want to perform for us, you ask?'

'Yes indeed, you goddam head case,' Savannah muttered.

'We are the Family,' Stanford thundered. 'We are the new world order. We have the arms, we have the people. The world is tired of the capitalist nightmare that's enslaved millions and done nothing but make the rich richer and the poor poorer.

Peace, love and understanding is not just a mindless mantra, it's real. Sadly, there will be casualties. That's inevitable. But the scourge of capitalism cannot be defeated at the ballot box. The reality is the ordinary citizens of America are hungry for change. In one coordinated attack we will take over the radio stations and television networks and believe me, when you control them and we tell the world what we have planned, hearts and minds will follow. The music of Dylan, the Byrds, the Beatles, the Rolling Stones and so many more already spreading the word. Just listen to the music of today. No wonder the establishment is scared. The youth of America have already discarded capitalism and the trappings of wealth. We will be the first of the glorious guerrillas, we will move amongst the people as the fish swims in the sea. Remember this, my brothers and sisters, political power grows out of the barrel of a gun. We have the guns and we have the people. Are you with me?'

CHAPTER 14
COUNTING THE LOOT

Stanford held court behind his huge oak desk. In one corner of the office stood an impressive floor to ceiling torch and drill resistant state of the art Chubb safe. Its massive heavy door was open, exposing stacks of $100 bills.

'Ok, Perez, you first. How much do you have?'

'Better than expected, Stanford.' Perez grinned as he handed over a stout old-fashioned leather steamer trunk. The three men in the room gasped at the neat bundles.

'Wow, compadre. How much?' Xavier asked.

'$90,000'

'Any problems, Perez?' Stanford tipped the bag upside down, bank notes spilling over the desk.

'Not really. Well sort of. The old guy was, well, he was old.'

'And?' Stanford asked.

'I smacked him around. Not that hard. He showed me where the money was and he had a heart attack. Sorry boss.'

'Don't worry, Perez, he was just another capitalist pig. He won't be missed. You cleaned up?'

'Yeah, like you showed me. No prints. No nothing.'

'Good work.'

'Ronny, how did the last bank job go?'

'Not bad. Unfortunately, Xavier shot the security guard.'

'Dead?'

'Hey Stanford, it wasn't my fault, The prick went for his gun,' Xavier whined.

'Don't worry about it, Xavier. The guard was as much a part of the money-making machine as the head of GMH. How much?'

'75 Gs.' Ronny replied.

'Not bad. But that's not all.' Stanford nodded his approval.

'The insurance money?' Ronny smiled.

'You got it. Joshua Phelps's policy paid out $150,000. Courtesy of Bankers Life and Fidelity of Indiana and Marty Ferguson paid $120,000 from Allied and General of Philadelphia.'

'That was one smart move, Stanford, insuring those guys. No problems?' Ronny asked.

'No, so long as we only get people who don't have any known close relatives there shouldn't be a problem.'

'That's a sweet deal, Stanford. Are there any more prospects from our bunch of happy campers?' Ronny asked.

'As it happens, there are two new ones. When they have outlived their usefulness they'll be next. They're brother and sister.'

CHAPTER 15

TWO TIRED FIELD HANDS

Spencer and Savannah slumped in their steamer chairs, the twilight fading into a comfortable black. Examining the callouses on his hands, Spencer realised he hadn't minded the work; he reckoned he was fitter than he'd ever been. But where was it all going? So far there was nothing other than another "save the world" cult, albeit with some nasty criminal adherents. Surely Delaware's grandiose revolution was only talk? Was Ronny Delgado now a reformed criminal? Surely not, after the state they'd found Agent Tod in. But then there was that nasty bastard Perez and that "no questions" guy Xavier. Something was definitely off.

'Penny for them?'

'Huh?' Spencer knew his mind was elsewhere. He was now thinking of home, his wife Michiyo and his daughter Trilby. He and Michiyo had been discussing a holiday to England, taking Trilby with them. Home, he thought, should be a place of safety above all, but he knew that he, Spencer Marlowe, could be wrenched back in time at any moment. First the vivid colours, then the noise, the sensation of tumbling, it was no longer a surprise. He now accepted this was his life. How it would end, or even if it would end, he had no idea. *You can only deal with cards you've been dealt.*

'What did you say? Something about cards?'

'Nothing. I think I was falling asleep. I'm worn out.'

'Working as a field hand is hard work. Some of Stanford's fruit drink would be nice,' Savannah grumbled.

Spencer had to smile at the normally neat and tidy Savannah, sitting there in stained jeans and a worn plaid shirt. She was rubbing the blisters on her bare feet.

'You're telling me. I'm walking like my limbs don't really belong to me and each step is a negotiation rather than an order. Everything hurts now. Every bloody thing. I wince to cross the floor. I don't know how long we're supposed to keep this charade up. So far all I can determine is Stanford is a grade A nutter and that guy Perez is a nasty piece of work, but that's not a crime. Bloody hell I'm sore,' Spencer complained.

'And what about that creep, Xavier? If he hasn't done some serious jail time I'd be surprised.'

'There's something else. A couple of things, actually.'

Savannah yawned. 'Let's hear it.'

'Remember when we first met Stanford in his trailer, and we more or less swallowed his bullshit, and we left all starry eyed?'

'Yeah, sure. But we've figured out it was something to do with that blasted orange fruit drink,' Savannah replied.

'Whatever is in that drink it's pretty obvious that's what's being used to keep everyone compliant. It's being drunk every day by everyone, as far as I can see. So, what could be in it. You must have covered this sort of stuff in your FBI training?'

Savannah sat bolt upright. 'You're right. It could be a cocktail in fact. And I have an idea; I could be wrong...'

'Go for it.'

'Spencer, have you ever heard of scopolamine?'

'Isn't that a truth drug? Used for interrogations?'

'It is, but there's more to it than that. It has an interesting nickname.'

'Tell me more.'

She did. It was also known as "Devil's Breath". She vaguely recalled that it was derived from the borrachero shrub, either the flower or the leaf, she couldn't recall. It was common in one South American country or another. She wanted to say

Columbia. It wasn't even a controlled substance. The thing with scopolamine was it didn't necessarily enable the perpetrator to control the victim's mind like a puppet master; the induced state of confusion and compliance can make the victim way more susceptible to suggestion. The downside is that it generally brought about quite a degree of lethargy.

'Well, there's certainly no sign of that, everyone seems to be working hard. Not a lot of lethargy on display.'

'Oh yeah but…'

Spencer had risen to grab some water from the fridge, though he'd been hoping for some beer. 'But?'

'This is hush hush, but I do know the boffins at the FBI were working on a goddam cocktail with this stuff.'

'Why would they do that?'

'Jesus, Spencer, how would I know? My guess is they might want to keep someone compliant but still completely with it. Anyway, what they came up with was a mixture of scopolamine, amphetamines and some other drug, I forget exactly.'

'So, the thing is that's probably not even particularly illegal. Not like coke or heroin?'

She shrugged and sagged into the chair. 'I don't know. It'd be a hard one.'

'Ok, moving along. What is it with the Beatles?' He crossed the room and peeked out of the curtains at the deepening gloom toward Delaware's mansion. Their suspicion about the orange drink made him uneasy, so Delaware's obsession with the Beatles grew even stranger. 'I mean, there's photos of them everywhere. Stanford spoke like they were gods. That's seriously weird. Then there was the band playing their songs where we had dinner. Actually, those band members are part of the commune. I saw a couple of them working in the field. The bass player was driving a tractor.'

'Yuk, I hate their goddam music.' Savannah screwed up her face.

'I can't see anything sinister in that. Weird, certainly but I can't see how that can go anywhere.'

'Agreed. But I'd prefer it if he enjoyed Tony Bennett.'

'You're definitely not a groovy flower power gal, are you? Anyway, we're going to have to keep Dale informed. I haven't seen a phone anywhere. Who knows how far we'll have to go to find one? As soon as we have a day off, we're going to have to go for a drive to the nearest town, wherever that is.'

Savannah peered into the gloom.

'It looks like we have a visitor.'

A tall, lean figure approached.

'That's Roberto, I wonder what he wants?'

'Good evening, muchachos,' a smiling Roberto said.

'Nice to see you, Roberto. What can we do for you?' Spencer asked. He thought lanky, gaunt Roberto seemed a little friendlier today.

'I'm here to pick up the papers I left. Have you filled them out with your details?'

'Gosh, sorry. We've both been working so hard, I must confess I think we both simply forgot. Savannah?'

'Spencer's right. How about we do that tonight and can you pick them up, say tomorrow night?'

'Sure, not a problem. Buenas noches.'

'Oh, there is one thing, Roberto,' Spencer said.

'Yes?'

'My sister and I thought we might take our vehicle out for a drive to the nearest town on our day off. Where is our Volkswagen? In a garage somewhere, I guess?'

'Why do you want to leave? Everything you need is here?'

'Hang on, Roberto, we're not leaving. We just want to do some exploring. You know, tourist stuff.'

'I see. As you say, your Kombi is in a garage with a lot of other automobiles. I'm pretty sure it had a flat tire, and it's parked behind a heap of other vehicles. It'd be very difficult to get it out. How about I let you know when the other cars and trucks are moved out.'

'And when would that be Roberto?' Savannah asked, her eyes narrowing.

'Señora, please. At the moment we are very busy. If it can just wait a few days. I tell you what, as soon as our mechanic has a moment I'll get him to change your tire, and he'll drive the Kombi to your cabin. How would that be, eh?'

CHAPTER 16

INTERESTING PAPERWORK

Spencer and Savannah took a seat at the kitchen table and began poring over the stack of papers.

'Bloody hell, they certainly want to know our details. We're going to have to tell a few porkies.'

'Porkies?'

'Sorry, Savannah, an Australianism. Porkies, pork pies. Lies. Get it?' Rhyming slang.'

'Silly me. If ever I have the misfortune to go to your home country, I don't think I'll understand a goddam word. How about some coffee before we start?'

Climbing wearily to her feet, Savannah filled the kettle and plugged it in. Opening the well-stocked pantry, she grabbed the French press and spooned in coffee from a ceramic container.

'You can't complain about the way this place is organised. We have everything. Have you had a good look? We have bacon, eggs, cereal, bread, butter. And plenty of that damn cordial. The kitchen is well equipped.'

'It's amazing. They have a bakery, a butcher, it seems like it's a completely self-sufficient little town. Maybe that's why Roberto wanted to know why we needed to go exploring?'

'You really believe that?' Savannah glared.

'No. Not really.'

Savannah took a sip of her coffee.

'Spencer, have you read all of this stuff? I have. They want all details of our next of kin. They want our height, weight, any medical history, our age. This's seriously weird. I'm not telling them my darn weight. It's none of their business.'

Spencer examined the documents closely.

'Do you know what this looks like?'

'You mean apart from being an invasion of our privacy?'

'Apart from that. This reminds me of when I filled out forms when I applied for a life insurance policy.'

***

Spencer sat bolt upright in bed, waking with a start. Heart racing, he slid from nightmare to reality as he rubbed his eyes, trying to focus on the room around him. He shivered at the now fading image of a ghoulish Stanford Delaware, dripping fangs and a bloody scalpel in hand, looming over him as he lay helpless and unable to move. Right at that moment he wished he'd woken up in the next century, with his beautiful wife, Michiyo, by his side, but he knew the puppeteer had other plans.

His shaking hand reached for the bedside lamp, clicking it on. A vague fear still haunting him, he tried to shake it off as he checked his Bulova watch for the time; 5.25 am, just enough time for a shower and a quick breakfast before the truck packed with workers would arrive like clockwork at 6 am.

Groggily climbing out of bed he peered through the window. He enjoyed waking up to skies lit by the wintry sun. He thought of it as a sort of visual poetry and a stark contrast to the images that had tormented him in his nightmare. What had it meant? Had it just been an aberrant dream... or did it warn of something more foreboding?

'Wake up, Savannah, bacon eggs toast and coffee in fifteen,' Spencer yelled, making his way to the bathroom.

She groaned. 'Do you mind if I take the day off? Joking of course.''

Spencer busied about the kitchen, allowing the routine of cooking to take him to a meditative state. Stanford Delaware, time travel, Michiyo, Trilby, and the deepening wrongness about this place vanished beneath seasoning the eggs, flipping the bacon, and brewing a pot of joe. It was a welcome distraction from the unidentifiable danger they'd embedded themselves into. Two loaded plates and steaming cups later, his reverie was over.

'There you go, girl, eggs over easy, crispy bacon, just as you like it, and coffee.'

'Thanks, Spencer.' Savannah leaned down and laced up her shoes. 'This looks great.' She took a slurp of her coffee. 'What's on the agenda today?'

'Spreading mulch, weeding. I think they want to plant some spuds.'

'And I suppose you might thump poor old Perez again. Bully!'

Spencer grinned.

'I'm sure dear Perez won't be difficult. It'll be a nice day, at one with nature.'

'Frankly I've just about had all the nature I can stand. We don't seem to be making a lot of progress.'

'What about those papers we filled out? You don't think...?'

Savannah interrupted. 'C'mon, Spencer. A bit farfetched. Stanford insures his workers and then knocks them off. That's like a bad movie.'

'And the scopolamine?'

'It's only a theory, and even if I'm right I'm not sure that would fly. If that's the best we can come up with it's hardly the smoking gun that would have the Feds swarming over the joint. Frankly, I'd like to ask Dale if we can pull out.'

'You're forgetting something.'

'That is?'

'We still don't seem to have our trusty vee dub.'

'Rubbish. It's obvious that it's as Roberto said, it's parked with a lot of other vehicles and it's hard to get to. Anyway, he said the mechanic would sort it out. I'm sure if we insist, we can go and get it. There won't be a problem. Let's go, the truck's here.'

CHAPTER 17
PEREZ HAS A BAD DAY

Spencer helped Savannah onto the back of the old green international pickup. He recognised Grady and one of the musicians from the other night. And a scowling Perez. *What a miserable-looking sod.*

'G'day, Grady.'

'Yo, Spencer, Savannah.' Grady waved and gave them a cheerful grin.

Savannah squeezed onto the crowded bench. Spencer held out a hand to the Beatle lookalike.

'G'day, mate. Spencer, and this is my sister, Savannah. We both loved your music.'

'Thanks, buddy. I'm the lead guitarist. Obviously, we're not as good as the real Beatles, but I guess you'll see that for yourself, soon enough.'

'Yep, I guess we will.'

Savannah leaned into Spencer whispering, 'What the hell is he on about?'

Spencer shrugged and whispered, 'No idea. I think he's been eating too many magic mushrooms. But it's uncanny, Grady is the lead guitar and he looks just like George Harrison.'

'Who?'

'George, he's one of the Beatles. The lead guitar, coincidentally enough.'

'Really? Fascinating.' Savannah yawned.

'Hey. you're here to work, not talk.' Perez scowled.

'Hang on, Perez, we're not there yet. What's wrong with a bit of chat?' Spencer snapped.

'Shut it. I won't be so gentle with you next time.'

Spencer's jaw dropped. It was all he could do to not laugh.

'I'll bear that in mind. Thanks, Perez.'

Randy giggled, prompting a scowl from Perez. Spencer managed to cram in next to Savannah.

'I'm sure he has you worried.' Savannah was trying hard not to laugh.

'Let's not upset the moron. Anyway, look over there, if ever we want to go for a drive, check that out.' Spencer pointed.

Parked next to a big garage and workshop a Hispanic woman wearing blue coveralls, her hair covered with a bright red bandanna, was polishing Stanford Delaware's Rolls Royce. The pickup truck lurched to a stop.

'Everybody out and let's get some work done. We got lots to do,' Perez barked.

In front of them a mountain of mulch waited. There were at least two dozen men and women hard at work, planting potatoes, weeding, and spraying. In spite of Perez, Spencer felt good as the dawn chorus of melodic birdsong drifted in. The rising sun cast a rosy hue across the morning sky. Golden fingers of sunlight lit up the scene.

'Jesus, I really shouldn't have come out today. My blisters are killing me,' Grady complained, as he sat on a stack of paving bricks and removed his boot.

'Have a look at this, Spencer.' His toes were bleeding and his heels were red raw.

'You can't work with that foot, Grady. Hey Perez, do you have any liniment or band aids in the truck that Grady can use?'

'What the fuck! Why didn't you sort this out before you arrived, you dumb son of a bitch?' Perez screamed, spittle flying from his mouth.

'Hey. C'mon, Perez. Calm down,' Spencer entreated.

'Who do you think you're talking to?' Perez yelled again.

All the workers stopped and turned placid faces on the combatants. Then everything changed. Perez reached into his coat and yanked out a small silver automatic. Grady cowered as Perez held the pistol an inch from his head.

'You're a useless piece of shit.'

The gunshot sounded more like the boom of a cannon in the still morning air. Grady fell backwards, a neat hole in his head, between his eyes. As Perez turned the gun, Spencer erupted with the Mae Geri jumping kick. Perez flew backwards, his skull splitting against the stack of paving bricks. Momentarily stunned, Spencer gaped.

'Oh shit. We really can't take you anywhere can we, Spencer? Serves him right. Nasty little prick. Is there a second act?' Savannah quipped.

'Enough with the jokes. I think it may be time to leave.'

The workers stood like a group of open-mouthed statues, saying nothing. Spencer didn't bother checking pulses. He knew Grady and Perez were dead.

'I think the keys are still in the truck.'

Spencer's mind was in a whirl as they climbed into the pickup. The keys were in the ignition. The Dodge roared into life. Spencer jammed the gear into first and accelerated.

'So much for thinking this was just a slightly offbeat commune with a slightly wacky leader.' Spencer glanced at the fuel gauge. 'Bloody hell, it's showing just over empty.'

Spencer drove along a cornfield and made a right, taking them past the garage.

'Hey, Spencer, look.'

'I think we might be leaving in style.'

The Hispanic lady looked up, her eyes wide as she paused polishing the long hood of the Rolls Royce.

'We don't want to hurt her, but if she has the keys, she's going to have to hand them over. Ok, Spencer?'

Spencer nodded as he pulled in front of the Rolls. They both climbed out.

'Buenas mañanas,' Savannah said breezily, as she stepped up to the driver's door. 'Do you have the keys?'

'Si.' Her face paled in fright. 'I heard a gunshot. What do you want with the Prophet's car?'

'What's your name?' Savannah asked gently.

'Maria, Ma'am.'

'Maria, there has been some trouble and you must hand over the keys. I don't have time to explain.'

'Where are you going? There's a guard post.'

'Yes, we know that. The keys?' Savannah held out her hand.

Maria dropped her chamois. Retrieving keys from her pocket, she placed them in Savannah's hand.

'Take me with you?'

'Maria, I don't understand. If you're not happy, why don't you just leave?' Spencer asked.

'Señor, you can't leave. But please, we must hurry. There are men with guns. Xavier, Perez, they are bad men.'

CHAPTER 18
WHAT'S NEXT, A FERRARI?

The Rolls Royce sat as if it were formed from flowing metal, aquatic yet feminine with its curves. A thing of beauty.

'I'm driving,' Savannah said firmly as she folded herself into the driver's seat.

Even Spencer, who decidedly wasn't a car person, couldn't help but be impressed with the cream Connolly hide seats and the burled walnut dash.

'Seeing as we're now car thieves we've certainly started our new career on a high note. What's next, a Ferrari? Are you OK, Maria?'

Maria cowered into the corner of the rear seat, gazing fearfully at the two gringos. 'Si señor. I'm just worried they will come for us. These men, they are very cruel.'

Savannah glanced sideways at Spencer.

'I'm beginning to think we might have underestimated exactly how bad this organisation is.'

'I think you might be right. Let's just leave our belongings and get the hell out of Dodge. We're getting some strange looks.'

Labourers in the fields stopped work as the majestic Rolls Royce cruised past.

'Have a look, there's the man himself. Shall I wave?' Spencer grinned as they passed the mansion. Stanford Delaware had been watching the workers. They saw him spring up from his easy chair and gesticulate.

'Maria, do you know if the man at the guard post has a gun?'

'Si, yes. I think. I don't know for sure. I am sorry, señor,' Maria began to cry.

They had passed the haberdashery and the dining hall and were now speeding towards the guard house. They could just see the man's distinctive top hat. He appeared to be on the phone.

'Shit, he's been told, 'Savannah swore, as the man dropped his phone, bolting out of his little hut, pistol in hand.

'Go for it, Savannah.' Spencer turned to Maria. 'Keep your head down.'

Savannah put her foot to the floor. The big British limousine, true to the advertising, hardly murmured as the rear wheels spun and the sedan rocketed forward. The steel barrier smashed off its hinges, two rounds from the guard's pistol ricocheted off the heavy steel body.

'Where the hell are we going? Any ideas Savannah?'

'Look, there's a sign, Clayton. It's a small town, I don't know but I thinks it has about 10,000 people. It's right at the foot of the Diablo mountains. We can phone Dale and tell him what's happened.'

'I'm not looking forward to that; he just hates it when we kill people.'

Savannah grinned. 'Oi, less of the "we", partner.'

'I vote we head to Clayton, phone Dale, check into a motel, and wait for the cavalry. How are you off for cash, Savannah? Maria, do you have relatives, friends in the US?' Spencer asked.

'No, señor, my husband and I came from Mexico a year ago. It hasn't been possible for me to contact anyone. It wasn't allowed.'

'And where is your husband?' Savannah enquired, reaching for her wallet.

It was obvious from her body language Maria had begun to relax but at the mention of her husband her face crumpled. 'My el marido, my…'

'Your husband?' Savannah asked.

'Si, my husband, Santiago, died.' She began to cry again.

Savannah handed her a handkerchief. 'What happened, Maria?'

'They said it was a heart attack. It happened while he was working in the field. But he was strong, fit. There was nothing wrong with him.'

'Excuse me for a minute, Maria. Spencer, I have $20 and some quarters and dimes. You?'

'$35 and some nickels and dimes. Enough for some rooms and a bite to eat.'

'But there was something else,' Maria piped up.

'What was that something, Maria?'

She twisted the handkerchief.

'The day before Santiago died, he got into a fight with Perez. When he came home that night he was scared. I think Perez killed him.'

'Perez isn't going to kill anybody else, Maria. He's dead.' Savannah reached back and took Maria's hand.

'Who did this thing?'

Savannah gave Maria a reassuring smile. 'This hombre, his name is Spencer. My name is Savannah.'

CHAPTER 19
CLAYTON

The whisper-quiet Rolls glided down Mt Diablo. Nestled in the valley below lay the small town of Clayton. They passed the usual welcome signs; apparently The Lions and Rotary were there to help. Savannah slowed at the corner of Oak and Main.

'Where to now, Spencer?'

'We have a sign.' Spencer pointed.

'The Platinum Palisade Motel. Wow, they have television and a pool.' Savanah snickered at the "amenities".

Five minutes later they paused in the parking lot of the motel, engine running, aircon blasting heat as they scanned the surrounds for anything out of the usual. The motel lobby was illuminated with a soft and welcoming light as if it were a sunshine in gentle pastel hue. Savannah asked for two rooms. The clerk, a tall man with high cheekbones and a handlebar moustache, pushed the register towards them.

'Sign here. That'll be twelve bucks even, for the rooms. That your car out there?' He nodded at the Rolls parked in the under croft by the front door.

'No such luck. It's the boss's car. We are, um, delivering it for him.' Spencer smiled disarmingly.

'You don't say? Here's the keys. Check out's at ten.'

The rooms each had two bay windows with a front door in between. Spencer took number 4, Savannah and Maria were at the far end in number 18. Spencer entered and shut the door. The motel, he decided, was the kraft dinner of hospitality. It did the job, pleasant enough, yet absolutely a microwave meal of a place.

The desk clerk picked up the phone as he watched the Rolls Royce park outside of room 18.

CHAPTER 20
A WAITING GAME

Spencer lay on the comfortable king-size bed and switched on the television, flicking through the channels to see if he or Savannah had made it on to America's most wanted. Reaching into his pocket, he felt the faint buzz as his fingers touched the cornicello. His constant companion had been a present given to him by a grateful soldier, Bert Weadley, back in wartime Australia in the 1940s. His only link with the past and future. He remembered vividly when he and Michiyo had travelled to Singapore and the mysterious fortune teller, Madame Zu, had fled the room almost in a panic after examining the trinket.

What had it revealed?

He splashed water on his face and ran a hand over his bristly beard and listened for any unusual noise. Satisfied nothing was amiss, he sprung up, thrusting the cornicello firmly back into his jeans and opened the front door. Nothing had changed. He saw the same motley collection of vehicles in the parking lot. Feeling exposed, he made his way to room 18.

'Who is it?' Savannah answered as he rapped on the door.

Bona fides established, Spencer entered the room. Maria sat on one bed, looking tired and drawn.

'What now, Savannah?' Spencer asked.

'I've called Dale. He's on his way with a few gun-toting agents. He didn't sound too happy. He won't make it until tomorrow, so we'll just have to wait, I guess. I'm going to order room service, and that's it. I feel naked without a weapon.'

'A rare experience.' Spencer chuckled. 'Are you ok, Maria?'

'Si, but Señor Spencer, we are not safe. The Prophet has spies everywhere.'

Spencer didn't know how to respond to that. 'Maria, I have some questions for you.'

Maria nodded.

'Did you see anything suspicious at the commune? Anything that scared you?'

The maid considered this for a time before nodding. 'Yes, si. I had the job of cleaning out this big brick building.'

'Is that the one with the tall chimney?' Savannah asked.

Maria wrung her hands, nodding. 'There was often blood on the floor. It made me scared. I'd heard stories. At first, I didn't believe.'

'What sort of stories, Maria?' Spencer probed.

'I heard that bad things happened there. People died. And then it was said they burnt the bodies. Every time we saw smoke from the tubo de lampera…'

'Sorry, Maria, tubo…?'

'Yes, it's the chimney.'

Spencer and Savannah locked eyes. They had their own crematorium. That wasn't suspicious in the slightest.

'Do you have any proof of these bad things?' Savannah asked.

'No, only I would find stuff. Once I found a passport. And some bank documents from someone who'd been living at the commune and had left suddenly.'

Savannah glance sideways at Spencer.

'Is there anything else, Maria?'

'There is one other thing.'

'What is that?' Spencer asked.

'There is a cabin in the woods. It's hidden away; you have to drive down a narrow track behind the big shed at the end of the cornfields.'

'What is the cabin used for?' Savannah asked.

'I was told to clean it. I had to walk, because I don't drive. It took me a half an hour, and it was all uphill and it was hot.'

'What was in the cabin, Maria?'

'It was terrible. The cabin had a large cell with steel bars. There was blood all over the floor. I think someone had died there.' She began to cry yet again.

'Try and forget all of this, Maria. You are with us now. I'm sorry to keep on asking you stuff, but there is one other small thing.' Spencer still couldn't figure out the rock and roll obsession. 'I'm puzzled about all of the references to "The Beatles". Everywhere there are pictures of them. Delaware seems to be obsessed with them. Grady…' He trailed off, about to say "one of the guitar players in the band that played the other night," but Grady was dead now. 'Grady said that the Beatles will be performing at the commune. What in hell is that all about? Why would a world-famous English rock and roll band come to see the Prophet, and perform there? It doesn't make sense.'

'I don't know, Señor Spencer, but everyone has been talking about it. I do not know this music, but if the Prophet says they will come, they will come.'

'C'mon, Spencer, who cares? We know Stanford is as crazy as a kite with a broken string. I mean, seriously?'

***

Being on the run hadn't diminished anyone's appetite. There was only one slice left of the pepperoni pizza left from the three family size offerings from Skipolini's Italian. Savannah and Spencer had washed it down with cold Budweisers; Maria had Coca Cola.

Spencer burped. 'That was great. Let's hope Dale turns up soon. Meanwhile I'll go back to my unit, watch some TV, and see if we've been featured in the news. You OK, Maria?'

'Si, but I'm scared.'

'It'll soon be over, Maria. Don't worry. When our friends arrive, we'll organise for you to go back to Mexico, OK?' Savannah spoke gently.

Maria tried to smile. Again, Spencer scanned the parking area before making his way to Unit 4.

CHAPTER 21

THE PROPHET IS NOT HAPPY

Ronny BBQ Delgado shivered, sitting next to Xavier Martinez on the sofa in the Prophet's mansion. He had never seen Delaware angry before. Nothing about the stormy expression, the pacing, or the hands clasped behind the man's back helped his nerves in the slightest. He already felt judged and found guilty, but likelihood of imminent punishment was the worst.

'You have both failed me.'

'Stanford, it's not my fault.' Ronny realised his voice sounded like a whine.

'A man can fail many times, Ronny, but he isn't a failure until he begins to blame somebody else.'

'Stanford, I…'

'Be quiet. Just listen. I have new information. What is done, is done. I can't believe it that Perez is dead. But on reflection he's no great loss. It seems he shot that beautiful and talented guitarist, Grady Chamberlin, and then Marlowe killed him. It's beginning to look like maybe Marlowe is something more than just an Australian journalist, which means his supposed sister may not be what she claims to be. One thing's for sure; they have to be removed from the picture.'

Xavier and Ronny nodded their assent. He was eager to act, to be away from this Stanford Delaware, to deliver good news, and eager to erase this look from the Prophet's face.

'Stanford, what are you going to say to those other idiot band members about Chamberlin?' Ronny asked.

'Good point, Ronny. We can't really tell them exactly what happened.'

'I have an idea.' Xavier eyed the other two.

'Let's hear it,' Stanford said.

'There are too many witnesses to shut them all up. Everyone in the commune knows that we are going to have a revolution. It's perfectly believable that Marlowe and his sister were actually government agents sent to investigate, and Grady Chamberlin was one of them. Perez figured that out, a fight happened and Perez and the guitar player died. Marlowe and the woman are on the run. Heaps of the members saw them drive away in your Rolls with that puta, Maria. We'll tell them she was kidnapped. What do you think?'

'Hell, Xavier, it's a bit thin.' Ronny snorted.

Stanford nodded contemplatively. 'I think that would work. Everybody was dosed up on happy juice. Anyway, we'll run with that. If anyone argues…'

'Got it,' Ronny interrupted.

'All right then. Next on the agenda, Xavier. Ronny, do you remember the man who was the lookout in San Francisco when Jimbo Kline was shot? When you and he were interrogating that FBI undercover operative? What was his name again?'

'Um, Ryan Tod or Bruce Murray. Prick didn't give much away. He must have died, I reckon. He was a real mess after I worked him over, I tell you. But our lookout, Axel Haraldsson, he was one tough mother. He just disappeared. It's weird.'

'Not so weird. He's being held in the San Bruno Jail, San Mateo County, in solitary.'

'I don't get it how…' Xavier cut in.

'Just listen, we have precious little time," Delaware said. "One of the guards at San Mateo is a Family member. He had no idea who Axel was until they spoke to one another. He's in remand, charged with kidnapping, so it's SFPD, but for some reason no one seems to know anything. My sources been less than helpful. Anyway, Axel says that he was jumped by a tall guy, pretending to be a drunk, and there was a woman. He's a bit hazy but the two he saw sounded like Spencer Marlowe and his supposed sister, Savannah Steele. I thought at the time their story was a little odd. Marlowe said they were half sister and brother. He's Australian and she's from South Dakota. Anyway, it's them. Who or what they are I cannot be sure. They certainly aren't related. More likely they are romantically bound.'

'Wow, Stanford, this is really something,' Ronny said admiringly.

Stanford nodded as if that was self-evident. 'Yes. There's more. As you know they stole the Rolls and Bertie the guard said that wetback Maria was with them. She's with them.'

'What the fuck is that all about, Stanford? A hostage?' Xavier asked.

'That doesn't make a lot of sense. Bertie said she was in the back of the car. She could have jumped out if she'd wanted to. I reckon she went willingly. She was polishing my car when those two turned up.'

'What do you know about her, Ronny?'

'Maria, Maria, let me think. Oh yeah, her husband was that annoying little prick, Santiago. Santiago Gomez. That's the one.'

'Refresh my memory, Ronny.'

'Little bastard always complained. Anyway, he'd been bitching about something. Said he wanted to leave. They'd signed the papers; I think they were covered by Mutual of Idaho. $150 grand, as I recall. I remember inviting him into our little crematorium. Christ, you should have seen him, down on his knees crying. I shot him in the head. I told him I was gonna fuck his wife as well.'

'You are very crude, Ronny. You know how I feel about that sort of thing.'

'Sorry, Stanford, but she has nice, big…'

The telephone rang, stopping the conversation. Perez and Ronny shared a look while Stanford sat stoically, absorbing news from whoever was on the other end. Finally, Stanford put the handset down without a word.

'I have news,' Stanford growled. 'One of our people is the desk clerk at the Platinum Palisade Motel in Clayton. The three of them are there. That woman, Maria, and the female who calls herself Savannah, are in room 18. Spencer Marlowe is in room 4. Grab Eddie Strode, he's working in the garage.'

'Hang on, Stanford, Eddie is a goddam loose cannon. He's likely to blast anyone who upsets him.'

'He'll be OK. Perez is dead so he's the next choice.'

'What exactly do you want us to do?' Xavier asked.

'What do you want us to do?' Stanford mimicked, then pinched the bridge of his nose and heaved a great sigh. 'Give me strength. Get some appropriate weapons from Roberto, handguns are all you need. Grab that green Dodge Van with the blacked-out windows. There's no way that you're likely to meet too much resistance. Eddie is ex-special forces, Green Berets, or the Seals, I forget which. No one can get past him.'

'Goddammit, Stanford, Xavier and I don't need any help.'

'Do as you're told. Two women and one man, unarmed, aren't likely to present a problem, but you never know.'

'So, I guess we knock on the door, whack them and leave? Right, Stanford?'

'I worry about you, Ronny. Really I do. When the revolution is successful, I'm going to need all manner of people. Smart people. We're going to need mayors, chiefs of police, administrators, all types of officials. If you want to be one of the movers and shakers you're going to have to smarten your ideas up. Of course I don't want them killed. You bring them back in the van.'

'And then what, Stanford?' Ronny asked.

'And then, Ronny dear, you are going to go to work on them. I want to know exactly who they are. And who they work for. We must know everything before the twenty-ninth of August.'

'What about the two women?'

'All of them. Use your imagination. You have a free hand. Do whatever you want. Understand?'

CHAPTER 22

THREE MEN ON A MISSION

Ronny Delgado had to admit Eddy Strode sure looked the part. He was huge. Tall, with a thick neck and a blonde buzz cut that looked like a lawnmower had been run over his head. They'd found him out splitting firewood and keeping the other Family members well clear with pure animalistic rage. Wearing his combat gear and examining his 9mm Beretta, Eddy grunted.

'This should be OK. What are you guys packing?'

'We both have 0.38s. Also rolls of duct tape, a box cutter and ropes.' Xavier answered.

'Cool. Wake me up when we get there.'

Ronny thought Eddy was like a person that got beamed in from Mars as a full adult. He thought it was odd that he had no idea who his parents were, what his childhood was like, if he had any siblings. The only clue to his past was a photograph of a blonde-haired girl on his bedside table. She was sitting astride a Harley Davidson chopper, thin legs dangling and a big grin on her face. Ronny had asked about her and he'd simply smiled. All he would say is "Pretty, ain't she?"

Stanford had hinted that Eddy had done time and he'd been a contract killer. Whether that had been Stanford Delaware bullshit, Ronny didn't know. But he thought Eddy Strode was one scary guy. A nutcase.

Xavier had one hand on the wheel and a can of Budweiser in the other. He burped loudly then whispered to Ronny.

'What do you know about…?' he directed a thumb at Eddy.

'He and Stanford go back a long way; he's been mixed up in some heavy shit.'

'Yeah, well, haven't we all?' Xavier chuckled.

'I know you did some time. What was that for?'

'Don't remind me. I was just a kid. I'd joined this gang, The Lords of Frisco. I guess I wanted to impress them. I held up a young guy in the Tenderloin in San Francisco. Stupid prick tried to grab my gun.'

'And…?'

'Yeah, the gun went off. And he was dead. Just like that.'

'They got you, huh?'

'My buddy ratted me out. Son of a bitch.'

'That would have been some serious time surely?'

'No, the public defender was fucking clever, I tell you. Had the jury was eating out of his hand. Actually, I think he was a faggot. I sort of led him on a bit.'

'Did you…?'

'Did I what?' Xavier said angrily.

'I mean, you know. Did you help him out?'

'Fuck no. I'd rather do twenty years than suck some guy's dick. Jesus, I hate fags. What about you?'

'What do you mean?'

'So, how do you feel about homosexuals, Big Ronny BBQ Delgado? How do you feel about queers?'

Ronny's face reddened.

Gentle snores emanated from Eddy as he lay full length on the rear seat of the Dodge Van. Ronny had a cassette, softly playing the Beatles' brand new album, Revolver. Worn wipers scratched across the windscreen, as big fat drops descended from the heavens, hammering the roof of the van. Ronny turned up the volume.

'Hey, a man's trying to sleep here. Turn that racket off, BBQ!' Eddy Strode yelled. 'Fucking hell, how does anyone get a handle like that? BBQ, Jesus, give me a break!'

Ronny BBQ Delgado grinned at Xavier.

Xavier smiled in return. 'The prick's got a mouth, hasn't he?'

'What was that? You sonofabitch. So, I've got a mouth, have I?'

'Hey Eddy, calm down. Just cool it, Xavier. Ok?'

'Don't tell me to fucking cool it, you spic cunt.' Eddy grabbed Xavier by his black ponytail, jerking it back and jamming his pistol into his neck.

'C'mon, Eddy, no offence was intended.' BBQ was shaking.

'Shut the fuck up and pull over. Look, over there.' Eddy pointed to a lay-by with a huge sign, featuring a picture of a happy family drinking Coca Cola and the message "Things go better with Coke."

Ronny and Xavier stumbled out of the van onto a large, potholed asphalt area. Wooden trestle tables were scattered around the picnic grounds. A resting place, nestled in the Diablo Mountains, surrounded by beautiful big leaf maples. Not a soul in sight.

'C'mon, Eddy. What the fuck are you doing?' Ronny was shaking.

'On your knees,' Eddy commanded.

'Eddy, please.' Tough guy BBQ Ronny Delgado had wet himself.

Xavier closed his eyes and mumbled a prayer. Two shots exploded into the trees. Not a sound could be heard in the aftermath. Ronny's ears were ringing, but eventually he heard wheezing laughter that rose in volume.

Eddy Strode roared with laughter. 'Scared the shit outta you, didn't I?'

'Is that it?' Xavier stammered.

'Yeah, you little wetback prick. C'mon, both of you, on your feet, we got a job to do.'

Ronny found his voice. 'What the fuck was that all about?'

'I'll tell you what it was all about, motherfuckers. I'm the boss, watch your mouth, do as you're told. I'm running this little op. Upset me and next time will be for real. Understand?'

Ronny glanced sideways at Xavier. 'Yeah sure, Eddy, you're the boss.'

'Good, no hard feeling then.' Eddy clapped BBQ on the shoulder. 'Ok boys, a half an hour and we hit Clayton. We won't have any problems, I can assure you. Just leave it to Eddy. Geez, you stink, Ronny.'

Still shaking, Xavier and Ronny took their places in the front of the van. Eddy was soon snoring on the back seat. Ronny squirmed in his seat; his pants sodden. He was not happy. Xavier's two hands were on the wheel, his jaw tensed, his nostrils flared, the very picture of terror fuelled rage. Eddy stirred when Xavier changed up to third gear and the van laboured noisily up a hill. Ronny quietly snapped open the glove box, grabbing his revolver. The sharp punchy sound of the two 0.38 rounds hurt their ears, the acrid smell of gunpowder made their eyes water.

Xavier turned a wild grin on Ronny. 'Fuck, that was loud.'

Two close range head shots had certainly made a mess. Blood and brain matter spilled out of Eddy's head, spattering over the seat, the rear window and even the hood lining.

'How about you pull over, Xavier, and we dump the body before we get to Clayton.'

'Hang on, Ronny, hang on. What the fuck are we gonna tell Stanford, eh?'

CHAPTER 23
THE PLAN

Spread out before them lay the small Californian town of Clayton, a peaceful little municipality where sudden violent death rarely visited. The hotel was easily recognizable and not far off, flanked by greenery and the sign sticking up like a middle finger. Several neon letters flickered.

'C'mon, BBQ, you got any ideas? What the fuck do we do with Eddy?'

'I'm thinking! Look, the best I can come up with is we dump Strode at the motel and look, I don't know, we blame this guy Marlowe. That's really all I can think of.'

'Oh yeah. But Stanford is gonna be there when we interrogate these pricks and they're gonna deny it.'

'All right, smart ass, you come up with a better idea. Anyway, we're here, the Rolls is parked outside of number 4. As far as we know the two dames are in 18, so we grab them first and then we grab Marlowe.'

'What about Eddy?'

'Give me a hand. We'll dump him here,' Ronny ordered.

'Is that smart?'

'Just do as you're told. It's gonna look like Marlowe did it.'

'Jesus, Ronny. I don't know…'

The water in the motel parking lot potholes shimmered by the glow of the dim yellow motel lights. Eddy Strode's body was as lifeless as the fallen leaves surrounding the lone small tree they left him leaning against. Xavier edged the van midway between the units and parked at the front of Unit 12. No lights were burning. The two men climbed out, scanning the parking lot.

'Now what?' A not-so-confident Xavier asked.

'Easy peasy,' Ronny replied. 'Grab that roll of duct tape and the ropes. Pass me that knife.'

Ronny tested the blade of the box cutter before stuffing it into his jacket. Guns in hand, they crept up to the door. The soft light of the television flickered through the drapes. They could hear the drum roll intro to Hogan's Heroes. Ronny nodded at Xavier, hesitating at the front door equipped with two impressive, good quality locks. The door itself was maybe thirty years old, probably mahogany. Same for the frame. Cheaply made at the time, damp and swelled through a lot of summers, dry and contracted through as many winters, and no match for ex-Dallas Cowboys Ronny BBQ Delgado's size 15 boot. The sharp crack of the timber shattering sounded like a grenade exploding. Ronny and Xavier burst into the room, guns in hand. Savannah dozed on an armchair; Maria screamed as she sprung up from one of the two single beds.

Immediately motel lights flashed on. A hoarse male voice yelled something unintelligible.

'OK, ladies, do as you're told and you won't get hurt,' Ronny snarled.

Instantly awake, Savannah jumped up, only to be met by Ronny's ham-like fist smashing into her jaw. Momentarily stunned, Savannah groaned as Xavier wound the duct tape around her wrists, ankles and over her mouth.

'Hey you, face down on the bed.' Tears sluicing down her face, Maria did as she was told.

'Like I said. Easy peasy.' BBQ smiled.

Savannah lay on the floor, hands, feet and mouth duct taped. Ronny rolled her over.

'I'm gonna take the tape off your mouth. If you scream, I'm gonna cut your goddam tits off.'

He nicked the boxcutter blade against Savannah's neck until a drop of blood appeared.

'OK bitch, now talk to me. Who the fuck are you? Who exactly is Spencer Marlowe? Don't tell me he's your brother, that's bullshit.'

Ronny picked her up and threw her onto the bed. Savannah yelped as he ripped the duct tape off her mouth. His strong dark eyebrows gave his face a fierce look. He moved his menacing bulk closer, his teeth bared. Revolver in hand he grunted.

'Talk to me, bitch. Who exactly are you and Marlowe? Your answers are important. It's not about life and death; it's more about how you die. You follow?'

Savannah's mind travelled at a hundred miles per hour. She wished she and Spencer had planned a cover story.

'We're journalists.'

'No kidding? So, what's the story with Marlowe? He's not your brother, that's for sure.'

'Spencer works for a newspaper in Australia. His editor had heard about the Family and contacted my editor at the New York Times. It was agreed we'd work together posing as brother and sister. We thought it'd sound credible.'

'So, I imagine he's fucking you? Colleagues with benefit, eh?'

Savannah had the glimmer of an idea. 'None of your goddam business.'

'Everything is my business, you stupid slut.' Ronny leaned over and slapped her face hard.

'Hey, Ronny. How about we have a little fun? I'll have the Mexican and you…' Xavier leered at Maria.

'For God's sake, Xavier, save that until we get back home. We're in a hurry; somebody might have already called the police. You can do whatever you want then. I'm sure the ladies won't mind. Will you, girls?'

He leered at the bound ladies, but that leer definitely didn't invite an answer.

'What now, Ronny? Time's-a-wasting. We gotta grab Marlowe. I don't wanna kick in another door. We can't risk someone calling the cops.'

'Like I said before, Xavier, easy peasy. We leave the Mexican here for the moment and Savannah is going to help us with Marlowe. On your feet, darling.'

Xavier jerked Savannah upright, removing the tape from her feet. It had begun to rain again as a tight little triangle of two men and a woman in lockstep made their way to Unit 4.

Ronny whispered, 'Now, tell him you want to join him. You're lonely and amorous, got it? Make it good.'

Reclining on his single bed Spencer half-dozed as he tried to follow a television crime story. FBI, starring Efrem Zimbalist Junior as lantern-jawed Special Agent Lewis Erskine. The black and white TV with its dark grey screen and false wood panelling looked like it belonged in a museum. He bolted upright as he heard a noise at the door, then a firm rat-a-tat-tat.

Not the way Savannah knocked.

He sprung to his feet. Soft lamplight filtered through ivory curtains casting gentle shadows across the pale green carpet. Special Agent Lewis Erskine barked orders at Agent Tom Colby.

Moving noiselessly, he stood against the wall closest to the door.

'Who is it?'

'It's me, Spencer darling. May I come in?'

'Of course you can, sweetheart. Are you alone?'

'I am. Maria finally went to sleep. Poor thing. We can have a nice time before she wakes up. Would you like that?'

'Yes please.' Spencer leaned over and flicked the latch. 'The door's open. Come in. I'm going to the bathroom to freshen up.'

Savannah hurtled through the door, screaming, propelled by Xavier's boot. Gun in hand, Xavier followed, two hands on his pistol, crouched ready to shoot. Spencer's fist slammed into the side of his head. Xavier folded into a heap.

'Nice one, tough guy.' Ronny chuckled. His 0.38 pointed unwaveringly at Spencer's chest.

'What the hell's going on in there? I'm calling the cops,' an angry voice yelled from the adjoining unit.

Xavier groaned. 'What was...?'

'You walked into that one. Get up. We may not have a lot of time,' Ronny snarled.

'Where's Maria. Is she…?'

'It's OK, Spencer. She's tied up in the room.' Savannah glared at Ronny.

'Shut the fuck up. Here's what's gonna happen. You two, on your feet. We're going to grab the Mexican woman and we're all going to head back to the commune. Stanford wants to have a talk.'

The *wee wah* of police sirens rang menacingly.

'That was fucking quick. Shit, Ronny, what the fuck are we gonna do? The cops must have been just up the road. Let's just shoot them and leave.'

At the far end of the parking lot, the blue and red lights were little more than smudgy illuminations in the slanting rain. But beneath their glow they could see the black and white bodywork of two police cars.

'Too late, boss wants 'em alive. Another day.'

Spencer watched helplessly as Ronny and Xavier ran towards the other end of the parking lot. He heard the rattle of a motor and the crunch of gears. Peering into the pelting rain, he watched as two police cars quietly rolled closer.

CHAPTER 24

I FOUGHT THE LAW

Savannah swore as Spencer ripped off the last of the tape binding her wrists and ankles. Four police officers, guns drawn, burst into the room.

Outside, a light ran had begun pattering down, but the forecast had promised a full downpour.

Savannah grinned. 'Whoever said there was never a cop when you need one?'

A fifth officer wearing a captain's uniform sauntered in behind them. Spencer observed an overweight older man with hanging jowls, a slack, loose mouth and a thick, brown moustache gone to gray, his fingers as thick as sausages. Nicotine stained the first and second fingers of his left hand.

Spencer grinned. 'Boy oh boy, are we ever glad to see you guys.'

'You are, are you?' The captain sneered.

Savannah spoke. 'Captain, if you hadn't arrived when you did, we were going to be executed.'

'Shut the fuck up. First of all, where is the woman you kidnapped, Maria Gomez?'

'Captain, I can assure you Maria wasn't kidnapped. You'll find her tied up in Unit 18,' Savannah said, trying to show the abrasions on her wrists from where she'd torn off the duct tape. The captain wasn't paying attention.

'For God's sake, just listen to yourself. Not kidnapped but she's tied up. Give me a break. Luke, and you, Keith, go and check Unit 18. Be careful, there may be some accomplices.

And you, Dante.' The captain nodded at a swarthy, youthful Hispanic officer.

'Slap the cuffs on these two, then secure the complex. Check the parking lot and see if there's anything amiss.'

'You got it, Captain.'

Spencer said nothing, holding out his hands.

Savannah wasn't so compliant. 'Listen to me, Captain, this isn't what it seems.'

'If I had a dollar for every perp that said that.' The captain sighed as he plonked heavily onto one of the chairs. Reaching into his coat pocket he pulled out a packet of Marlboros and a chrome Zippo.

'You don't mind if I smoke? Like I give a fuck.'

'Captain, you really need to hear what we have to say,' Spencer snapped.

'You'll get your chance, but meanwhile, you have the right to remain silent, the right to have a lawyer present during questioning, the right to have a lawyer appointed if you can't afford one, the right to stop answering questions at any time. Do you understand?'

'Captain...' Savannah began.

'Do you understand?' The captain yelled.

'We understand,' Spencer acknowledged.

'Ok, now, I'll tell you what's happening. First of all, you.' He pointed a finger at Spencer. 'You're Spencer Marlowe, correct? And you're Savannah Steele.'

'Yes,' they both said, sharing a glance at one another. Had this police captain ever had a taste of Stanford Delaware's happy juice? Spencer would place money on yes.

The captain turned to Spencer.

'Well, I gotta tell you son, you're looking at the gas chamber. First of all, we have the capital murder of one Grady Chamberlin.'

'You're joking. He was...' Spencer gasped.

'Shut it. Like I said, Grady Chamberlin. And before you waste your breath, we have witnesses. Next, Jesus, I gotta say you are one evil dude, next is Perez Garcia. Head split open like a goddam watermelon, they said.'

Spencer realised it was pointless to protest.

'Hey Captain, you're not gonna believe this.' A breathless Officer Dante rushed into the room.

'Calm down, Officer Dante. Talk to me.'

'We found a body in the parking lot. He…he's been shot. In the head.'

'No kidding. Let me guess, you two know nothing about it, right?'

Spencer glanced sideways at Savannah who was perched on the bed, her cuffed hands in front of her. She rolled her eyes and shrugged.

'You see a gun around here?' she asked, voice heavily laden with sarcasm.

'Got it in one, Captain.' Spencer was beyond being surprised. 'We don't know anything about it.'

'Oh, and Captain, Mr Delaware's stolen Rolls Royce is in the parking lot,' Officer Dante added.

'Grand theft auto is the least of your worries. Although, I do have some good news for you both.' The captain chuckled.

'Really?' Savannah spoke, her voice laden with sarcasm.

'Yeah, the good news is we can only gas you once. Doesn't seem fair really.'

They all stared at the doorway as Maria's sobs could be heard. Officer Luke entered followed by Maria and a stern-looking Officer Keith.

'Maria, are you OK?' Savannah sprang up from the bed.

'Si, Savannah. I'm fine.'

'Captain, the lady here bears out what these two have said.'

'Is that so? This puts a whole different complexion on things.' The captain tapped out another cigarette from the pack and lit it. 'First things first, Keith, get on the two-way.

We want more officers out here. We need the technicians, forensics and everyone else, you know what to do. You never know, there might be more bodies lying around. And Luke, go wake the manager, and see if he has anything to add.'

'Roger, Captain.' Luke hurried off.

'So little lady, you're saying that these two characters are innocent? We have witnesses to say Spencer Marlowe has murdered at least two people and now it looks like there is a third body in the car park, and you came here with them willingly in a vehicle belonging to one Stanford Delaware that you would have known was stolen. Is that correct.'

'Si, yes but it is, how you say, it's not seeming how it is.'

'Well, sweetheart. I wasn't born yesterday, and I've never met a wetback that wasn't a stinking liar. So, it's obvious to me you are part of the gang, so to speak.'

'No sir, you are wrong, it's not…'

'Listen to me, woman. I have no idea exactly what your part in this is, but there may be a plea deal for you. I can't say for sure. But meanwhile you're under arrest. Hey, Dante, you need some practice, read Maria Gomez her rights.'

***

First came the sound of multiple car engines. Doors slammed. Approaching footsteps clip clopped across the tarmac. A muffled, brusque voice could be heard issuing orders. Officer Dante drew his revolver when he heard the sharp banging on the door. The captain jumped to his feet.

'Who is it?'

'Don't worry, Captain Mackey, we come in peace.'

'What the fuck? Officer Dante, open the door. Be careful.'

A smiling Dale Fletcher entered the room followed by Agent Tyrone Brookman.

'My gosh, it's wet out there.' Dale removed his sodden fedora and placed it carefully on the kitchen bench.

Spencer smiled in relief. 'Dale, Ty, you're both a sight for sore eyes.'

He and Savannah had worked with Agent Ty Brookman and Agent Gus Horslay when they were all undercover in South Dakota in a sting to take down outlaw bikers.

'Who the hell are you two, and how do you know my name?' Mackey barked.

'Do I smell cigarette smoke?' Dale Fletcher asked.

'What? Yeah. So?'

'I'm not supposed to, but I'd love a cig.' Dale smiled winningly.

The captain reluctantly offered his soft pack and a light.

'Thanks, Captain. Much appreciated. My wife, I tell you…'

'OK, who in hell are you and what do you want?'

Dale smiled contentedly as he drew on the Marlboro.

'I prefer Camels, but this is pretty darn good. Right, where to start? How do I know your name? Well, I guess you could say that's my job.'

'Which is?'

'Sorry, I should have said.' Dale flashed his badge. 'This is Agent Ty Brookman and I'm Special Agent Dale Fletcher of the FBI.'

'Feds. I should have guessed. Well, *Special Agent Dale Freeman,* we pretty much have this thing under control. We have the perps dead to rights. We don't need your help, so…'

'Fletcher.'

'What?'

'My name. It's Special Agent Dale Fletcher,'

'Good, so, it's real nice of you fellas to drop by, but I'm kinda busy. So, if you don't mind…?'

'Sorry, Captain Mackey, I should explain. I'm here to take Spencer Marlowe and Savannah Steele off your hands. This is an FBI matter. Oh, and we'll be taking the Gomez lady as well.'

'Who the fuck do you think you are? You can't just waltz in and take our prisoners, just like that.'
'Wanna bet?'

CHAPTER 25

DALE'S AGENDA

The quartet of unmarked FBI Chevrolets drove past upmarket shopping malls and a lot of elegant stucco homes. But it seemed even Palo Alto had its share of slums. This was definitely not where the millionaires had their mansions. Savannah and Maria travelled with a charming FBI Special Agent who said her name was Jenny Smith. With her straight black hair, olive skin and lithe body, there was something of the gypsy about her. She didn't strike Savannah as a typical FBI Agent and either she didn't know much, or she wasn't prepared to discuss the case as she expertly directed the conversation towards basketball and how the Lakers were currently performing.

'I tell you, Savannah, Rudy La Russo is the best player the Lakers have, and what a hunk. What do you reckon?'

Maria dozed in the back seat. Savannah had about as much interest in basketball as she had in knitting baby booties. 'Yeah, he's a hunk all right. Where exactly are we going, Jenny?'

'Oh, I thought you knew. It's a safe house. Didn't Special Agent Fletcher tell you? Anyway, we're here.'

***

Dale ushered the trio into the slightly run-down stucco bungalow. Once inside, Spencer was surprised to see a spacious family home. It was welcoming from the open door to the wide hallway. Upon the walls were photographs of children. The floor was an old-fashioned parquet with a blend of deep homely browns and the walls were the greens of summer gardens. Spencer grinned at Savannah and mouthed 'nice huh?'

'Well, folks. this is home. Well, at least for a while. You'll find the kitchen is well stocked. Hey, we even have a colour TV. Give Jenny your clothes size and tomorrow we'll get you kitted out. Probably Walmart, I imagine. There are four bedrooms and even a goddam pool. How about that, eh?'

'What about me?' Maria asked anxiously.

'I'm sorry, Mrs Gomez, we haven't quite figured that one out. Clearly you can't go back to the commune. For the time being you're safe. Don't worry, we'll look after you.' Dale glanced at his watch. 'It's late. I suggest you select a bedroom and try and get some sleep. I need to have a chat in private with Savannah and Spencer.'

Savannah hugged Maria; they watched in silence as she retreated down a hallway to where the bedrooms were.

'How about a beer, folks? I'm parched.'

'I'll get them, Dale.' Spencer padded into the spotlessly clean kitchen, scrupulously organised with plenty of work surfaces. He gazed in awe at the refrigerator standing like a great silver monolith, a testimony to the extravagance of western lifestyle. Jerking open the steel door, he was surprised to see it was full of cheese, cream and cold meat slices and gallons of chilled milk along with Californian white wine and Budweiser beer. Spencer was aware that quid pro quo was a part of FBI tactics. *Nice house, great food. What's the trade off?*

Spencer had a sinking feeling that Dale had plans. He'd sort of figured now Stanford Delaware knew they weren't exactly brother and sister hippies seeking enlightenment that their mission had effectively been terminated.

'Cheers, happy days.' Dale clinked their bottles. 'Darn, I'd love another cigarette. It's my wife, she's like a dog with a bone. I mean, even my doctor smokes. In fact, I've read that the medical profession recommends Chesterfields.'

Spencer glanced at his Bulova; he'd heard it all before.

'Yeah, sorry, folks, I guess you're all tuckered out. Look, I'll tell you what I'm thinking. Well, not just me you understand. I mean, I take orders just like everybody. I mean we all have to answer to somebody, don't we? You may think I make all the decisions, but, no, it's not like that. I mean, take my wife, hey, that sounds like one of those jokes, you know, the comedian says "take my wife. Please." And our marriage isn't like that at all, no sir. I mean Edna is a fine …'

'Dale!' Savannah rolled her eyes.

'Right, right. Um, OK. Another beer? There's plenty there. Oh, and there's an envelope in the desk in the study with a couple of hundred dollars, for any immediate expenses. And Savannah, you'll find a plastic case with a brand new 0.357 Magnum a shoulder holster and five boxes of cartridges. Yes, and for you Spencer, a second hand 0.38. I know guns aren't really your thing.'

'Point?' Savannah snapped.

'Sorry, what?' Dale pursed his lips.

'Dale, what Savannah is saying, is please get to the point.'

'You got me. First of all, how about you two tell me how you read the situation with Stanford Delaware?'

Savannah glanced at Spencer and nodded.

'Well, it seems pretty straightforward to Spencer and me. Doesn't it, Spencer?' Spencer nodded but felt that sinking feeling again.

'Go on.'

'Where do we start? Spencer saw this guy Perez shoot a man called Grady Chamberlin. There were at least, I don't know, maybe ten witnesses. Then in self-defence, Spencer hit Perez Garcia who unfortunately was deceased after his head hit a pile of bricks. Once again there were the same witnesses. Ronny Delgado and a guy called Xavier burst into my motel room, assaulted me, gagged me and Maria and then forced me to go to Spencer's room where they would have either killed us or kidnapped us and taken us all back to the commune where we would certainly have been murdered. Oh, and as a kicker, there was a deceased gunshot victim found in the carpark of the motel, who would certainly have been murdered by the lovely Ronny or Xavier. How does it sound so far, Dale?'

'Yeah, I get you, but?'

'But what, Dale?' Spencer's eyes narrowed.

'OK, for starters. All those witnesses? Well, guess what, they're all singing from a different song sheet.'

'You're kidding?' Savannah swore.

'Oh, and it gets worse. I'd murder a cigarette. We have the witnesses saying you, Spencer, shot Grady Chamberlin and when Perez tried to wrest the gun from you, he was thrown onto the bricks and his skull cracked. Then you two forcibly stole the Rolls Royce, kidnapping Maria Gomez.'

Spencer shook his head. 'Anything else?'

'One more thing, you tried to run over their security guard, Bertie someone. So that's an attempted murder. You might get away with a reckless driving charge on that one.'

'What about BBQ and Xavier kicking in the door of our motel and all the rest of that? Christ, that bastard Delgado punched and slapped me. Come on, Dale?'

'Two desperate killers on the run make up a nonsense story. You don't have any damn witnesses.'

'What about Maria?' Savannah snapped.

'The captain's running with the story Maria was a part of it. Get this. Stanford Delaware is saying Maria Gomez had been suspected of theft, and if she'd been charged, she'd have been deported at the very least. Although it's still a kidnapping, then she, for whatever reason, decided to throw in with you two.'

'This is bloody nonsense, Dale. You know that. Also, Maria has told us she suspected her late husband, Santiago Gomez, was murdered by Stanford or one of his goons.' Spencer stared hard at Dale.

This new information seemed to put Dale on a knife edge. Spencer watched him struggling for control, pacing up and down the living room floor, compulsively patting pockets for cigarettes that weren't there.

'Hell, it just gets worse, Spencer said. 'Let me guess, he was reported as dying of natural causes and it was signed off by a doctor or coroner, and she never went to the police, am I right?'

Savannah glanced sideways at Spencer.

'Actually, we haven't had time to really question Maria about her late husband, but I reckon you could guarantee that would be the case and, you're not going to believe this, Spencer and I suspected Stanford may have been insuring undocumented arrivals, killing them and collecting the payouts.'

'C'mon, you suspect? What evidence do you have?'

'You're right, Dale, it was more of a gut feeling. Spencer and I were asked, well, more than asked I guess, to fill out forms that looked just like an application for a life insurance policy, but, of course, that's not evidence so forget that for the moment.'

'Ok, anything else?'

Spencer cleared his throat. 'Um, yeah, Dale, there is. But I think you may laugh.'

'Try me.'

'I'll admit this sounds silly; Stanford is obsessed with the Beatles.'

'What? You mean like weevils, grubs, insects?'

'No, I mean like the English rock and roll band.'

'You mean those stupid long-haired freaks whose music sounds like a direct hit on a guitar factory? Give me a break, Spencer. So, he likes their music, what has this have to do with anything?'

'I'm sorry, Dale, but seriously Stanford has more loose screws than a hardware store in an earthquake. I tell you he's capable of anything.'

'Capable of what? So, he likes their music. I don't have time for this.'

'Hear him out, please, Dale,' Savanna urged.

Dale sighed. 'Go on, Spencer. If you must.'

'Here's the thing, Dale. Stanford has announced at their gatherings that the Beatles will be coming to the commune. Everyone you talk to accepts it as an absolute. They've built four nice houses beside Delaware's mansion, just for the four band members to stay. Whether you like them or not, the Beatles are the biggest thing in the world today. I can't see how Stanford Delaware, as wealthy as he may be, can talk their management into having them perform at the commune, but the fact remains he thinks they will. It doesn't make sense. For a start they're in England.'

'Oh, my God.' Savannah put her hand over her mouth.

'What is it, Savannah?' Spencer asked.

'Remember the stupid Beat Box record store on Haight? And poor Agent Tod?'

Spencer nodded.

'I don't really know why I of all people would notice, but there was a day bill stuck on the window advertising that the Beatles would be performing at Candlestick Park in San Francisco in August.'

Spencer turned his attention back to Dale, eyebrows raised.

'Enough already,'' Dale said, and downed the last of his beer. 'There's your answer. The Beatles are coming to San Francisco and Delaware reckons he can get them to add an extra play date to perform at his commune. And perhaps he can, he'd have enough money, that's for sure. Anyway, you two, who cares, let's focus on what I need to tell you, OK?'

'Yeah, all right. Go ahead, something seems to be bothering you,' Savannah grunted.

'Where to start? Spencer, Savannah, face reality, Stanford Delaware is a very wealthy man with a lot of influence. The "Family" appears to have moles and conscripts permeating through every level of government. He probably has judges and certainly police in his pocket.'

'That's a given. Tell us something we don't know. As far as Savannah and I are concerned this operation has just about run out of legs. We're definitely persona non grata with Stanford, so I guess if you just pull us out and we move on. Right?' Savannah nodded her agreement.

'Actually, it's not that simple.'

Spencer had a feeling he knew where this was going.

'As you know, we, that is, the FBI have a lot of influence, but...?'

Savannah glanced sideways at Spencer. 'But?'

'What I'm trying to say, is these charges are not going to go away. We can't make them go away. The fact is there are too many dead people. Too many witnesses to say you two committed at least two felony murders. We don't have anything of substance against Stanford, or Ronny or that other guy, what's his name? Yeah, Xavier. Captain Mackey wasn't pleased when I took you guys away. You can guarantee he'll be asking questions. If this gets leaked to the press, which I'm sure it will, the FBI is going to be placed in an untenable position.'

'Dale, what was the story about the body the police found at the motel grounds?' Spencer asked.

'Oh yeah, that was the lovable Edward Strode, an absolute psychopath. Definitely a Family member, ever since he got out of San Quentin.'

'What was he in for?' Savannah asked.

Dale shook his head.

'This was an awful case. He killed his ten-year-old daughter, Katie.'

Spencer looked horrified. 'How come he was out of prison?'

'The lawyer managed to convince the jury it was involuntary manslaughter. He served three years. We believe the truth was he murdered her in a fit of rage because his wife, Jaquie, threatened to leave him.'

'How the hell did he get an involuntary?' Savannah's eyebrows raised.

'Apparently the girl and her mother fled the car Edward was driving and dear Eddy ran over Katie. The prosecutor said it was deliberate, the defence said it was an accident.'

Savannah scowled. 'Some bleeding-heart jury members no doubt.'

'In this case I suspect you're correct, Savannah. But, well, it looks like he got his comeuppance, didn't it?' Dale grinned.

Spencer stood up, yawning.

'No loss obviously, Dale, but how did he die?'

'Two gunshot wounds to the head at close range.'

'So, who did it and how come no one heard the shots?' Savannah asked.

'Stop yawning, Spencer, it's contagious. Who did it? Had to be Ronny or Xavier. Why? Eddy Strode was a nasty guy with a very short fuse. I reckon there was a falling out and well, we can guess the rest. The coroner said he wasn't killed at the motel. They probably shot him in the vehicle they were traveling in. That's pure conjecture, of course. But as far as Captain Mackey is concerned, he's convinced you two are the culprits.'

Savannah sat forward in her chair.

'Whoa, for Chrissake, Dale, you want us to take the rap for all of this? You gotta be kidding? They have the death penalty in California.'

Dale didn't answer straight away. The room was totally silent. Like a wake. Flatline.

'We do have a plan.'

'Jesus, Dale, you've been stalling all bloody night.' Spencer locked eyes with Savannah. 'I have a feeling we're not going to like this.'

CHAPTER 26

HOW TO AVOID THE DEATH PENALTY

Scattered across the coffee table lay an untidy collection of empty beer bottles and plates. Savannah had rustled up cheese and crackers. Dale rummaged through an empty box of Cracker Jack, finally giving up in disgust he threw the box down. Sitting forward as if newly energised, he spoke:

'Just listen, everything will be OK. Like I said, we have a tiny problem in as much as we don't have any real evidence against Stanford. Sure, we could go in guns blazing...'

'Guns blazing, really?' Savannah said hopefully.

Dale moved in his chair and spoke.

'That was a metaphor, Savannah. No, what I mean is, we could descend on the commune in force, but here's the problem. We really think that The Family is a vicious cult with a lot of seriously brainwashed people. We suspect they're also a heavily armed militia. If we went in with law enforcement, the belief is it could become a real firefight with women and children at risk.'

Spencer yawned again, glancing at his watch.

'We're still waiting for the punchline.'

'Yes, it is rather late. Well, one word sort of sums things up.'

'Dale!' Savannah glared at her boss.

'That word is—bait.'

For Spencer, the penny dropped, all that was needed were the details. Savannah glanced sideways at Spencer. The same penny. Savannah jumped up.

'Good one, Dale. Now we know why it took so long to tell us. Who was the genius who came up with this idea? So, we sit somewhere and wait for some of Stanford's crew to turn up and blast us. Terrific.'

'Hang on just a minute, Agent Steele, just consider things for a minute. OK?'

'Let's hear what you have, Dale,' Spencer interrupted.

'Stanford believes you two are sort of undercover journalists who are going to write a nasty sabotage piece exposing what you know or suspect about the Family. He knows journalists play fast and loose with the truth, and you could write something quite lurid, and the last thing he wants is the spotlight turned on his outfit.'

'Yeah, sure, but…'

'Savannah, hear me out. He has absolutely no idea the FBI is involved, and he would see two journos as being no problem. He'll probably send someone like Delgado or that Xavier guy, or both of them. He'd see it as being a quick hit, disguised as a random robbery gone wrong, something like that.'

'How would Stanford know where we are?'

'That's easy, Spencer. We'll tell him.'

Spencer glanced sideways at Savannah.

'Wonderful, Dale. You tell him. He sends in his assassins; we get shot and you arrest Stanford Delaware. Sounds perfect.'

'Hardly. The idea is that we leak the information. We have agents watching the house. When the hitmen or…'

'Or women.' Savannah interjected.

'For God's sake, Savannah.'

'It was a joke, Dale.'

'Anyway, the general idea is that whoever has been hired to do the hit is arrested and we'll use the old plea bargain routine. It's an oldie but a goodie. We offer him or them a deal in exchange for Stanford.'

'C'mon, Dale, that's pretty thin. I can see where you're coming from but there's too many variables. They or him could have been hired by a third party with no connection to Delaware.'

'We realize that. But this is all we have. However, there is another deal on the table.'

CHAPTER 27
NO DEAL

Bored with the process Savannah grabbed an old, battered tome *The Gun and its Development* by WW Greener from the bookcase, leafing through the pages and stifling a yawn.

'Agent Steele, am I keeping you awake?'

'Hell in a handbasket, Dale, you've been taking all night to come up with this little gem. What I, and I'm sure, Spencer, can see, is a distinct lack of gratitude and given what the first plan was, I have little faith in what else you and the mental giants at DC have dreamed up.'

Spencer was stunned at the outburst at her superior. He remembered the insecure, newly minted agent when they had first met in New York in1955. She had morphed into a no-nonsense, hard-edged law enforcement officer who seemed to have smashed the glass ceiling into a million shards and Dale had to try hard to not get cut on the fragments.

'Witness protection.'

'What on earth are you talking about, Dale? Witness protection for who exactly?' Spencer frowned.

'You two. All I'm saying is, just think about it. As I said, we can't just pull you both out and say to the press, Stanford Delaware, Captain Mackey, and anyone else who asks, "sorry, folks, it was just a game and it's over. Spencer and Savannah didn't kill anyone and our apologies for thinking nasty thoughts about The Family."'

'You're serious. You want Spencer and me to go into witness protection? I don't believe it.'

'Like I said, witness protection would work. We'd tell Mackey that you are both helping us with our enquiries. We relocate you with new names and identities. Hell, it wouldn't be hard for you, Spencer. We've never really figured out exactly who you are, *Mr It's a Long Story.*

Spencer always felt uncomfortable when he came under scrutiny.

'Dale, forget it. I'm not doing it, and I'm sure Spencer doesn't like the idea. Right, Spencer?'

Spencer nodded.

'Actually, I hoped you'd say that. But the alternative simply has to be that you two are as I said, going to be, that is, not to put too fine a point to it...'

'Bait. Lovely word that, Dale.' Spencer rolled his eyes. He was having an internal debate whether to grab another beer or fall asleep with Dale talking.

'So, what do you tell Captain Mackey if he asks what we've been charged with?' Savannah asked.

'Leave him to me. I'll tell him you're both in custody, taken to another state to face other charges. After all, we are the FBI, and we're not restricted to any one jurisdiction.'

'That sounds OK, but what about Stanford and his merry men? What are they going to think?'

'I know exactly what they'll think. They'll think you're hiding out. And they're going to find out exactly where.' Dale smirked.

'You look like the cat that got the cream.' Savannah wasn't smiling.

'Indeed. I told Mackey what a great job he's done, and that Washington may have bigger plans for him than just being a captain in Hicksville, California. Anyway, he's given the press a statement that they have no idea who the body is that they found in the parking lot and they don't have any leads.'

'No kidding.' Spencer was impressed. 'What about the Rolls Royce?'

'The Roller? Well, we just sort of made it disappear.'

'What about the motel desk clerk?' Savannah asked.

'That should be OK. I got the captain to quiz the guy about you two and to say that you both left before the cops arrived. It's all tied up in a pretty neat pink bow.' Dale grinned.

'Wonderful, Dale. But don't forget: Spencer, Maria and I will be sitting ducks.'

CHAPTER 28
UNHAPPY

Huddled on the cream divan, Ronny and Xavier went over the story they'd concocted, but Ronny was still worried. Sitting bolt upright, he glanced at his watch. Stanford had kept them waiting for twenty minutes, the logs in the fireplace had become glowing embers. Grabbing a poker, he jumped up and stoked the flickering coals, bending down to grab some small chunks of timber, and placing them in the andiron.

'Just look at those poor bastards working their butts off, Xavier.'

It gave Ronny a sense of pride every time he stared out of the picture window and looked down on the valley and saw the workers toiling. Beyond that, laid out like a Van Gogh painting, he could see the fields and the sizeable complex of cabins, sheds and all the buildings that made the commune into what was a small town. He and Xavier were like barons in this little kingdom. And the king…

He glanced anxiously down the dark hallway leading off the lounge room where Stanford's master bedroom and study were located. *What's keeping him?*

They heard voices.

'I'm sure you're going to find at the commune all that you're seeking, Chase. And don't forget, if you have any questions, any at all, you're welcome to come and see me anytime.'

'Yes sir,' the boy stammered.

Ronny glared at the youngster. He wasn't the first the Prophet had taken an interest in, but this one was, well, different from all the others. He was handsome, not perhaps in the conventional sense, but he had the appearance which could make him stand out in the crowd. He was fair, almost pale white. His golden-brown eyes contrasted with his light-toned face. Ronny looked at his own expanding figure. A tight knot formed in his stomach.

Stanford looked fondly at the retreating figure of Chase as the boy picked up his rucksack, making his way to the cabins on the lee side of the corn field.

'Fine young man.' Stanford beamed. 'He's going to be an asset. A real asset.'

'Does he have family, Stanford?' Ronny asked casually.

Stanford spun around.

'Yes, maybe. I don't know. But you can forget about that. An insurance payout is not on the agenda. OK?'

'Sure, Stanford, I understand. But you know, sometimes accidents happen on a working farm. I mean he could get run over by a tractor…'

'If that happens, I will be very unhappy. You don't want that, do you, Ronny?'

Ronny's fists were clenched at his sides. He glared at Stanford.

'I'm sure your new *friend* will fit in perfectly.'

The Prophet ignored the dripping sarcasm. 'That's the spirit. Now how about some refreshment? The usual?'

Xavier had watched the interaction with interest, and now spoke up. 'Not for me, Stanford. We gotta talk.'

Ronny spoke. 'Yeah, Stanford. We have some problems.'

'We do, don't we?' Stanford lowered himself onto his handmade dragon chair. Made of leather and hand sculpted wood, Ronny knew it'd cost a small fortune.

'Stanford, things didn't go as planned…'

'Really? Spencer Marlowe and that Savannah woman are not with you and neither is Eddy Strode. You two have some explaining to do.'

'It was Eddy Strode's fault. Wasn't it, Xavier?'

Xavier nodded. 'Yeah, that's right, Stanford.'

'Yeah, Stanford. This is how it went down. We got to the motel. Everything was cool. Xavier and I wanted to take care of the women first. We thought if we…'

'Come on, Ronny. I don't care what might have happened or what you thought. OK?'

'Sure thing. Anyway, the rest of it's real simple. Eddy had his pistol. The silly fucker went and banged on Marlowe's door. The door opened, we could see Eddy with his gun in his hand.'

'Was he pointing the gun, was it by his side, which?'

'Oh, ahh, I don't remember. Xavier?'

'I think he was pointing it. No, hang on, it was by his side.'

'Really? Is that a fact? Neither of you remember a critical thing like that? Amazing. Carry on. What's next? Hang on, let me guess. Eddy's standing there like a dummy and Marlowe shot him. Is that what you're saying? Eddy Strode, more professional than anyone I know, stands there waiting to be shot, and the Australian journalist, who probably doesn't know one end of a gun from another, figuring that someone was going to knock on his door, is all ready and waiting. And what about the two women, Steele and the Mexican?'

'Well, like I said, Stanford, Eddy knocked on Marlowe's door. He got shot. All the lights in the motel came on. People were hollering.'

'Yeah, Stanford,' Xavier cut in. 'They were yelling, screaming call the cops. It woulda been suicide to grab the two dames.'

'Now, tell me. What really happened?'

Ronny felt beads of sweat on his brow.

'Honest, Stanford. That's the truth.'

The face of The Prophet was an unreadable, terrifying blank. He spoke without a hint of emotion. 'Get out. Both of you. I need time alone, to think.'

'Stanford?' Ronny pleaded.
'Get out!'

CHAPTER 29

RONNY GETS NEWS

Ronny BBQ Delgado lay on his bed halfway through a bottle of Early Times. The picture window of his comfortable room held sweeping views of the commune and Stanford's palatial mansion. Ronny was proud of his home. His comfy king-size bed got most of the sun. To the left of the bed sat a small bedside table with a gray shaded lamp. To the right was a set of wood-stained patterned drawers with a collection of his Cowboys trophies crammed on top. On the righthand wall as you walked in, bright Dallas Cowboys posters and flags boasting of Ronny Delgado's glory days dominated the room. But at that moment he wasn't thinking about football.

He'd seen the young man enter the Prophet's home. Bile rose in his throat as he watched Stanford place an arm over Chase's shoulder, before the door shut. Two days and nights had passed and Stanford hadn't called. August was drawing near and Ronny despaired. He'd put the word out. If Spencer and Savannah were anywhere in California, someone would see them. Someone *had* to see them. Ronny needed this to happen. He needed to be back in Stanford's good graces, to see a smile light up those hypnotic eyes.

The phone suddenly rang.

'Hey, BBQ, I heard you was lookin' for a couple of cats. That right, man?'

'Who's this?'

'You remember me. Booker. Perez and me was buddies. He introduced us at that Family meet in Oakland. I heard about what happened. Real shame, he was a cool dude.'

Ronny vaguely remembered a tall black guy with an outrageous afro.

'Oh yeah. I remember. How did you get my number?'

'Hey man, you remember, you said if ever I wanted to join the Family give you a call. You wrote your number on my arm. We smoked some shit together.'

'Yeah, yeah. What can I do for you?'

'I heard you was lookin' for a tall guy, an Aussie and his bitch.'

Suddenly sober, Ronny sat bolt upright. 'Where are you, ahh, Booker…?'

'Hey man. Like I say, I heard about Perez. Did this guy ice him? I mean Perez was one tough…'

'It's a long story, Booker. But I gotta find them. Where did you see them?'

'I work at the 7-Eleven, 708 Colorado Avenue, Palo Alto. And they come here, regular. You know? Buy the usual shit. Is there some dollars in it?'

'Yeah sure, Booker, but where do they live, exactly?'

'Hey man, am I a postman? How the fuck do I know? But they walk here. Can't live far.'

'That's all you got, Booker?'

'Yeah. But like I said. I expect some green. You know what I'm sayin?'

'We'll be seeing you, Booker. Gotta go.'

Ronny's chest swelled; he punched the air. 'Yes!' he yelled.

Jumping off his bed, he yanked on his boots and grabbed his coat. He'd been spreading the word among the underbelly of San Francisco's counterculture, hoping that at the mention of the Family all the up-and-coming revolutionaries and disaffected youth would keep an eye open. He felt a surge of pride. Stanford would be pleased.

'You have done well. Very well indeed, Ronny. I'm still not convinced you and Xavier have exactly been honest with me. But let's move on. I believe you that Strode is dead, but I'm not convinced it happened exactly as you said.'

'Honest, Stanford…'

'I said, we are moving on, Ronny. Go to the garage and see Roberto. He'll give you any weapons you think you may need. Take the van again, because this time you'll have hostages, won't you?'

'You can count on me.'

'Take Xavier with you, and that new guy, Wilbur. He's working in the garage with Roberto. He's only been out of Attica for a few months and he's keen. I see a big future for him. He's a good-looking fellow, butter wouldn't melt. He's got quite a rap sheet. Ex-marine.'

'You're kidding? Ex-marine? He looks like a pussy. And that haircut. You're kidding.'

'Really, just because he works out and you can see the results? You should think about doing some exercise, Ronny. It's most unbecoming when someone lets themselves go. It's weakness, laziness, and I can't abide either.'

'I'm gonna lose weight, honest, but Wilbur…?'

'Enough. Wilbur has got what it takes. He has nerves of steel. He's done time for an aggravated robbery, and I believe he has a couple of kills to his credit.'

'How come he's out then?'

Ronny and slim-hipped Wilbur hadn't hit it off. Wilbur Miracle hadn't been particularly impressed when Ronny had started to tell Wilbur, over a few beers, about his football career.

'I'm not without influence, Ronny dear. I assured the parole board that by taking Wilbur Miracle…'

'Miracle? That's his handle?'

'Yes, Ronny, that's his name.'

'When do you want us to go, Stanford?'

Stanford glanced at his watch.

'No time like the present. I reckon it's about three hours, give or take, to Palo Alto.'

***

Ronny watched Wilbur Miracle. Oxy welder in hand he was cutting through steel plate, sparks showered across the garage. Wilbur had a Mohican cut and scythe-shaped eyebrows, accentuated by the black welder's goggles. His Roman nose and high cheekbones sat above a chiselled jaw. Ronny kept watching as he turned off the control valves and laid the torch body down on an upturned metal drum. Nodding at Ronny, he ripped off his goggles, wiping sweat off his face with a dirty towel. Walking with a tiger-like tread he padded over to the bench, grabbed a bottle of water, and unscrewed the top. Upending the bottle and pouring the contents down his throat, he winked.

'Seen enough?'

Ronny blushed.

'I, ahh, I didn't want to interrupt.'

'You here to talk about football.'

'Nothing like that. We got a job to do. The Prophet reckons you're the man.'

'Whatever he wants is OK with me. I owe him big time.'

Ronny waited to tell Wilbur the details until they were in the van. Xavier powered the old Dodge van through the winding mountain road. Wilbur just grunted, and didn't seem at all concerned as Ronny explained that they were going to kidnap three people.

'A guy and two women, huh? Is the dude going to be a problem? Are they carrying?'

'Nah, no problem. The guy and one of the women are journalists and the other is a Mexican woman. There's no way they'd be armed.'

Ronny opened the glove department and grabbed a Beretta 9mm semi-automatic pistol.

'You familiar with one of these?' He handed it to Wilbur.

'Yeah, standard issue for the Marines.'

Wilbur and Xavier sat in the front while sprawled on the back seat, Ronny pored over the National Geographic Road atlas and began to realise finding their prey had a needle in the haystack feel about it. Stanford had an uncanny ability to condense arguments and not get involved with the fine details.

'I'll bet you guys don't know why these are called the Diablo Mountains,' Wilbur said out of the blue.

Ronny yawned. 'I have a sneaking suspicion you're gonna tell us.'

'Of course. In 1805 or 6 or whatever soldiers tried to capture some Indians in a marsh near Concord. The Indians simply disappeared into the woods in the middle of the night, the soldiers named the area 'Monte Diablo' which means thicket of the devil.'

'How the hell would you know shit like that?' Xavier asked.

'I'll tell you. When I was told I'd make parole and I'd be living with you guys in the Diablo Mountains I went to the prison library and read up on it.'

'Thanks for sharing. Not.' Ronny rolled his eyes. On the other hand, he was thrilled Wilbur wasn't a trigger-happy psychopath like Eddy. He hadn't seen his impending death even once so far, and they'd been on the road for going on three hours.

'Can you guys fill me in on something?'

Wilbur turned his head to look at Ronny.

'Sure, if we can.'

'What the hell is it with the Prophet's thing about the Beatles? He's obsessed. And everyone says they'll be playing at the commune. And then there's the band that performs at night after chow. I mean, they're great. They look and sound like the Beatles. What's the story?'

'I guess it's OK to tell you.' Xavier glanced back at Ronny.

'Can it, Xavier,' Ronny barked. 'Let Stanford tell Wilbur about it in his own sweet time.'

'I just thought…'

'Stop thinking, Xavier, it's not good for you. Look, we're about to enter San Jose.'

Ronny turned to Wilbur.

'The thing is, Wilbur, you know the broad detail of what the Prophet's plan is. Some of the finer details are a bit of a secret. But the main goal is to escape the tyranny of America and its justice system. Hell, you'd know a bit about that?'

'Folsom wasn't a lot of fun.'

'I'm sure it wasn't. We are going to be drawing our own borders. The commune is just the first. We have land in Arizona, Montana and more. It's going to be a different America.'

'How's it gonna be different?'

Ronny's eyes blazed with patriotic zeal.

'We're going to have proper freedoms, proper laws. No more fucking cops acting for crooked politicians. We want our country back. We have well-armed militias in several states. Just listen to the music *The Times They Are A-Changing*. It's not just a song. Did you listen to the message in the *Eve of Destruction?* The music of today is reaching out and drawing people in.'

'No kidding?'

'I tell you, we're serious. We're going to change everything. Wall Street, the crooked bankers. They won't know what fucking hit them. We send billions overseas when we have poverty here. It's a goddam disgrace. Remember we had a revolution in 1775? That started with a few patriots just like us.'

'I'm listening. But what the fuck have the Beatles got to do with this?'

'Like I said, they're a small cog in the upcoming miracle. Do you like that, Wilbur Miracle?'

'Yeah sure. Love it. Hey guys, we got time for a burger? I don't give a fuck about the Beatles. Whatever the Prophet has planned is OK with me.'

Ronny glanced at his watch.

'Yeah, we gotta eat.'

'Before I went inside I used to go to the Burger Bar in First street. Great eats. Is that OK?' Wilbur asked.

***

Xavier swung the van into the parking lot.

'I been here before. Great burritos.'

The old burger barn looked like it was preserved in time on South First Street, like an insect trapped in amber, with its old-time drive-in exterior, a marquee reading *BURGERS 5 FOR A BUCK* and the unmistakable diner-fried food aroma wafting through the ample parking lot.

They slid into a booth overlooking the parking lot and ordered popcorn shrimp, fish and chips and burritos from a smiling waitress in jeans, tie-dyed T-shirt, beads and sandals.

'Hey man, I love your cool hair. It's a groove.' She smiled, holding eye contact. Wilbur grinned, boldly taking her hand and kissing it.

'I finish my shift at eight,' she whispered in his ear.

Ronny glared at her, until she scurried off.

Smiling again at Wilbur, ten minutes later, the server placed their orders in front of them. Ronny wasn't pleased at the great big smile Wilbur gave her in return, or how blatant he was in watching her walk back to the kitchen.

'Keep your mind on the job, Wilbur. Let's get down to business. We're only a few minutes away from the Seven Eleven.'

'What the fuck do we do then, Ronny? We got no idea where these pricks live.' Xavier spoke through a mouthful of burrito.

Suddenly Ronny wasn't so confident. What if their prey had already left Palo Alto? They could've gone anywhere. He figured Stanford wouldn't be happy with another failure.

***

Xavier made a left into Colorado Avenue, which appeared to be divided into three parts by intersections. The architecture was typical California, both sides of the street were made up of three-storey blocks of buildings which were uniformly square, old-looking with grimy walls. Their colours of green, yellow and faded pink made the street appear slightly tawdry. At the far end of the avenue a lone single-level, shabby stucco home with an overgrown garden stood out. As they drove quietly along, they passed an old people's home and a liquor store and then the Seven Eleven featuring a rectangular flower bed with some bedraggled blooms and a wood bench covered in graffiti.

'I thought Palo Alto was supposed to be pretty fancy?' Xavier's lip curled as he reversed the van into a spot in-between an old Simca and a battered 59 Ford Galaxie.

***

The Seven Eleven looked like any other, with countless aisles standing anonymously, in perfect symmetry. Masses of snacks and candy piled onto each shelf. Ronny counted about five staff members, and maybe the same number of customers. Xavier stayed in the van. Wilbur strolled in and threw some fruit into a bag.

A slim Mexican woman with a trolley piled high seemed to be studying rows of cosmetics. Behind the checkout looking cool, leaned a tall black guy with an afro.

'Hey, Booker.' Ronny and Booker slapped skin.

Booker grinned. 'Hey. What's up, my man?'

Ronny pulled out his wallet and slipped a fifty into the black man's hand.

Booker winked, stuffing the note into his top pocket. Wilbur strolled up to the counter with a bag of apples.

'Booker, this here is Wilbur. He's one of ours. Know what I mean?'

Wilbur and Booker bumped fists as Wilbur placed the fruit on the scales.

'Nah man. You good. On the house.'

'Any more clues on what we looking for, Booker?'

Booker leaned forward whispering.

'See that Mexican chick? She come in with them all the time. Know what I'm sayin?'

Ronny spun around; the woman had her back towards him as she pushed her trolley up the aisle. He knew who she was.

'Thanks, Booker, you been a great help. C'mon Wilbur. Gotta go.'

'Hey man, what's happening?' Wilbur asked as they climbed into the van.

'Yeah, Ronny?' Xavier asked.

'Thank God she didn't see me. The Mexican chicana, Maria, is in the store.'

'Hey, no kidding?' Wilbur smiled as he opened the glove box, grabbing his pistol.

'For fuck's sake, Xavier, move the fucking van. She'll be coming out in a minute. She can't live far away. We don't want her to see us. We're gonna find out where she lives. Stanford's gonna be happy. Man, I tell you. We can't lose. We'll be back at the commune tonight with three happy little hostages.'

CHAPTER 30
THE MAGNUM

Maria left the Seven Eleven, a carry bag in each hand. She'd purchased the ingredients for her homemade chilli. Garlic, onion, peppers, cilantro, black beans and ground beef. She wanted to thank Spencer and Savannah with a memorable Mexican dinner. A glimpse of two men scrambling into an old Dodge Van had her on high alert. Savannah and Spencer had warned her to be wary. Placing her bags on the ground, she perched on the bench at the front of the Seven Eleven. She peered at the small mirror after retrieving a lipstick and a compact from her bag.

Her stomach lurched. Xavier Matinez in the driver's seat had his head bowed. Next to him sat the frightening Wilbur Miracle with his distinctive mohawk. She recognized them immediately.

Her hand shook as she snapped her compact shut. At the end of the street, she could just see the house. So near and yet so far. She sat quivering with fear. Had they recognised her? Minutes passed; she remained frozen.

***

Savannah glanced at her watch, then over at where Spencer was engrossed in campy superhero hijinks.

'I'm not sure it was such a good idea, Maria going to the store.'

'You may be right, but she was very restless, she just needed to get out. She was really keen to prepare a meal for us. The Seven Eleven is just up the road, surely…'

'Surely what, dammit? I'm going to check on her.'

Savannah grabbed her pistol, checking the load before strapping on the shoulder holster.

'Oh hell, I might as well join you.'

'Are you sure you can leave Batman?'

Spencer padded over to the television and reluctantly switched it off.

'The Riddler was just about to do something dastardly. Never mind, I'm sure Batman and Robin will come out on top.'

They grabbed their coats and stepped outside, cautiously scanning the street.

'Hey, look, I can see Maria, she's sitting on the seat outside of the store.' Savannah pointed.

'I guess she's OK. I might go back inside and see what the Riddler is up to?'

'Hang on, Spencer. Take a look.'

Maria rose from her seat, bags in hand. As she strode off in their direction, they saw a Dodge van pull out and slowly follow.

'C'mon, Spencer, I don't like the look of this. Have you got your 0.38?'

'No.'

'Good, you'd probably hit a passer-by anyway.'

They strode off in the direction of the van. Maria saw them and broke into a run.

***

'Wilbur, Xavier, look, those two fucking journalists are heading this way. Wilbur, jump out and grab that wetback bitch. Put your gun to her fucking head. They'll get the message. Xavier, get ready. You've got your pistol? How good is this?'

'Hang on a minute, Ronny. I don't believe it, that Savannah broad has a fucking gun. Jesus, since when did fucking journalists carry a gun?' Wilbur yelled.

'Just do as you're told, Wilbur, there's no way in hell she could hit you from there. No one is that good. Particularly a fucking woman.'

Wilbur threw open the passenger door and shot towards Maria. She screamed and dropped her bags, breaking into a sprint.

'No, you fucking don't, you Mexican slut.' Wilbur grabbed her by her coat collar. She screamed again.

Spencer had seen it all before. It would remain etched in his mind like a movie played in slow motion. Savannah, legs apart and the Magnum in both hands, squeezed off a round. The 0.357 Magnum round, travelling at 1800 feet per second, punched its way through Wilbur's chest, leaving a gaping hole quickly filling with blood and gushing like a fountain. He fell to the ground, the pool of red forming around him, soaking into his clothes as he choked to death.

The van stopped, then reversed at high speed up the street. Savannah loosed off two quick shots as the Dodge careened backwards, but it swerved just in time to save the driver from her aim. Smashing into a parked car, the van swung in an arc and roared off.

CHAPTER 31

THE AUDITION

Stanford ushered the young man into the lounge area.

'Let me give you a hand,' he offered, grabbing the compact Vox AC 30 amplifier by its handle.

'Thanks, Mr Delaware, this's a real honour. I've been looking for a regular gig for a while. It's tough in San Francisco. Everyone's a guitar player.'

'Has anyone ever said you look just like George Harrison?'

'Yeah, I get that all the time. I can even do the accent. "Thank you very mooch. I'm glad you liked the show."'

Stanford clapped his hands. 'That was wonderful, Caspar. Now let's see what you can do.'

'Here? Now?'

'Yep, right now. Get your guitar out. What is it?'

'It's a Strat, Stratocaster, Fender, Mr Delaware. It's…'

'Yeah, I'm familiar with the Fender. I think both John Lennon and George Harrison use them.'

Caspar opened his guitar case and pulled out a well-worn and scratched sunburst Stratocaster. He then plugged it and the amplifier in. Stanford sat behind his gleaming black Steinway.

'OK, I'm going to play some twelve bar in E. Just follow.'

The compelling, fluid sound of a walking bass line flowed out of the piano. Caspar grinned and slid into a riff that sounded like an amalgam of Chuck Berry and some Mississippi Delta blues. Soon the two players were lost in the beat. The Stratocaster howled with a blistering solo. The beat changed. Caspar's fingers danced over the fret board. Workers in the fields below stopped as the sounds rung out over the valley.

Finally, Stanford took his hands off the keyboard.

'That was great. Just great. You've got the job. Wow, it's thirsty work. How about a drink, Caspar? Non-alcoholic, of course. And I'll explain what it's all about.'

Caspar thirstily quaffed the orange liquid.

'Say, Mr Delaware, this's nice. What is it?'

'I guess you could say it's an old family recipe.' Stanford topped up Caspar's glass.

Now glassy eyed, Caspar asked, 'So, what exactly is the gig, Mr Delaware?'

'I'm not in a position to disclose all the details, but I will say this. It will be the biggest show you have ever done. The biggest crowd. The eyes of the world will be on you.'

'Wow. No kidding? Can you tell me where, at least?'

'San Francisco. But I really can't say more at the moment.'

'So, what happens in the meantime, Mr Delaware? I mean, I have expenses. When does it happen?'

Stanford laughed and stood up.

'Just look out there, Caspar. This is our wonderful commune, and you're now a part of it.'

'Yeah, it's real nice but…'

'I can see you're confused. Here's what's happening. You'll need to rehearse with our band. They only play Beatles songs.'

'Do you mean sort of like a tribute thing?'

'Exactly. I'll admit it's a little unusual. You'll have your own cabin. I expect you to work in the fields along with everyone else, and then at night you'll play a set with our group. They're great, good players. Nice guys.'

'I don't know, Mr Delaware. This isn't what I…'

'Of course, I understand. But you'll be paid $150 a week and everything will be supplied, and after the big gig, the offers will start rolling in. I'll give you a clue. A television series.'

'Wow, I've heard rumours of a television series about a rock and roll band. They were auditioning in LA. Is this what it's all about, Mr Delaware?'

Stanford had been a little uneasy when he told the other band members about Grady Chamberlin. On reflection he wasn't surprised they'd swallowed the story. Their thirst for fame had been far greater than their concern for anyone but themselves. *A pity, he really was a lovely young man.*

Stanford held a finger to his lips.

'I've told you too much already. But yes. The reason I want you here in the band, is you will need to get to know the other guys. This'll be a show about four struggling musicians trying to hit the big time.'

CHAPTER 32

ON THE MOVE

Dale's Pontiac and three pale blue Ford Galaxies crammed close as if to form a protective barrier at the front of the safe house.

Inside the Seven Eleven, a well-built police sergeant tried to interview a reluctant Booker.

'You must have seen something. For Chrissake, how about a bit of cooperation? We can take you back to the precinct if I say so. Make you spend the rest of the day going over mugshots? We can make your life difficult if we want.' He turned to his deputy. 'Hey, Gordon, you find anything in the back room?'

The deputy had spent the last twenty minutes in the storeroom and lunchroom rifling through the Seven Eleven employees' bags and belongings. Booker had thanked his lucky stars he'd had the forethought to flush some baggies of coke down the toilet.

'C'mon, guys. You got a warrant? You can't just do this crap,' Booker protested.

'Listen to me, dipshit, in case you hadn't noticed there's been a homicide. We don't need a warrant. Now, I'll ask you once again. Who were those people who came into the store?'

'Which people?'

'Witnesses have said, two guys, one a Latino, the other a tall white guy, came in and you were talking to them like they were old friends.'

Booker didn't like the cops and he particularly didn't like the sergeant. Booker also had a basic criminal understanding of his rights.

'Listen, man, I told you I didn't see nothing. And guess what, I've heard about the fifth amendment. So, charge me or get the hell out of my store.'

He thought he heard the deputy mumble *fucking nigger* as he put his hand on his nightstick.

'Leave it, Gordon,' the sergeant snapped.

***

Dale paced up and down the living room. Two agents sat in their cars, scoping the street. One bustled around the kitchen making coffee and rummaging through the refrigerator on the hunt for food. Savannah had offered to make sandwiches but Clint, an agent built like a Mack Truck, smiled and said, *'that's OK, Ma'am'*, as he continued his search. She stormed out of the kitchen not knowing whether she was most annoyed being referred to as Ma'am and not her FBI rank or the cavalier way he seemed to make the house his own.

'Just tell your agents to make themselves at home, Dale, su casa mi casa,' she snarled, plonking onto the lounge next to Spencer.

'What?'

'Su casa…Oh hell, it's Spanish.'

'OK, Spanish, huh? Good. Now let's talk about what's happening. Where's Maria now?'

'She's in her room,' Spencer replied. That woman had had a rough go of it.

'Best place for her at the moment. Now where were we? Hang on, it looks like we have company.'

'May I come in?' A voice boomed from the front door. Spencer grinned at Savannah.

'As I live and breathe. Gus Horslay. How the hell are you?'

145

Spencer jumped up as the big guy entered the room and wrapped his huge arms around him. Gus disengaged, laughing and grabbed Savannah's outstretched hand.

'And, of course, Special Agent Savannah Steele. It's great to see you both again. I see the tats have disappeared. That's a shame.' Gus grinned from ear to ear.

'My days of being a biker old lady are thankfully over, and the fake tats were scrubbed off.'

'We didn't have a chance to talk at the motel in Clayton. You still riding that panhead?' Spencer asked.

'No, no. I bought one of the first new Harley Shovelheads. Straight out of Milwaukee. I tell you, it's gorgeous. Leaks oil like you wouldn't believe. But then it wouldn't be a Harley if it didn't. What about you, Spencer, you still got that chopper?'

'No Gus, sadly it belonged to the bureau. I tell you I miss it.'

Gus turned to Dale.

'Greetings, Special Agent Fletcher. Gus Horslay reporting for duty. Good to see you, Dale.' Gus saluted with a grin.

'Good to see you again, Gus. Ty wasn't available apparently.'

'Nah, silly sod fell off his goddam bike. Broken leg.'

'Sorry to hear that. Sit down, we'll tell you what's happening,'

Clint entered the room with a tray of mugs, a pot of coffee and ham sandwiches.

'Here we go, folks.' He turned to Savannah. 'I'd sorta hoped there'd be some pastrami or mustard, even some Swiss Cheese.'

'Gee, sorry about that. I'll dash down to the Seven Eleven right now.'

'No, no. Stay where you are. We'll manage.' Obviously, Clint wasn't the most perceptive of agents, and missed the sarcasm.

'Excuse me, boss.' Special Agent Jax came in through the front door. Spencer thought he looked like a parking meter. He noticed the agent's heavy metal cufflinks and wondered if he wore them as an anchor. A strong wind would have blown him away.

'What is it?' Dale snapped.

'There's a police officer talking to Orson. He wants some answers. I think he's probably figured the Feds are involved.'

'OK, show him in.'

'It's they, actually. He has a deputy as well.'

'Wonderful. That's all we need. Show them both in.'

Gus winked at Spencer.

'This should be interesting.'

The sergeant led the way. Big, bluff, red-faced and no nonsense.

'I'm Sergeant Biggerstaff, Palo Alto Police. This here's my deputy, Gordon Slye.'

'Biggerstaff? You're kidding?' Savannah whispered sotto voce, nudging Spencer in the ribs.

'Hey, Sarge. Someone here has questions to answer.' Deputy Slye stared hard at Savannah.

'Thanks for dropping by, Sergeant and Deputy Slye. I'm FBI Special Agent Fletcher. This's federal business. I'm very sorry about what's happened, but as I'm sure you're aware the deceased was shot as he attempted a kidnapping.' Dale flashed his badge.

'Hey, hang on a minute, Foster...'

'Fletcher.'

'Yeah, of course, Fletcher, who gives a... witnesses had the impression it may have been a domestic. A guy and his wife...Maybe she'd run away. Something like that.'

Deputy Slye stepped forward. 'Hey you.' He pointed at Savannah. 'You fit the description of the suspect who shot the guy in cold blood. Let's see some ID. How the fuck do we know you're FBI?'

Savannah roared with laughter.

'Hey Dale, I just love this guy. He's like a man with a fork, in a world of soup. Room temperature IQ.'

'You listen to me, you better…'

'Deputy, go and play with the traffic. I'll handle this,' Biggerstaff snarled.

Silence descended as the deputy stomped out of the room. The sergeant continued.

'Sorry about that, Ma'am. I gather you're the one who fired the round. And you are?'

'I am none of your business.'

Beet red, Biggerstaff turned to Dale.

'I'm a patient man, Fletcher, but a bit of cooperation would be nice. We have a dead body and a lot of loose ends that aren't going to just disappear. How about you give me a clue as to what's going on? For a start, this woman here and the guy next to her, are they FBI? If so, can I see some sort of ID?'

'I'm sorry, Sergeant Biggerstaff. Sadly security concerns make it impossible to supply more details. Would you care for a sandwich?'

CHAPTER 33

FAMILY IS FOREVER

Slurping his coffee and moodily chomping on a ham sandwich, Dale moaned.

'Heck, this wasn't the way I thought things would pan out. Gosh, I thought they'd never leave. Biggerstaff could be a real problem. Anyway, no point worrying I guess.'

Over the next hour Dale had outlined to Gus all they knew and what they suspected.

'What a surprise. Savannah Steele's at it again.' Gus had laughed when told about Savannah shooting Wilbur Miracle.

'Gus, I didn't have a choice.'

Savannah, Spencer, Dale and Gus sat at the kitchen table. Spencer nursed a Modelo Beer. Savannah's coffee had long gone cold. The other FBI agents were invisible.

'It would have been a far better outcome if you hadn't shot the late Mr Miracle.' Dale scowled.

'Silly me. I don't know why, but I thought seeing as he'd grabbed Maria and held a gun to her head that would constitute probable cause.'

'Don't be so gosh darn sensitive, Steele. I know you had to do it; it just wasn't the outcome I wanted.'

'I can see you're upset, Dale.' Spencer chortled. 'I mean a 'heck' and a 'gosh darn'. That says a lot.'

'Yeah, I know I'm a bit of a square. Anyway, a change of plans. It turns out Maria Gomez is an illegal immigrant, so she's going back to Mexico.'

Savannah frowned. 'That's a bit rough, Dale. Surely she could apply for citizenship?' Maria had been abducted once, tied up and nearly abducted a second time, only to have The Family try for a third. In the last case she'd had a man die feet from her from a sucking chest wound. She deserved better than to be casually tossed back to Mexico.

'Yes, she could. But we don't know what Delaware's next move is and I don't have the resources to protect her.'

'C'mon, Dale, she can be with us, surely,' Spencer snapped.

'Enough. It's settled. Special Agent Jenny Smith is going to drive her to Tijuana. The Mexican authorities will take it from there. It's for the best.'

'Wouldn't it be easier if you put Maria on a flight to Mexico?' Savannah asked.

'Thought about it, but Delaware seems to have people everywhere. There's a chance, slim perhaps, that he may have San Francisco Airport watched. If Agent Smith takes her by car there's no way they are going to be able to know that's happening. Trust me, Savannah, I know what I'm doing, OK?'

Maria gave Savannah a hug before climbing into Special Agent Jenny Smith's cream Chevrolet.

***

The old van, now with a badly dented side panel, peeled off into the traffic. They'd gotten lucky that the woman's hand cannon had ricocheted off the steel pillar and not punched holes in the windscreen or the window. Wilber hadn't been as lucky…

'I don't get it, Ronny, why are we following the beaner broad? I mean what the fuck has she got to do with anything?'

'I just hate it when you think, Xavier. Let me explain. I've phoned the Prophet, and we are in agreement something stinks. Whoever the woman was who shot Wilbur, she sure as hell isn't a journalist. You saw the cops go to the house where they're living.'

'You took a goddam chance watching the house. We coulda…'

'Shut the fuck up, Xavier, they didn't think we were going to be so close. Anyway, just look at what happened, the cops showed up, then all those cars. I reckon Marlowe and Steele are Feds.'

'You think?' Xavier clearly didn't believe him, and Ronny didn't blame him. An Aussie, a Fed? 'Hang on, Marlowe is an Aussie. There's no way he's FBI.'

It didn't make sense on its face, but there was no other explanation. Their terrible luck only fuelled Ronny's anger.

'Give it a rest, Xavier. Who knows what the exact story is? But I'm telling you Steele at least isn't a fucking journalist. Who or what exactly Marlowe is remains a mystery.'

'So, what does the Prophet want with the Mexican?'

'If we can grab her, she'll talk. We have to know what's going on. August is getting closer. If the Feds have got wind of what's going down, we'll have to abort.'

That could not happen. Stanford would lose his fucking mind, and the target of his rage would be Ronny.

'Ok, I get the picture. I'm not a fucking idiot. So what's going on? We're following that Chev, there's a woman driving, the Mexican's in the front seat with her. What do you want to do? Run them off the street, grab the Mexican and take off?'

'The driver has to be a Fed; she'll be armed. If we try anything she'll shoot and we'll have a firefight on a busy street. Not a great idea.'

'So, what then, Ronny?'

'They may be going to another safe house. They may be going to an FBI office. Who the hell knows? My idea is just follow and see what sort of opportunity presents itself. It's getting dark. They're not going to drive all fucking night.'

***

Maria gazed fearfully at the traffic as Jenny expertly sped onto US-101 South and then turned into Leavesley Road in Gilroy.

'I'm worried, Jenny. Perhaps they might follow us.' Maria and Special agent Jenny Smith had immediately bonded.

'I don't think so, Maria. They're not interested in you. It's Spencer and Savannah they're after. And remember, I have a gun.'

Jenny opened her jacket, exposing a revolver nestled in a slim black shoulder holster. The air had become an anxious swirl of drops, the windscreen wipers slapped across the screen.

'When I was a little girl in Mexico, I used to love the rain.'

'Where in Mexico did you live?'

'Popotla. It's about fifteen minutes from Rosarito.'

'And that's close to Tijuana, right? Is it nice?'

Jenny had visited Tijuana as a child, with her family. She had a scattered, cheerful memory of swarthy moustachioed men, sombreros and fish tacos.

'Si, but my family was poor. It's a half hour drive from Tijuana. My father was a fisherman, but he died. Our house had a view of the ocean. Why I have to go back to Mexico if you say these people are not after me?'

Jenny didn't really have an answer.

'How long before we get to San Diego, Jenny?'

Maria's question reminded Jenny of when she was on a family road trip and her younger brother Brad would constantly ask the same question. *Are we nearly there, Dad?*

'Sorry, love, it's a long drive. Seven hours give or take.'

'Diablos, I'm so tired.'

'I know you are. You can get some sleep here and now if you like. We're going to stop at a motel in San Luis Obispo for the night and then make an early start for the border. I know a great little Mexican restaurant there. We can have a nice meal, maybe some Cerveza. How does that sound?'

'Oh yes. I'd like that. I wish I didn't have to go back to Mexico. I miss my husband so much.'

Jenny Smith had been the runner up in the Miss California Beauty Pageant in 1962 and had screen test offers from tinsel town. She was considering taking one of them, but after her younger brother Brad had been shot in a late-night robbery in Tenderloin, a neighbourhood in San Francisco, movies were out of the question. She decided to join law enforcement instead.

CHAPTER 34

SAN LUIS OBISPO

Jenny swung the car off Route 101 and on to Monterey Street.

'We'll be staying the night at the Motel Inn, Maria. I used to stay here with my mom and dad and my late brother Brad, years ago. I remember Dad saying it was the very first motel in the whole wide world. Would you believe it was actually built in 1925? How about that?'

'What happened to your brother?' Maria didn't seem to be interested in motel history.

'It was terrible. A young punk, a gang member in 'The Lords of Frisco', shot him and stole his wallet. A lousy 10 bucks was all Brad had on him.'

'Did they catch the bandito?'

'Yeah, they got him. He did some time in San Quentin but because he was young and a first offender he only got a few years. Bleeding heart jury as always. Nothing ever seems to change. His name was Juan Garcia.'

***

'How about a margarita, Maria?'

Seated in the noisy barn-like Morenos Taqueria in Dolliver Street, Pismo Beach, Maria gazed in wonderment at the vaulted wooden ceilings and the casual chic of this family run eatery. The tantalising lively aroma of sauteing peppers, grilled meats, salsas and herbs wafted from the kitchen.

'This is a very fancy restaurant. Is it expensive?' Maria asked nervously.

'Don't you worry about a thing, Maria. The bureau is paying. The fish tacos look good. And chicken enchiladas, wow. We're going to have a feast.'

Over the next hour Maria poured out her story.

'Santiago and I left Mexico.' She pronounced it Meh-hico. 'There is no future. Everyone is poor. Our first stop was San Diego. I remember we climbed out of the bus; we had one small suitcase each. Oh Jenny, we couldn't believe our eyes. It was a city of wide avenues, and small places to sit and eat or, or just to relax. It was so clean. And the sky towers in the centre, we discovered parks and wild spaces.'

'How did you manage for money?'

'Oh, straight away I found a job as a server in the Casa De Reyes restaurant in Calhoun Street. Do you know it, Jenny?'

'No, can't say as I do.'

They paused as the waiter, a dashing, good-looking guy in a traditional charro suit with its tight decorated pants, short jacket and black silk tie, placed their order in front of them.

'Two beautiful tacos for two beautiful ladies.'

Jenny stifled a laugh. Maria blushed, glancing at his retreating figure.

'He is very good looking.'

'And what did Santiago do?'

'Santiago? He got a job in same restaurant, washing dishes. He was jealous. I make so much more money. Americanos so generous. The tips. I could not believe. Sometimes they give me twenty dollar.'

Maria and Jenny laughed as they ate and drank cold beers. The restaurant carried a happy vibe of noisy chatter interwoven with the aroma of their meal.

'We stayed at a cheap motel. It was OK. It had a television.'

'Tell me about the Prophet.'

'Jenny, it was like something out of a movie. We went to Balboa Park, the Starlight Bowl. There was a band, The Mothers and their Fathers.'

'Really? Are you sure? I think you mean the Mamas and the Papas.'

'Si, oh yes. A big lady. Such a lovely voice. We listened to the band and a nice man, started talking to us. He told us about the "Family" and how they were going to change the world. They had like, big signs and pretty girls were handing out pieces of paper with the writing about the "Family" and there was free hamburgers and Coca Cola.'

'What happened then?'

'The Prophet had this lovely big trailer, and the man we were talking to asked us if we'd like to meet him.'

'You mean, meet the Prophet?'

'Yes, si, we couldn't believe it. I was so nervous. He was very nice. The trailer was so quiet. We sat down and he gave us a drink of a sort of fruit drink. He was like a God. He asked us if we'd like to join their commune in the Diablo Mountains. We had no doubts. At first it was just as we expected. Santiago worked in the fields. I did cleaning and some cooking. It was hard work, but it was friendly, the food was good. Santiago and I had our own cabin.'

Jenny took a bite of her fish taco. 'Wow, that's about as good as it gets.' She wiped her mouth with a serviette. 'They are messy. You said at first it was OK. What changed?'

'It was small things. There was one man. A nice guy, from Alaska I think, he was complaining.'

'About what?'

'Silly things really. The food. The work was too hard. That sort of thing.'

Jenny's eyes narrowed. 'So, what happened?'

'There was this man. Eduardo, he had a Mexican gang tattoo. I remember he shoved this Alaskan man; I think his name was Jackson, up against the wall and held a knife against his throat.'

'Not very nice. And what happened after that?'

'He wasn't hurt. Eduardo slapped him and whispered something. And then Eduardo, he walked away. I remember this guy Jackson was terrified. Then he was just gone. One of my jobs was cleaning the cabins. I was told to clean his cabin. But all his stuff was still there.'

'You mean Jackson disappeared?'

'Si.'

'What do you think happened to him?'

Maria shivered. 'I don't know. I think they may have killed him.'

The crowd started to thin.

'Would you like another beer, Maria?'

'No thank you, Jenny.'

***

Ronny checked his watch. It was nudging ten pm. The air was filled with the melody of car horns, voices and footsteps.

'Doesn't anybody sleep around here?' Xavier grumbled.

'Just wait, it's starting to quiet down.'

Heaving a sigh of relief, Ronny smiled as a number of noisy teenagers left the restaurant, laughing and singing. Car doors slammed, radios blared rock music, noisy exhausts bellowed as their vehicles roared out of the parking lot. Ronny and Xavier had been impatiently watching Morenos Taqueria in Dolliver Street, Pismo Beach from the vast parking area. They could see the cream Chevrolet at the far end, at least two hundred yards from the restaurant entrance.

'Well, they won't be going anywhere soon.' Ronny laughed. He'd punctured two tires on the Chev with his trusty switchblade.

'Hey look.' Xavier pointed as Jenny and Maria sauntered out of the restaurant.

'OK amigo, you know what to do.'

Ronny started the Dodge and reversed out from where they had been parked between an Austin Healey sports car and an old puke-green Studebaker. With no pedestrians now in sight, the van crawled towards the two ladies who appeared to be chatting happily. Ronny put his foot down, accelerating to where a stunned Jenny Smith spun around and Maria screamed. Xavier had jumped out of the Dodge, gun in hand. Jamming the gun into Maria's side he grabbed her hand, yanking her towards the van. Jenny's hand went to her shoulder holster.

'Don't even think about it, bitch!' Xavier screamed.

Now viciously grabbing Maria's long hair he dragged her towards the Dodge, effectively blocking Jenny's line of fire. Jenny watched helplessly as Xavier threw Maria into the open side door of the van. As he slammed the door shut and tried to climb in after her, Jenny Smith saw her chance, firing her first shots in anger as an FBI agent.

CHAPTER 35

THE HUNTERS BECOME THE HUNTED

Waving his pistol, Ronny screamed at Maria cowering on the rear seat of the van.

'Don't you fucking move. Comprende?'

'Si, but why, what do you want?'

'Shut it. You'll know soon enough.'

'Ronny, I been hit. You gotta get me to a hospital,' Xavier moaned.

'Where did the slug go?'

'Ronny, it's in my stomach. It fucking hurts.'

'Yeah, sorry about that, amigo. We gotta get back to the commune. We'll get someone there to check you out.'

'Ronny, I'm not gonna make it. You gotta get me to a hospital. Please, buddy, please.' Xavier coughed up blood.

'Hey look, I'm sorry, but tell me how the hell would that work? What do I do with the Mexican slut when I get to the hospital, eh? What do I tell them? My buddy's been shot? They're gonna call the cops. You're just going to have to hang on. It's about 6 hours away.'

***

Jenny swore when she noticed the flat tires.

'Bastards.'

Just as the restaurant ushered out the last customers Jenny tore up to the front door flashing her badge.

'I need to use your phone.'

'We're just closing.' The handsome waiter tried to push the door shut. 'What's the problem, sweetheart?'

'I'm certainly not your sweetheart. I'm FBI and I'm going to be here for some time, I have calls to make and you're just going to have to stick around. You must have heard the gunshots, for Chrissake. Now what you can do, *sweetheart,* is get me a cup of coffee, black. Now move it. Where's your phone?'

She had no success calling the helpful San Diego Police department or the local hospitals. She knew she'd hit one of the kidnappers and it should have been a life-threatening wound, but as an hour of failed calls passed, she had to admit defeat. She finally gave in and called a sleepy Dale Fletcher with the bad news.

***

The light of dawn had already seeped into the kitchen at Colorado Avenue when Dale, Spencer and Savannah sat dejectedly drinking coffee.

'So, Dale, where exactly are we at?' Spencer needed the caffeine hit.

'Jenny described the van, California plates, but we know who it was of course.'

'And you say Jenny shot one them?' Savannah asked.

161

'Yep, and the local cops found a pool of bright red blood. This would tend to corroborate Jenny's belief that it was a stomach wound. It definitely sounds like arterial bleeding, and I think it could be a major artery to the abdomen.'

'And the local hospitals haven't admitted anyone with a gunshot wound?'

Spencer padded over to the coffee maker and poured himself another cup after offering it to Dale and Savannah.

'Not matching the description she gave. Delgado wouldn't care too much about poor old Xavier Martinez.'

'You think he'd just let him die?' Spencer cocked an eyebrow.

'Oh yeah, I wouldn't doubt it. Delgado's lost a lot of people, and he might have been responsible for the death of Strode. Let me tell you, I doubt Delaware or Delgado would consider dear Xavier a great loss. He'd done time. Actually, I haven't got his record here, but he'd changed his name. I don't remember what it was. It's always a good ploy. It's amazing how often law enforcement don't check name changes.'

'What now, Dale? I'm hungry, I'm going to fix some eggs. Any takers?'

Spencer and Dale declined.

'What now? Jenny Smith is on her way back here. She's pretty upset. It's been her biggest assignment and I gather she blames herself.' Dale grimaced as he drank the last of his cold coffee. 'She's organised a BOLO on the Dodge van but once it hits the turnpikes of Los Angeles it'd be like looking for a needle in a haystack...'

'We ran the plates?' Savannah asked from where she was cooking.

Dale snorted ruefully. 'They belonged on that VW Kombi we issued you at the beginning of this fiasco. Delgado must have the plates of everyone they suckered into joining their cult. If I were him I'd have changed them out already.'

'You think he'll go through LA?' Spencer asked.

'I don't know for sure but I think Ronny will hightail it back to the commune, and he'll go through Los Angeles.'

'What does the future hold for Maria?' Savannah thought she knew the answer.

Dale stood up and rummaged through the drawers.

'You don't suppose there'd be some cigarettes here, do you?'

'No, Dale. No cigarettes.' Savannah rolled her eyes. 'They're bad for you, remember? Let's talk about Maria?'

'Of course. First of all, I need to impress upon you both that the "Family" is far bigger and has tentacles that we now think are even in other countries. But locally we know he's infiltrated the police, and we suspect even the judiciary. Possibly some politicians as well.'

'C'mon, Dale, seriously? He's just a nutter.' Spencer scowled.

'Sure, and so was Hitler. There are a lot of disaffected people. Every rally Stanford holds keep drawing more and more folk. And often any disturbance is nipped in the bud by seemingly compliant local cops. I tell you this is far bigger than you can imagine.'

Spencer remembered how quickly the police were on the scene at the rally in San Francisco when the father of a young man who'd died at the commune tried to shoot Delaware.

'And what about Maria?' Savannah piled scrambled eggs on to her plate and buttered some toast.

'Maria, yes. This really isn't good. Clearly Stanford is worried about you two. He would certainly realise you're not journalists or even brother and sister. So, he'll do whatever it takes to get Maria to tell him all she knows.'

'What then?' Savannah paused holding a slice of toast in her hand.

'He'll kill her.

***

Spencer checked his watch. At 11.30 am a bevy of grim-faced FBI agents had grabbed every available seat in the spacious lounge. Gus Horslay gave Spencer and Savannah a wave. Having driven through the night a weary Jenny Smith plonked herself on a recliner chair.

Savannah brought her a toasted sandwich and a cup of coffee.

'Listen up. everyone. First of all, Jenny, thanks for turning up, you really should have got some sleep.' Dale had dark circles under his eyes.

'I wouldn't have slept. I'm disgusted with myself for allowing this to happen.'

Dale reassured her that there was no real way for them to see this coming, and asked if there was any further information she hadn't given them previously. There was not. She suspected the large shape of the driver was Ronny Delgado, and the man she'd hit fit the description of Xavier. The van was the one Savannah and Spencer had seen at the Seven

Eleven and the hotel, a 1963 Dodge A-100 Sportsman with California plates.

Dale frowned over the lack of anything new, or new leads. 'Where was I? Here's what I believe. Does anybody have…?'

Special Agent Rory Branson grinned as he held out a soft pack of Lucky Strikes.

'Thanks, Rory.' Dale cupped his hand as the Zippo clicked. 'As I was saying, I believe Delgado will hot foot it back to the commune with Maria Gomez so that she can be interrogated by Delaware.'

'Do you think she may be tortured?' asked Special Agent Andy Morgan, a trim guy in a lightweight blue suit.

'Probably not. She will certainly tell them what she knows. She'll tell them Spencer and Savannah are FBI and we're on to them. She knows my name and a few of you as well.' He nodded to Gus. 'It's obvious she's not a player. I believe they'll get the info and then dispose of her.'

'Seriously, Dale, do you think they're going to risk taking Maria back to the commune? I mean kidnapping is one hell of a charge.' Spencer leaned against a wall, coffee in hand.

'I do. First of all, Delaware feels invincible. The press love him. His influence with law enforcement and the judiciary can't be overstated. And also the commune is so vast Maria Gomez could be hidden away easily enough, in a cellar or somewhere in the surrounding woods.'

'What a goddam mess,' Savannah muttered.

'It is that, Agent Steele, so we are going to fix that mess. Right?' Dale grinned at the agents who responded with cheers. 'We're going to head off shortly to the commune. We're going to go in hard, fast and noisy. We have AR 15s, shotguns, long guns and of course our sidearms. We also have Special Agent Bryce Fraser here who is a sniper. Welcome to the team, Bryce.'

A tall gaunt officer, in jeans a white shirt and a check sport jacket, gave them a wave.

'That's great, Dale, but sometimes these militia-change-the-world nuts are very well armed and fortified. We may need the army to take them down.' And that meant collateral damage. A name popped into Spencer's mind: Waco, Texas, but he squashed it.

'Certainly, a possibility, Spencer. If we encounter overwhelming force, we'll withdraw and do that. But I can't now call in the army or the California National Guard for what is just a kidnapping. If that's all, people, let's get going, we'll meet up a mile before the entrance. There is one more thing. Spencer, Savannah, you won't be joining us.'

'Are you serious, Dale?' Savannah snarled.

'I'm with Savannah, Dale. We know what's at the commune. If Maria and Ronny Delgado are hidden away, we would have more chance of finding them.'

'Golly, I understand you two want to be in on the kill so to speak, but look at the goddam…'

'Goddam? Wow.' Spencer chuckled.

'Blast, just listen.' Dale turned back to Rory and plucked another Lucky Strike out of the pack, then lit it. 'Remember we still don't have anything tying Delaware into anything. The fact that Eddy Strode and Wilbur Miracle, now both deceased, were living at the commune doesn't specifically mean Delaware is connected. It won't be going to court in the first place, and if it did, it'd get laughed right back out.'

'C'mon, Dale, they both had long rap sheets. You're kidding me,' Savannah barked.

'Don't go off half-cocked, Savannah, just follow the dots. Stanford Delaware makes a big thing about rehabilitating criminals; he would argue that he doesn't keep them locked up and if they stray off the straight and narrow, it's not his fault.'

'That doesn't explain why Savannah and I can't come along.'

'I was getting to that. Delaware by now believes that you two are FBI, but he doesn't know that absolutely. What he does know is that you,' Dale jabbed a finger, 'you, Spencer, killed Perez. He also knows you two stole his Rolls Royce and drove off with Maria Gomez.'

'So…how do you explain to Delaware how come the FBI is investigating Maria's kidnapping allegedly by Ronny Delgado and Xavier?'

'For God's sake, Spencer, do you think I'm interested in explaining anything to Delaware? All he'll be told is that Maria Gomez, an undocumented alien, was being driven to Mexico by one of our people and she was kidnapped. That's it. But if on the other hand he sees you and Savannah with the rest of our team he's going to be on the blower to local law enforcement, the press, politicians, and anyone he can think of. So that's it. You're both out for the time being. Got it?'

CHAPTER 36

XAVIER'S LAST ROAD TRIP

Xavier's moaning was beginning to get on Ronny's nerves. Maria's crying didn't help. Ronny climbed into the back, gagging and tying Maria's hands and feet.

'Ronny. for God's sake, take me to hospital. I'm dying.' He certainly sounded like it, Ronny thought. He'd been begging for a hospital for hours now.

As the van approached Pasa Robles Ronny saw a McDonalds, conveniently placed in a fairly deserted parking area next to a mall, its famous golden Arches igniting his hunger pangs.

'I'm stopping for a burger, Xavier. You want anything? Silly question, I guess.'

Ronny drove to the deserted far side of the parking area to munch on his burger and fries.'

'Ronny, please.' Xavier's moan was accompanied by a low rough grunt. A dribble of blood leaked from his mouth.

'I think you're right, Xavier. You're not gonna make it.' Ronny quickly scanned the vacant parking area before grabbing his pistol. Xavier didn't flinch as the 0.38 slug slammed into his skull. Ronny heard Maria thrashing around in the back of the van. Chewing thoughtfully on the last of his burger, Ronny drove through the suburbs looking for a payphone.

'Stanford, we need to talk.'

'Why do I have the feeling that you've fucked up again, Ronny? Talk to me.'

'The good news is I got the girl.'

'And the bad news?'

'Xavier's dead.'

'For Chrissake, Ronny…'

'No, listen, Stanford. It was his own fucking fault. He grabbed the silly bitch when the FBI broad was with her. I fucking told him we should have waited, but no, the idiot grabbed the Mexican, and just as he pushed her into the van the FBI woman opened fire.'

'And hit Xavier?'

'Yeah, Stanford. He'd just climbed into the van when she opened fire. That was it, he died almost immediately. What do you want me to do?'

'Let me think…OK, here's what to do. Dump the body and head back here. I'd imagine the Feds will be all over us any time now.'

'So, what about the Mexican? We can't…'

'Of course, take her to the old cabin, it's pretty well hidden. The Feds aren't likely to find it. I'll send Eduardo to babysit her. As soon as things have died down, I'm going to question her. I want to know exactly who Steele and Marlowe are and exactly which government agency they're aligned to.'

'What about me?'

'Did anyone actually see you? Savannah Steele or Spencer Marlowe, for instance?'

'No, I don't think so.'

'All right, like I said, take her to the cabin. Eduardo will be waiting, then go and get Roberto. He can follow you to the old quarry. Set fire to the van, that should take care of any evidence and then come back here and keep out of sight. They don't have anything on you. I need to make some pre-emptive phone calls.'

CHAPTER 37
WE ALL HAVE STORIES

The road stretched onward, hugging the land, taking each turn in easy stride. Gus Horslay and Jenny Smith were in the last Ford Galaxie. All together, twenty well-armed agents in a phalanx of sedans were about to descend on the commune.

Jenny drove while a relaxed Gus admired the scenery. The road was a smooth black river, the scenery took on an almost meditative quality, the light igniting the hues of the big leaf maples and redwoods.

Jenny told Gus about her early days and the decision to join the bureau after her brother Brad had been murdered. Gus proved to be a good listener.

'What about you, Gus? What's your story? Why did you join the FBI? How do you know Spencer and Savannah?'

'Just like a cop, you're asking a lot of questions.'

Jenny blushed. 'Sorry. I guess it's none of my business.'

'No, that's OK. Where to start? A bit like you, only I didn't win a beauty competition.'

Jenny giggled.

'No, my wife was an innocent bystander when a bank was held up. There was a shootout. She'd been a hostage when the robber left the bank. The guy was high and holding her hand, pulling her close. Melanie made a break for it. A sharpshooter took the guy out, but he didn't die immediately.'

Gus choked on his words. 'Wait a sec…he…he hit the ground…hit in the chest…the last thing he did was shoot Melanie in the head. All the cops opened fire. He took fifteen rounds. But Melanie was dead.'

Jenny grabbed his hand. 'I'm so sorry.'

'Yeah, but…this is where it gets hard. It's difficult to talk about it. Melanie was pregnant. A boy. I was a schoolteacher. I'd always thought it was a worthwhile career. After that, all I wanted was to take down bad guys.'

'Oh, Gus.'

Silence reigned.

CHAPTER 38

THE FBI MEETS THE PROPHET

The procession of cars glided up to the barrier. Special Agent Jax whispered to Dale, 'Just check this guy out.'

Dale had to smile at the tattered jeans, the flip flops and the ridiculous top hat.

'It doesn't look like he's armed.'

Dale glanced warily around as he climbed out of the car, badge in hand.

'FBI. We're here to see Stanford Delaware. Open the gate.'

'FBI. No kidding?' The phlegmatic guard spat out a gob of tobacco juice. 'You got an appointment?'

Jax jumped out of the driver's seat. 'Open the gate now, you son of a bitch.'

'Language, Jax, please,' Dale remonstrated.

'Keep your shirt on.' The guard swung the gate open, but took his time about it.

Jax and Dale scanned the area before climbing back into their vehicle.

'It's quiet. Too quiet.' Jax said with a grin.

In the back of the car, Agents Clint and Orson chuckled.

'You got that line from a John Wayne movie, Jax, didn't you?' Dale asked, smiling. Internally though, he was hoping

173

for a nice, calming cigarette before they confronted Delaware. He was always twitchy and anxious without his coffin nail.

'Yeah, Jax, let's head em off at the pass.' Clint chortled.

As the cars roared through, they could see the guard with a phone in hand.

'OK, Jax, just follow the road around. Spencer and Savannah have explained the layout. We should be able to see Delaware's mansion in a minute. It's pretty hard to miss apparently.'

Dale hoped he wasn't showing any of the fears gnawing his insides. He knew it was possible Delaware may have armed gunman waiting in ambush. His 0.38 had never been fired at a criminal and he didn't know how he'd react in a firefight. Plus, he needed a blasted cigarette.

Orson pointed. 'Wow, that's gotta be Delaware's pile.'

As arranged, they all parked at the front of the mansion. Like warlike clones the dark suited aviator-shaded agents stepped out of their vehicles, eagle eyes scanning the surrounds for signs of trouble. Below in the fields workers downed their tools, silently watching.

The weather was pleasantly warm, with just enough sunshine to feel invigorating without being too hot. The scenery was lush and green with fields of peas and corn spread before them in well-tended symmetry.

'Come with me, Jax, and keep your trap shut.'

Dale rang the bell. Through the stained-glass side panels Dale could see the distorted image of two people huddled together. Immediately his hand went to his pancake holster. *Are they standing close because they're discussing an attack plan?*

One half of the polished oak door swung open. Dale was surprised to see a slim youth with long hair carrying a guitar case, standing close to Delaware.

'As you can see, Caspar, we have two lovely gentlemen from the FBI here for a chat. We had a nice time today, didn't we?' Stanford addressed the youth.

'It was wonderful, Mr Delaware.'

'Off you go, lad, unless these gentlemen want to interrogate you. Do you gentleman wish to…?'

'No, Mr Delaware, but we may wish to talk to him later. Jax, get his details please.'

Jax nodded and led the boy onto the veranda.

'Come in, come in…Special Agent…?'

'Dale Fletcher.'

'Dale Fletcher. Now that's a nice name. Please follow me into my study.'

'Thank you. Just a minute.' Dale held up a hand and moved to the front door. 'Jax, when you're done come in and join us in the study.'

Dale followed Stanford as they made their way down the hall. The front door slammed and Jax came trotting up to join them.

'I think I know what this must be about. But meanwhile, Dale Fletcher, do you know the meaning of your last name?' Delaware enquired.

'Fletcher? No, I don't think I do.' Things weren't going the way Dale had planned. Delaware was completely at ease.

'Yes, Fletcher. That in olden days was what an arrow maker was called. I imagine that particular trade became redundant many years ago.'

'Ahh, and we are now joined by…?' Delaware held out his hand.

'Special Agent Jax Fleetman, sir.'

'Fleetman. Another interesting title, fleet by name and fleet by nature, I judge, looking at your physique. You are a runner, are you not?'

'Mr Delaware, let's get down to business if you don't mind. We have some serious matters to discuss.' Dale felt his blood pressure rising.

'Of course, take a seat please, gentlemen.' Stanford pointed to two leather bound office chairs facing his desk. 'It's a warm day. A refreshing drink perhaps?'

'No thanks, we don't drink on duty.' Dale tried not to scowl.

'Very wise. Of course. But this is non-alcoholic.' Stanford rang a small bell.

Within two minutes a guy appeared wearing blue jeans and a T-shirt with a Beatles motif on it.

'Simon, please bring a pitcher of our fruit cordial and glasses.'

As Delaware turned his head Jax nudged Dale and frowned. Simon poured glasses of the drink. Dale drank thirstily.

'Drink up, Agent Fleetman. Now, gentlemen, tell me what this is all about?'

Dale placed his empty glass on a small table.

'What we are here to talk about is the attempted kidnapping of one of your followers—a Maria Gomez.'

Delaware laughed, a deep throaty chuckle.

'Dear me, aren't you supposed to read me my, what is it, my Miranda Rights?'

'Actually no, Mr Delaware, we only read the Miranda Rights prior to conducting a custodial interrogation. Asking questions in your home doesn't constitute a custodial interrogation.'

'I see. What I thought you were here about is the murder of two of our followers, Perez Sanchez and Grady Chamberlin. And of course, the kidnapping of Maria Gomez. A lovely lady, recently widowed. Oh, and the theft of my Rolls Royce. My understanding is that kidnapping is a federal offence. Now you tell me that one our brethren is responsible for the kidnapping of Gomez. You can understand my confusion when, with my own eyes I saw Maria Gomez being abducted by Spencer Marlowe, the same person who murdered Sanchez and Chamberlin.'

'We're not here to talk about those alleged matters. The facts are that one Wilbur Miracle, one of your flock, was shot dead while trying to kidnap Mrs Gomez.'

'Really? I have also heard, Special Agent Fletcher, that Spencer Marlowe and his sister, Savannah Steele, were in fact FBI operatives. Would you care to comment? I'm very confused.'

Dale found Stanford Delaware hard to dislike. He had such a kindness about him, and excellent taste in furniture and décor.

'I'm asking the questions. Tell me about Wilbur Miracle.'

'If you insist. It's my practice to take in convicted felons. To give them a new start. But they are free to come and go as they like. The "Family" is, above all, a peace-loving movement. We really do practice what we preach. Peace, love and understanding has become a cliché, but that is what we are about. We are a foil to the disastrous consequences of capitalism. Just look out of the window, agents Fleetman and Fletcher. What do you see? I'll tell you. Our extended family toiling in the fields. Honest work. We are a self-supporting community, free of crime, hate and prejudice. I might add we have support from the police, the judiciary and church leaders. In fact, I was just speaking to Tim Benson before you and your men turned up…'

Dale gasped. 'Tim Benson, the Governor?'

'Yes, Dale, may I call you that? I can see there has been an unfortunate misunderstanding. Tim and I go back a long way. In fact, I have his private number. Would you like to talk to him? As for Wilbur, I find what you are accusing him of a little hard to believe, but even if true it has nothing to do with me.' Dale found himself nodding along. 'In fact, it could be perhaps that he was trying to rescue Mrs Gomez, who I know was kidnapped from her home here. Frankly Dale, this is starting to look like a deep state conspiracy. It's very disturbing. I'm thinking the press would be very interested.'

***

A subdued Dale Fletcher and Jax Fleetman made their way to the car and the anxiously awaiting agents.

'Wow, this really is quite a place,' Dale remarked wistfully.

The four agents climbed into the car. Jax accelerated smoothly away. Dale didn't want to say, but in his heart of hearts he now knew absolutely Stanford Delaware was one of the good guys. They had such a lovely place out here! Idyllic, really. He wondered if perhaps he could take early retirement and he and Edna could move here. Working in the fields would be cathartic, he knew his FBI career had turned him into a hard-bitten cynic. Perhaps that was why his tobacco addiction had been so hard to kick. And what about Spencer and Savannah, had they been waging a war on this visionary guru? Savannah was gung-ho and quick to shoot. Perhaps they *were* guilty. Perhaps it was as Stanford had suggested, a deep state conspiracy. He felt pleasantly woozy as he gazed out of the car window.

'Special Agent Fletcher, are you awake?'

'What? Of course I'm awake.' Dale had become aware Jax was shaking him.

'What is it Jax? What do you want?'

'Sir, I tried to tell you not to drink that stuff.'

'What? What are you talking about? It was a fruit drink. Nothing odd about that. I noticed you didn't touch yours.'

'Didn't Marlowe or Steele tell you their conclusions about the beverage?'

'I have no idea what you're talking about.'

'Just listen, sir. They both said much the same thing. When they first met Stanford in his trailer and had some of that drink they drove away, sort of starry eyed. And even after they joined the commune. they said it felt like it was some sort of spell. It wasn't until they stopped drinking that stuff that they could see things seriously, honestly…'

'Jax, that's enough.'

'Sir.'

'I said that's enough. Delaware is clearly innocent, and I think we have to consider the possibility that Steele and Marlowe have gone rogue.' They had killed two people, and abducted Maria Sanchez, while also stealing that kindly man's Rolls Royce.

Clint glanced sideways at Orson, before speaking up.

'Dale, this is crap. I don't know what's happened to you, but you're wrong. Delaware is a monster. Savannah and Spencer have told us all about it. You can't...'

'Enough, all of you. I'm beginning to think you're all a part of this conspiracy. Tomorrow I'm getting to the bottom of it all. Meanwhile, I don't want to hear another word. And that's an order.'

Chapter 39
COOLING THEIR HEELS

Leafing through a heavy coffee table book, Spencer was absorbed in the photos of thatched rooves and ancient castles. There was nothing, he decided, quite like the pictures of patchwork hills, dramatic dales, ancient woodlands and winding country roads.

'Savannah, have you ever been to England?' he yelled.

Her Magnum and Spencer's 0.38 were in pieces on the kitchen table spread out on newspaper as she cleaned and oiled them.

'What? England, are you kidding? Why would I want to go there? Long haired musicians, warm beer and lousy food. It's always the same, the woman does the work while her husband lazes around. No, I've never been to goddam England.'

Spencer reluctantly laid the book on to the coffee table and sauntered into the kitchen.

'I am not and, never likely to be, your husband. What are you doing?'

'What does it look like I'm doing?'

'Dunno. I give up.'

'I'm cleaning, oiling and reassembling our handguns. I thought it would be obvious.'

'I didn't know they were dirty. Can I give you a hand?'

'Don't you dare. Jesus, if you got your grubby little hands on them they'd probably blow up in our faces. Go and read your stupid book or perhaps check out the refrigerator and use your culinary skills to whip up a nice dinner. Do something useful.'

'You are decidedly grumpy, woman.'

Savannah swore as she ran a cloth over the reassembled Magnum and laid it on the table. 'You're right. Sorry I bit your head off, but I'm not happy sitting around doing nothing.'

'How about I whip up a spag bol?'

'A what?'

'Spag bol. Spaghetti Bolognese.'

'You Aussies shorten everything. And your slang is incomprehensible. It's very annoying.' Savannah remarked darkly.

'Rubbish. I had a decko in the fridge this arvo and behind the coldies I found some ground beef and some pasta in a jar. And, by the way, I'm not Mutt 'n Jeff, OK?'

'Give me strength. I'm not going to ask you to explain all of that gibberish, but I gather we're going to have a nice spaghetti dinner.'

'Too right. It'll be bonza. Perhaps that'll cheer you up.'

Savannah slotted rounds into her Magnum. 'The fact is I hate this sitting around. I'm worried about Maria. I don't dare think what they may do to her.'

'I've been thinking. Dale and his merry men are going to the commune; there's no way Maria is going to be in plain sight. I've just thought of something. At the time with so much happening I didn't attach much importance to what she said.'

'Shoot.'

'Do you remember she told us about a cabin in the woods, with a barred cell inside it?'

'Come to think of it, yes. But we don't know exactly where it is. There's miles and miles of woods, ravines and gullies and God knows what. It'd be like looking for the proverbial needle.'

'Well, I think I sort of do. One day Perez asked me to dump some stuff in a disused quarry. I had to drive a Ford pickup along a narrow track right behind that big shed by the far cornfield. There was another trail, leading off that road and it had a sign saying 'Keep Out Private Property. It looked like a driveway to a house. And the thing was that the route to the quarry seemed to lead away from the commune. I'll bet quids it connected up to the main road.'

'Do you think that's where Maria could be?' Savannah placed the pistol back on the table, interested at the prospect of actually doing something.

'Who knows? She could be dead. But I think Delaware would have wanted to question her himself. I think we should go for a nice drive in the country. What do you think?'

Savannah held up the Magnum. 'Cleaned, oiled and ready for action.'

***

Spencer pored over the map while Savannah drove.

'Do you have it figured?' Savannah put her foot down, roaring past a Mack R series truck hauling rolls of shiny sheet metal.

183

'Not sure. Take exit 46B for Ygnacio road. It looks like there's an unmarked track that goes in a huge loop. And I'm sure that goes past the quarry.'

'Hm, yeah. I'm pretty sure there are a few hunters' cabins and getaway houses scattered through the area, as long as you know which one is the one we're after. I'm sorry we didn't get to eat your spag bol. Spag bol, for Chrissake. By the way, 'Mutt 'n Jeff?''

'What?'

'When you walked into the kitchen you said, 'I'm not Mutt 'n Jeff. What the hell was that?'

'Oh that. You were yelling at me, and I was just saying, I'm not Mutt 'n Jeff, not deaf.'

'Silly me. Every time I think I've got a handle on your Aussie speak, you throw a curveball.'

'Actually, just for the record, it's not Aussie–it's Cockney rhyming slang, so there.'

'Who gives a…'

'Language, Savannah.'

***

Savannah swung the wheel and cursed as the car bounced over the rutted surface. Pulling over, she put the transmission into park.

If you could get past the urgency of the situation and the fact that a woman's life was in danger, the scenery out here was gorgeous. Grasslands for ages, climbing over low but sharp hills, interspersed with stands of tall trees. And the sky simply colossal in scale.

'I hope you're right, Spencer. Nothing looks familiar coming by this route. Are you sure we're near the commune?'

'I'm sure. I think.'

'That's encouraging. Any thoughts about a plan? I'm not sure knocking on the door of the cabin would work. If we ever find it.'

'Look, coming up there's a letter box and a track that would take us to a house, I guess.' Spencer peered through the trees. 'No, that's not the cabin. We could ask these kids if they know any of the locals.'

Three young boys on bicycles skidded past, laughing.

'Too late, they've gone. Does anything look familiar, Spencer?'

'One tree really looks like another, doesn't it? Just go over this rise…Hey, look, there's the quarry. I think I'm getting my bearings.'

'Do you see what I see?' Savannah pointed.

'This isn't good.'

Savannah edged the car forward. It looked obscene, this man-made canyon. A quarry ripped out of the earth, with no regard for its attack on nature. That wasn't what drew the dismayed comment out of Spencer. Below them, next to a mound of gravel they saw a faded yellow excavator with its boom raised, as if it were about to devour the burnt-out skeleton of a Dodge Van.

'Oh my God, I just hope…' Spencer didn't finish.

'Shit, I'm going to have to drive down there. Damn.'

The steep slope was narrow and winding, its loose gravel surface treacherous and unforgiving.

'I don't like this.' Savannah scowled as the sedan slipped and skidded, trying to keep traction.

After a few minutes that felt like hours, the big sedan had reached the bottom, bouncing over the rough surface, sliding to a stop at the wreck.

'That's the van Delgado was driving.' Spencer said as he climbed out of the car, scanning the area.

Savannah jumped out of the car and strode to the burnt-out wreck, ripping open the scorched front door and peering inside.

'Thank God there's no corpse. I was sure we were going to find Maria's remains. That's a positive. But they obviously wanted to destroy any evidence, so, what evidence? Was Maria killed in the van? Was somebody else killed? It's a mystery.'

'I'll tell you what isn't a mystery.'

'What, Spencer? I'm all ears.'

'I know how to find the cabin. Go back up to the top. I remember now. Follow the road around the ridge and then just near that big redwood there's a bit of a track and about three hundred yards in there's another pathway leading to the cabin. Hey, and look. See that smoke? I'll bet you anything that's the abode we're looking for.'

'Clever boy. Now all I have to do is get the goddam car up to the top of the quarry without sliding off the side.'

The big V8 obviously preferred uphill. After a few tense seconds when the vehicle threatened to slew sideways, it made its way, slowly inching its way to the rim.

***

186

'This's definitely the place.'

'That's good, Superman. What do you suggest we do now?'

They could just make out, nestled in a copse of pines, the log wall and shingled roof of the hut at the end of a winding gravel path. As peaceful a scene as it was possible to be.

'You notice there's no vehicle. I'm betting that there's one guy. And hopefully he's guarding Maria.'

'Why do you think there's only one person, Spencer dear?'

'If Delaware or Ronny were here, they'd have a vehicle. I'm telling you. One guard and Maria's locked in the cell. Betcha.'

'Good one. But what if it's the wrong cabin and it's a retired lawyer up here for a weekend shooting.'

'Why a lawyer?'

'I don't know, Spencer. For God's sake, it could be anyone. So, what in hell do we do? If we knock on the door and it's one of Stanford's goons, he's going to come out shooting.'

'I have an idea. It's not great but...'

'Let's hear it.'

'Like I said, it's not the best of plans. You know how in the past I've been a tad critical of you executing anyone who upset you...'

'Not again. Jesus, Spencer, how many times have I saved your miserable hide?'

'Moving right along. I know this isn't very original...'

'It's certainly long winded,' Savannah groused.

'Listen. Damn you. I'm going to throw some of these pebbles onto the roof, and fair dinkum the guy will come out and you shoot him. There. That's it. What do you think?'

'What do I think? I think you're nuts. That's what I think.'

'Wait up. I think we know most of Delaware's heavies by sight. He has a hard core of thugs. We've both seen them strutting around the commune. Most of them sit together at mealtime. There's one guy always wears a red bandana. There's a bloke with a mohawk. No, hang on, you shot him. But another dude, short blond hair and a full beard. And there's that nasty bugger, I think his name is Eduardo, big, full beard. What about Xavier? He's a piece of work. We'd recognise most of these men.' On reflection, the Agent who'd been escorting Maria had claimed to hit a man matching Xavier's description.

'Suppose you're right and even if we recognise one of Delaware's bully boys, that doesn't mean he isn't at the cabin legitimately. A dirty weekend with his girlfriend perhaps.'

'Like I said. I know I've been critical in the past. But all I can say is we know, putting aside due process for a moment, that Stanford and his crew are downright evil. Just look at all that's happened. The motel, Perez casually executing Grady, the deaths and the insurance payouts, going after Maria several times. It's huge. And this guy and his organisation have to be stopped. And you and I are in a position to save a life. I'm sure Maria is locked up there, and I'm equally sure they're going to kill her when they've finished. And who knows what else they may have in store for her before they do?'

'I can't believe you're actually talking me into shooting someone.'

'How about that? Look, I'll throw some pebbles. We're about thirty yards from the front door, can you hit him from here?'

'I just hope you're right, Spencer. Of course I can damn well hit him.'

'If he's an old guy with a combover and holding a bible, don't shoot. OK? I'm going to move behind that redwood and start chucking. Get ready.'

The first pebble bounced lazily down the roof and fell onto the stoop. No reaction. Spencer threw four more in quick succession and peered through a dense ninebark shrub, as the stones rattled noisily down the roof. They watched as a curtain was pulled aside and a bearded face appeared momentarily.

'That's that jerk, Eduardo. Happy now?' Spencer whispered.

Savannah grinned and gave a thumbs up.

A volley of pebbles clattered down the shingles. Just as Spencer scrabbled for more stones, the front door jerked open and a scowling Eduardo stormed out brandishing a twelve gauge.

'Fuck off, you little bastards. I don't care how young you are, I'm gonna shoot. Don't make me come after you. You're going to regret it.'

'I'm going to give him the chance to surrender,' Savannah whispered.

'Suit yourself.'

Savannah jumped up from behind the bush.

'We're not kids, Eduardo, drop the shotgun.'

'Fuck you.'

Savannah stood legs apart, the revolver in both hands, the classic shooter's stance. The first round slammed into Eduardo's chest. Centre mass. Spencer thought he saw a flicker of surprise on his fleshy face. The shotgun clattered to the ground and exploded. Buckshot took out the branch of a lone maple. Savannah's second slug tore through Eduardo's throat. A small pool of blood leaked out. His heart had taken early retirement and had stopped pumping.

They heard a scream from the cabin.

'Maria, are you OK? '

'Si, Señor Spencer.'

'Are you alone?' Savannah yelled.

'Yes. I am alone.'

CHAPTER 40
HOW EMBARRASING

The sky was inky black. A weary Spencer turned the car into the drive at Palo Alto and killed the motor. A persistent thin drizzle had been their companion for the last thirty miles. The atmosphere, dark and heavy, a stillness hung over the street, the silence broken by a low crack of thunder. A streak of hot silver split the sky. Tall streetlamps dimly lit the rain-soaked dwellings, illuminating the ghostly outline of two Ford Galaxies. Maria had fallen asleep on the back seat. Savannah peered into the night, scanning for any movement.

'Looks OK.'

Spencer nudged Maria.

'Wake up, we're here.' He glanced at the second Galaxie. Something wasn't right. 'Savannah, just wait.'

'What is it?' Savannah grabbed her pistol.

'Look at the rear Ford. You can just make out the outline of whoever is in the front.'

'Yeah, so?'

'Why are they sitting so close together? They're almost on top of each other. They haven't even looked in our direction. Are we sure they are even Dale's people? I can see some movement. Hell, it could even be an assailant attacking an FBI guy.'

'It does looks odd. Grab your 0.38. You go to the driver's door, I'll take the other side. Be careful. Maria, everything's OK. Just wait.'

Maria nodded.

They stealthily climbed out of their vehicle and edged their way around the Ford. It appeared as if the occupants were grappling. Spencer nodded and wrenched open the driver's door, levelling his pistol.

'I don't believe it.'

At the same time, he heard Savannah cackle.

'Gus Horslay and Jenny Smith. Two intrepid FBI guardians.'

'Oh shit. Sorry, Spencer, Savannah. Don't tell Dale. Jenny and I, we, well I guess you could say we were, what's the term, necking?'

Spencer laughed.

'Is that what you call it? I'd suggest you put your neck away before you're arrested.'

***

Spencer awoke to the steady patter of rain upon his window. He'd been dreaming again about Michiyo and his daughter, Trilby. The coffee table book with its enticing photos of the bucolic English countryside had ignited a fierce desire to take his family on a holiday. *When I return. If I return.*

Checking his watch, he jumped out of bed in a hurry. Dale and the agents were due to arrive at seven am. He chuckled at the memory of Gus and Jenny *in flagrante delicto.*

Ten minutes later he was showered and dressed in a polo shirt, casual high-waisted flared pants and Cuban heeled boots, he smiled at the sight of his lengthening hair as he shaved. He figured he'd leave Maria asleep. He knocked on Savannah's door.

'Rise and shine. Dale and his crew are due in thirty minutes.'

Peering out of the window he noticed the Ford Galaxies had been replaced by three white Plymouth Furies: *the night shift.*

***

A good cup of coffee should be hot. Strong and smooth. It should have a rich flavour, not too bitter or too acidic. Whoever had stocked the larder knew their coffee. Spencer buttered toast and poured a cup for Savannah after making a fruitless search for his favourite condiment. *Yanks are so uncivilised. No Vegemite.*

Somewhere around an hour later, a dozen agents crammed into the living room. Spencer didn't recognise all of them. There was an intense looking guy, short and anxious. Spencer thought his name might have been Fred, or Ted. Fred or Ted smiled like a horse, showing off black gums and cloud gray teeth. He shook Spencer's hand vigorously and asked: 'How was your trip?' Spencer mumbled something in return, having no idea what the guy was talking about, and looked up to see an embarrassed looking Gus enter the room accompanied by a blushing Jenny.

193

'Excuse me,' he said to Fred. He was sure that was his name. 'Gus, Jenny, thanks so much for watching over us last night,' Spencer said. He always thought the Americans never did understand irony.

Gus leaned over, whispering, 'We found a room.'

A sombre Dale entered, brushing drops off his fedora. His charcoal grey suit looked rumpled, his white shirt with its narrow black tie made him look like a tired undertaker. With him was the thin agent Jax, followed by Clint and Olson. Spencer had never seen Dale look so worn and dispirited. He looked like a man who'd given up on life.

Maria, wearing a housecoat, bustled around with trays of refreshments. Spencer whispered to her as he accepted a coffee, 'How are you?'

'I am good, Señor Marlowe. I feel safe. Gracias a Dios,' she crossed herself.

As fresh as daisies, Jenny and Gus leaned against the far wall. They sipped their coffee, at the same time casting covert glances at each other. Spencer was pleased. He liked Gus enormously and what little he knew of Jenny Smith he admired.

'Listen up, everybody. We have a lot to talk about. First of all, I'd like to welcome again Ted Fredricks. He'll be helping out.' Dale pointed to horse teeth.

'As you know, we went and had a chat yesterday with Delaware. And …I have a sort of apology to make. It would appear that the man plied me with a… a sort of mind-altering substance.'

'LSD perhaps?' Gus piped up.

'Jeepers, Gus. No. Anyway I left the meeting convinced that Stanford Delaware was innocent of all wrongdoing. And sadly, while under the influence, I was guilty of making some totally unfair comments about Spencer Marlowe and Special Agent Steele. These ridiculous accusations were the result of imbibing this, whatever it was. I unreservedly apologise for these injudicious remarks.'

Spencer whispered to Savannah, 'Hell, we did tell Dale, didn't we?'

She nodded and rolled her eyes. She took a break from scowling and crossing her arms to gesture at Dale as if to say *can you believe this guy?*

'Anyway, the last few days have had some positives. Spencer and Savannah found Maria Gomez and rescued her. For those who haven't met Mrs Gomez, she's the lady serving us coffee.'

Dale then went on to describe the mission. On hearing about the death of Eduardo, all eyes were on Spencer and Savannah. A hushed silence fell over the room.

'There's more. Another development. As most of you are aware, Mrs Gomez was kidnapped at gunpoint while Special Agent Jenny Smith was taking her back to Mexico. We believe one of the perpetrators was Ronny, AKA BBQ, Delgado, the former star football player. The person who grabbed Mrs Gomez and forced her into a vehicle was Xavier Martinez, a convicted felon. Agent Smith was able to fire at Martinez. We now believe that shot hit Martinez but didn't initially kill him. Mr Martinez's body was found near a MacDonald's in Pasa Robles. Agent Smith fired one round, yet Martinez's body, on examination, had been hit twice. There was a fatal shot to the head with a different calibre slug. We believe Delgado figured an injured Martinez was a liability and finished him off. Just for the record, Martinez had killed before. As a juvenile gang member, he was convicted of involuntary manslaughter in San Francisco some years ago, but unfortunately the swine only served a short term. He was paroled and taken into care by Stanford Delaware, who suggested Martinez should change his name. Prior to this, his name was Juan Garcia.'

'Oh my God.' Jenny gasped and fainted, collapsing in a heap.

'What did I miss?' Spencer asked Gus.

'Pretty sure he was the guy who killed her brother,' Gus said.

CHAPTER 41
THE UNEXPECTED

2015

He was aware of a low-pitched hum surrounding him. Sort of a rumble. Spencer moved uncomfortably. *Why had Jenny collapsed? Will she be OK? Better get up and check. What's the time?* Suddenly awake he tried to sit up but his movement was constrained by something. A seatbelt. He glanced at his watch. The gold bezel of the Rolex glinted. It was 7.04. That familiar roar of jet engines and the stale smell of recycled air meant they were on a plane.

'Oh no. Not now. We're not done. Delaware has to be stopped.'

'Spencer, darling, they're about to serve breakfast. You've been asleep since we left Singapore. You've had me worried, talking in your sleep. Trilby even woke up.'

'Michiyo, and my beautiful Trilby. It's so good to see you both.' Unclipping his seatbelt, he hugged Michiyo and kissed her. His gaze turned to his daughter, fast asleep in the comfortable wide seat, her long black hair cascading, partly concealing her face. As he brushed away a few strands, Trilby opened her eyes.

'Hello Daddy. I was just dreaming about my karate lessons. Will I ever be as good as you?'

Before Spencer could answer, their meals arrived. In fact, he'd been stunned at Trilby's progress. Only fourteen and already with deadly skills, he believed she would eventually be a tenth Dan. Would he ever be able to tell her she was named after brave Trilby Lim, the extraordinary lady who'd helped him mine the Japanese ships in Singapore in 1942?

'Good morning, Mr and Mrs Marlowe, and of course Ms Trilby. We have scrambled egg with chicken chipolatas for the young lady. Kale and spinach frittata for Mrs Marlowe and for you, sir, spiced bean curd and peppers and of course your coffee and juice.'

Spencer pushed his tray forward to take the plates and drinks, at the same time noticing the server, an attractive Asian lady wearing a distinctive sarong kebaya uniform with its fitted blouse and flowing wrap skirt. Myriad thoughts hurtled through Spencer's mind. For the first time he felt cheated. It was too soon. More importantly, *where are we going?*

CHAPTER 42
BACK AGAIN

1967

The stench of cigarette smoke made Spencer cough. *I didn't think you were allowed to smoke on an aircraft.* He felt someone tap his shoulder.

'Kale and spinach. That's revolting.'

'For God's sake, Spencer, you dozed off while Dale was speaking. And what the hell has kale and spinach got to do with anything?' Savannah demanded.

Spencer sat bolt upright. He was back. What the hell was that all about? Not a dream, that's for sure. On one side he saw Savannah, on the other Ted Fredricks was setting fire to another Lucky Strike. Ted's halitosis made him flinch when he leaned close.

'Too many late nights, buddy, eh?'

'Yeah, Fred, I mean Ted. Sorry about that.'

Dale seemed to be wrapping up this debrief. The dark circles under his eyes told a story.

'Well, team, that's about all for now. Sorry if I've kept you up.' He glared at Spencer.

Spencer whispered to Savannah.

'Sorry, I guess things have caught up with me. It's all been a bit tense of late. Did I miss anything?'

'Where do I start? Did you hear that the cabin was blown sky high, Eduardo's body simply disappeared?'

'No kidding? I guess Delaware wanted to get rid of the evidence. What else?'

'The good news is Maria is allowed to stay in the US.'

'That's awesome. What about Jenny, is she…?'

'She's fine. No wonder she fainted. Here comes Gus and Jenny now.'

As the agents filed out of the room, Gus grabbed two chairs and turned them around facing Spencer and Savannah. Spencer thought Jenny was glowing and looking at Gus brought to mind cats and dairy produce. Jenny and Gus sat down.

'It seems like we're stymied. Apparently, the Governor himself has told Dale to back off.'

***

Savannah closed the door as the last agent disappeared and wandered into the living room where Spencer flicked through the television channels.

'This is a goddam joke. I've never seen Dale so dispirited. I can't believe Delaware is going to keep on doing what he's doing.' Savannah slouched onto one of the easy chairs.

'The question is, what happens next? Is Stanford going to be a problem? For us, I mean?' Spencer asked.

'I don't think so. Why would he? He obviously now knows we are FBI. He has the Governor in his pocket. We're irrelevant, I would imagine.'

'Do you have any suggestions?'

'Nothing springs to mind. It looks like Jenny and Gus are becoming an item. He's taking her to see the goddam Beatles at Candlestick Park tomorrow night.'

'How about that? Do you want to watch this?' Spencer pointed at the television. 'It's called Get Smart. It's about two FBI type agents. Actually, they're a bit like us. It's a cool show. In fact, Max's co-star Agent 99 looks a bit like you.' Spencer turned his attention to the opening scenes as Agent Max Smart made his way through a labyrinth of passageways and secret entrances.

'No, I damn well don't want to watch that show. It's ridiculous. I mean he talks into his shoe. I can't take my mind off Delgado and Delaware.'

Spencer reluctantly turned off the television. 'Why in hell can't we at least go after good old BBQ? Maria can positively identify him. She was a witness when he shot Xavier, or Juan or whatever his name was?'

'How long were you asleep? Maria is not prepared to testify, she's terrified. They found her at the hotel, and here, and down in San Diego for Chrissake. She knows that Delaware has people everywhere. I mean the Governor himself spoke to Dale. He's putting her into witness protection, change of name, the whole thing. I think Dale hopes that at some point she'll change her mind and testify. I can't see that happening, and who can blame her? Candlestick Park, the Beatles? That's interesting.'

'Don't tell me you want to go?' Spencer sniggered.

'I'd rather climb Mount Everest in ballet slippers, thank you very much.'

'Savannah, I agree the Beatles thing is interesting. I know Dale poo-poohed it when I mentioned Delaware's obsession with the Fab Four, but here's the thing, Maria is adamant the Beatles are going to the commune, which simply doesn't make any sense. The late guitar player, Grady, said to me when I spoke to him about the commune band and their resemblance to the real Beatles, that they, the Beatles were going to be living in those four mansions currently being built next to Delaware's monstrosity.'

'When I first asked him about the houses, he was a bit coy and said, *well, they are for royalty, rock and roll royalty.*'

'That could have been a throwaway line, surely? He actually said John, Paul, Gary and Bingo would be moving into those houses?'

'Yeah, I forget his exact words, but we spoke about a few things one night at dinner, and I said, I wonder who those houses would be for, they're fit for royalty. And it's George not Gary, and Ringo not Bingo.'

'Thank you so much for correcting me?'

'When I pressed him, he was adamant the Beatles were going to be joining the Family and Stanford was going to use them as a figurehead to launch his revolution. I didn't say much after that, I just put it down to, I don't know, just gossip, hearsay, something like that.'

'This makes my brain hurt. I can't see where this is going. So, Delaware is obsessed with a rock group. I can't for the life of me see any point to this discussion. I'll be glad when this mess is over and I can get back to Inez. Hell, I even miss Capone. He's a lovely old cat.'

'I'm not ready to let go of this. Let me run something past you, straight out of left field.' They were making their way through the kitchen to the expansive backyard, with its tall privacy fence. Several of the other agents were already out back, having drinks and chatting.

'If you must, Spencer.'

'I have had this idea for a while. I haven't mentioned it because it's totally nuts. But then I think, Stanford Delaware is totally nuts. The world's had plenty of head cases who've had delusions of grandeur and they cause a lot of damage. Look at the facts, the Family has grown from nothing, in a relatively short space of time, to a huge organisation with millions of dollars in assets. We know he has a huge following. You and I know he's a dangerous psychopath surrounded by some very nasty people. Frankly, I believe he's capable of just about anything.'

'Gotcha. You're building up to something weird, I just know it.'

'Don't laugh, OK?'

'Who me?' Savannah rolled her eyes.

They stepped off the large back deck and onto the soft grass. Spencer peered around at the foliage. It wasn't like the commune, going off forever in all directions, but the idyllic quiet and the bright summer sun were the same.

'I believe Delaware, or more specifically his henchman, Ronny and whoever else he has available, are going to kidnap the Beatles and take them back to the commune.'

'What's that Aussie saying—*a few roos short in the top paddock?*' Savannah laughed.

'It's not that crazy. Dale fell for his bullshit, hook line and sinker. And if you remember when we first saw him in his trailer, we walked away all starry-eyed. It was only when, due to unforeseen circumstances, we were deprived of the Love Potion Number 9 that we saw things with any clarity. Consider this, all of his flock are working in the fields or wherever else and all the time they're drinking happy juice. What's the bet if he gets the boys there, they may just see his point of view? Hell, John Lennon is always banging on about world peace.'

'Suppose, just suppose you're right. How the hell would it work?'

'Obviously there will be a big police presence. I've already checked; they're staying at the Hilton. They'll be going from there to Candlestick Park, on the Western shore of San Francisco Bay. I'd imagine they'd be travelling in a limo.'

'You really believe this rubbish, don't you? Have you stopped to consider, even if the plan worked, the city would go into lockdown and the limo with these English morons wouldn't get anywhere. There'd be choppers, motorbike cops, police cruisers. The whole goddam city would be on the case. No, not even Delaware would be that silly.'

He had a clear image in his mind of the four large houses beside Delaware's huge mansion, with the Rolls Royce parked out front.

'I haven't finished. Hear me out.'

'Ok, but honestly…'

'What if they didn't know the Beatles had been kidnapped?'

'Spencer, what have you been smoking? How in hell could they not know? *I'm sure we had an English rock and roll band here somewhere. I wonder where they could be.* Give me strength.'

'I've thought of all this. What do you think the point was about the band playing at the commune? They look like the Beatles; they sound like the Beatles.'

'Yeah, but they're not the Beatles. No one would mistake them for the real deal.' Savannah snorted.

'Really? Remember it'll be dark. Four long-haired guys. The cops, the press, the fans, are only going to catch a glimpse, and remember the eye often only sees what it wants to see.'

'Suppose you're right. What happens when they go on stage? Everybody will know.'

'Sure, but I have taken the trouble to research a few things. Listen to this. The Beatles always walk onto the stage in darkness, they plug in their guitars. Ringo's drums are on, like a pedestal. He takes a minute to sit, grab his sticks, whatever. They usually start their set with *Rock and Roll Music,* an old Chuck Berry number. Halfway through all the lights come on. Gradually the audience will realise something's wrong. But here's the good bit. At every Beatles concert the screaming is so bloody loud you can hardly hear the band. So, the organisers are going to take a little while to realise something's not right.'

'Great. So, end of story, the jig's up. What's the point?'

'I'll tell you what the point is. By the time that happens the real Beatles will be miles away, and no doubt drinking happy juice.' He cast a glance back over his shoulder at Jax and the other agents, commiserating over beers.

'What about the poor guys playing in the fake Beatles band? They'll be charged with aiding and abetting a kidnapping. They'll get twenty years.'

Spencer gestured out toward the trees and the more distant low mountain peaks, covered in greenery, visible over the tall privacy fence. 'Stanford couldn't care less; he's got what he wants. And remember, in his fantasy universe everything would be hunky dory. The Beatles will embrace Stanford's brave new world. He's a hero and they all live happily ever after.'

CHAPTER 43

THE ACTION

Savannah stared hard at Spencer.

'The Beatles concert is tonight. What can we do? I'm probably stupid, but you might just be right. You want to talk to Dale?'

'I know we should, but you saw him, he's thrown in the towel. What I suggest is we go to the Hilton, flash our badges and try and find out what the security is and take it from there. Hell, you're FBI—they'll take you seriously.'

'Just the two of us? If you're right we're going to need some help.' Savannah frowned.

'Gus and Jenny. They'll come on board, I'm sure.'

'Gus won't be happy; he's supposed to be taking Jenny to the concert, remember?'

Spencer laughed.

'What's the problem? We fill them in on what we think is going down. They follow us. If I'm wrong, they can go to the concert. If I'm right, there won't be a bloody concert anyway.'

***

The motel room was a study in muted elegance. Soft lamplight filtered through ivory curtains, casting gentle shadows across the plush invigorating green carpet. A teak dresser stood against one wall, adorned with a single vase of fresh lilies, their fragrance mingling with the subtle hint of lavender from the neatly made king-size bed. Jenny jumped up from an easy chair and embraced Savannah.

'Great to see you guys.'

Spencer shook Gus's hand.

'Nice motel. Doing it in style, eh?'

'Special place for a special lady.' Gus turned and smiled at Jenny.

'Gus, I have a sneaking suspicion this may not be entirely a social call. Am I right, Savannah?' Jenny frowned.

'Well…no…not exactly. Spencer, would you like to enlighten Jenny and Gus with your…shall we say, suspicions?' Savannah grinned as she plonked down on the bed.

'Have a seat, Gus. You might need to be sitting down.' Suddenly Spencer thought his idea may be farfetched.

Gus shrugged as he sat on the other chair. Spencer leaned against the wall and started going over it all again. He'd smoothed the wrinkles out of the retelling, though, and felt better about his delivery.

Gus handed around cold beers from the mini bar.

'That's it, Spencer? That's all?'

Spencer nodded.

'Hell, this takes a bit of getting your head around. What do you think, Jenny love?'

Jenny grimaced as she swigged her drink.

'I'm not really a beer lady, but under the circumstances… Anyway, I think the whole thing's crazy, but you may just be right, Spencer. Delaware is capable of anything. I mean it sounds weird but, remember a couple of years ago, Sinatra's son was kidnapped.'

Spencer heaved a sigh of relief, *maybe just maybe it's a goer.*

'So, let's run through it again, Spencer. We turn up at the Hilton, flash our badges, eyeball the security guys, and make sure they're kosher. Check out the limo driver, follow the Beatles to Candlestick Park, see them safely inside. I mean, there's no way anyone's going to snatch them once they're on the stage. What about on the return journey?'

Spencer shook his head.

'If I'm right, it makes sense that they grab the boys before the concert and Delaware uses the other band as a decoy. Maybe I'm completely wrong. If everything goes without a hitch, you and Jenny can attend the concert and that's that.'

CHAPTER 44

THEIR BIG EVENT

Three Beatles lookalikes admired their trendy velvet collared suits and highly polished black Cuban heeled boots. The fourth, a smiling Caspar, followed Stanford out of his bedroom and into the living room. A scowling Ronny Delgado, nursing a bourbon and ice, glared pure hatred at Caspar, smirking as he pushed his long hair back.

'OK boys, tonight's the big night. I'm going to tell you what the plan is. You're going to love it. This is where you make the leap into the big time. The eyes of the world will be on you. Ronny, pour the guys some of the usual, there's a good chap.' Stanford beamed.

Ronny mumbled something before slamming his tumbler down hard on the occasional table and slouching over to the drinks trolley, pouring out four long glasses of the orange drink.

'Here, help yourself, guys.' This time he glared at Stanford.

'Have a seat, fellas. Caspar, you sit next to me.' Stanford sat on the two-seater, patting the space next to him. 'Are you ready?'

The four mop tops nodded enthusiastically.

'Tonight, you're going to be the warm-up act for the Beatles at Candlestick Park.'

Ivan the beak-nosed drummer gasped. 'You're kidding.'

'No, Ivan, I'm not kidding. I have done a deal with their manager, a lovely fellow, Brian Epstein. We're going to open this very evening.'

'But how…?' Terry, the bass player, started to say.

A brief flash of annoyance appeared on the Prophet's smooth visage.

'Terry, this has been a long time in the planning. This is going to be filmed and used in the opening sequence of the television show I have hinted to you about. Broadly speaking, the series will be about four young lads who metamorphosise from ordinary suburban boys into become rock and roll stars. The footage of you at Candlestick Park will be a very important component and will be a very realistic and compelling intro. I have also hired the best songwriters from the Brill Building in New York. I trust you've all heard of this remarkable establishment?'

Terry, the rhythm guitarist, clapped and smiled broadly.

'Gee, Mr Delaware, this is just great. What sort of numbers? Complicated stuff?'

'All sorts of different styles, 12 bar rockers, simple catchy lyrics, ballads and a couple of really driving pieces with some memorable riffs. You're going to love them. From tonight on your lives are going to change forever. There will be television appearances across the Unites States, and the rest of the world. We'll start filming the television series in a month's time. Before that you'll be in the recording studio, we want to have an album ready for release to coincide with the first television release. Do you think you're all up to it, eh?'

'We can't thank you enough, Mr Delaware,' Ivan gushed.

'OK, boys. Your chariot awaits. Mr Delgado here will be your driver. The limo, of course, has very heavily tinted glass. There will be huge crowds of massed around the entrance. You'll be driven to the rear stage door at Candlestick Park. When you get there talk to no one. Run straight onto the stage. A warning, it will be fairly dark. Your instruments will be leaning against your amplifiers, all tuned and ready.'

Terry, the rhythm guitarist, spoke. 'The same equipment we've been using, Mr Delaware?'

'Of course, my boy. The amps are all Vox. The bass guitar is the Hofner violin model. Terry, you'll be playing the Rickenbacker and Caspar, dear boy, you'll be on the Gretsch Country Gentleman. Nice guitar, that one. And Ivan, the Ludwig kit is set up exactly as you've been using it here. Now boys, you remember your setlist? You play them exactly in the order I've told you.' All of them nodded along, glasses of happy juice in their hands. 'Now, this is important, you must ignore the fans, no matter what they say or do. All right, boys, your chariot awaits.'

CHAPTER 45

THE BEST LAID PLANS

Without awareness of the road or the rain, the car moved over the highway, lights on full beam. Savannah watched how the yellowed bright lights played on the droplets creating a splash of colour. She checked her watch.

'We should be at the Hilton in about a half an hour. I'm still thinking we must be nuts. The idea that Delaware could be considering doing this, it's…it's crazy.' She started fiddling with the radio.

'You said that already.' The gentle rhythmic *tick tick tick* of the indicator clicked as the sedan passed a Mack hauling logs.

'Sorry, let's change the subject. It's great to see Gus and Jenny getting it together. Hey, listen,' Savannah said, and pressed a button on the car radio, 'Sinatra's latest *Strangers in the Night*. This is what I call music. You know, I've been thinking, if you're right and Stanford is planning to kidnap those four long-haired creeps, he could be doing the world a real favour.'

'Now I know you're joking. We're coming up to the Hilton now. Speaking of Gus and Jenny, they're waiting for us at the entrance straight ahead.'

***

'I've told the concierge we're here to check on the Beatles. He was a bit suspicious. I think he thought we were press, trying to get an interview.' Gus looked embarrassed.

Jenny laughed. 'Yeah, he had a good look at our badges.'

'Apparently, they're still in their rooms. They have the whole of the top floor. I think you might have made a mistake, Spencer. Everything seems OK.' Gus shrugged.

They strolled self-consciously through the lobby, a lavish, sprawling area able to hold hundreds of people. Spencer admired the gleaming marble tiles, the multi-tiered chandeliers, and the tasteful water feature. Everything looked so normal. The long front desk was staffed with uniformed employees. The floor to ceiling massive windows and the hotel's name in gold lettering all screamed *nothing to see here, folks. This is the Hilton.*

The high-speed elevator was a plain silver box with plain silver buttons and plain silver doors. As it sped to the top floor Spencer felt decidedly foolish.

'OK, let's get this over and done with. You and Jenny will still make the concert.' Savannah punched Spencer playfully on the shoulder.

As they stepped out of the elevator and peered cautiously down the passage all was quiet. Nothing. No noise. No people.

'You would have thought there would have been some sort of activity. Some hangers on, some security.' Gus turned to Spencer, face full of astonishment. Was Spencer's insane hunch really playing out?

Jenny looked around. 'So, let's check some rooms.'

Spencer rapped loudly on the first door. No response. He tried the handle. The door swung open; the lights were on.

The hotel suite was a study in contrasts, its plush crimson curtains drawn tightly against the city lights, filtering through.

'Help!'

'What in hell?' Gus whipped his 0.38 out of its pancake holster.

'I think that came from that room over there.' Savannah pointed.

They were in what seemed to be a large well-equipped sitting room with a corridor running off it and a number of doors connecting to bedrooms. Empty beer bottles and used crockery and cutlery were strewn haphazardly on a table and the carpeted floor.

Guns drawn, they raced down the passage. Again, they heard a yell and something banging, like a foot on a wall or floor. The large double oak doors were locked. Spencer nodded at Gus before they launched themselves. 450 pounds of muscle exploded against the solid timber. The doors flew open, one completely off its hinge.

'Jesus, I don't believe it.' Savannah gasped.

Four burly uniformed men tied and gagged were lined up neatly against one wall.

'They've just gone. Minutes ago,' one of the men croaked as his gag was ripped off.

'How many minutes?' Gus demanded.

'Five, maybe ten.' A big guy with a handlebar moustache grunted.

'What do they look like?' Spencer asked.

'Just like us. There's two of them. Big guys. Same maroon uniform. That's why we fell for it. We thought the security company had sent back up, or replacements. They got guns.

You might be able to stop them. We'd been instructed to take the high-speed lift at the end of the corridor. I think they've taken our limo. I had to hand over my keys.'

'What make of vehicle?' Savannah asked.

An older guy with thinning hair and bad teeth spoke up. 'You can't miss it. It's a Mercedes Pullman. A big sucker. Black. The Beatles will be in the back, it's completely sealed to keep people out, but it also keeps them locked in. There's no way they're gonna get out. For Chrissake, you better hurry.'

Jenny ripped the rope off one of their wrists.

'OK, guys. You can free yourselves. Call the SFPD as soon as you can, OK?'

Gus frowned. 'I don't think we'll be going to the concert, Jenny.'

The speed of the service elevator was a surprise. The only indication was from the red-light indicator hovering above the door. The elevator moved so fast the lights didn't have the time to indicate every floor it passed. In total travel time was 75 floors in 58 seconds.

'Wow. That was fun.' Spencer tried to smile.

As they burst into the lobby, they heard raised voices, an argument. Spencer's stomach clenched.

'Hey. That's John Lennon.' Jenny pointed; her hand went to her mouth. Spencer's heart pounded. He scoped the lobby. A moment of panic. *Are we going to be outnumbered?* He had visions of a firefight with Savannah blazing away with her Magnum.

It took all of five seconds to figure out what was going on. Beatle John Lennon was signing autographs while the two bogus security guys sweated and tried to drag him away.

'C'mon, Mr Lennon, we're in a hurry. Your buddies are already in the limo waiting for you. We can't leave people waiting, now can we?'

Beads of sweat formed on the thug's brow as he harangued Lennon, at the same time scanning the lobby.

'Yes we can,' Lennon replied languidly. 'We're early. These people want autographs and they're going to get them.'

'Mr Lennon, I'm telling you…' The goon's voice raised as he grabbed Lennon's jacket.

Lennon angrily shook the hand away.

'And I'm telling you, fook off, you git.'

'Do you recognise those two clowns?' Spencer whispered to Savannah. She nodded.

'One false move and I'll shoot the sons of bitches.' Her hand slipped under her jacket.

Spencer didn't know their names but he'd seen them swaggering around the commune. Big guys, lots of muscle, but not a lot upstairs.

'How do you want to handle this?' Gus turned to Spencer.

'Easy as,' Spencer replied, faking confidence.

The four strode purposefully across the floor.

'Excuse me, folks.' Spencer beamed.

Captivated by a strikingly beautiful young fan, John Lennon moved away from the two would-be kidnappers as he chatted and signed autographs for her and another miniskirted stunner. Spencer and Savannah simultaneously shoved their pistols into the stomachs of the two thugs.

'Remember us?' Savannah whispered. 'Just give me a reason.'

Probably acting on a reflex, the biggest villain lunged at Savannah. Like a bolt of lightning, with fingers like tensile steel, Spencer jabbed his throat. Collapsing on the floor the man writhed, trying to breathe, eyes bulging.

Alarmed, Lennon turned. 'Is he OK?'

'He'll be OK, John. He's, um, epileptic. This lovely lady here will be driving you to the concert.' Spencer pointed at Jenny.

Gus held out a hand to the other tough guy, who stood blank-faced.

'The keys, please.'

***

The doorman's suit was as crisp as a new banknote and dyed to a uniform shade of sombre gray. If he thought anything was amiss, he didn't show it.

Spencer, Savannah and Gus watched as the heavy door on the Mercedes long wheelbase Pullman Limousine clicked shut. They could just make out the other Beatles through the heavily tinted glass. A moment of panic on Jenny's face as she searched for the ignition. A wave, a jaunty grin and the limo peeled off into the traffic. Spencer heaved a sigh of relief, his hands still shaking.

The throng of screaming, tearful girls had been adroitly, smoothly herded to one side by security guys as skilled as toreadors duelling with Spanish fighting bulls.

***

Savannah cracked a smile. 'Just wait till Dale hears about this.'

'It's not over,' Spencer reminded her.

'No, we still have to make sure everything is OK at the concert. By the way, that fingers to the throat trick worked pretty well, but you might have killed him,' Savannah said.

'Nah, just a love tap. If I'd been serious, he'd be in a body bag on his way to the morgue. Gus, your car's right here, hopefully we can get to Candlestick Park in time to sort out whatever's going to happen.'

'Spencer, Delaware might have squads of goons at the performance to oversee things. It could turn into a firefight with the SFPD. Who knows just what this nutcase has planned for?'

'Fucking unbelievable,' Gus muttered.

Spencer shook his head.

'What can I say, Gus? We know Delaware wanted to kidnap the Beatles. From here, the bogus band are simply a diversion. Unless he had some spies or informants at the Hilton who have called him, but we don't have any way of knowing that. I'm hoping he's sitting back just waiting for the Beatles to turn up at the commune. He'd certainly have some heavies waiting when they arrive. When that happens, the Beatles are going to be confused and scared. Obviously, they would've figured out something was amiss. About now Delaware would be thinking they'd be screaming and yelling in their limo trying to get out. Fat chance of that. Those Mercedes Limos are the vehicles of choice for at risk dictators. Rats in a trap.'

'Sure, but once they're at the commune the Beatles would never cooperate with him, surely?' Gus replied.

'I'm not sure Delaware sees it that way. If he can convince the boys there has actually been a revolution and he's the big white chief, well…'

Savannah interrupted. 'The thing is, Gus, he really believes his own crap. And remember, all of his followers have swallowed the story, hook line and sinker. And it's obvious there are God knows how many true believers scattered throughout the community. I know it's hard for you to grasp but when Spencer and I first arrived at the commune, worked in the fields, listened to his propaganda…'

'And drank that blasted cordial,' Spencer added. 'I tell you, Gus, we were well on the way to indoctrination. But meanwhile I'm as sure as I can be that the other band will turn up at Candlestick Park, the security will usher them in. The fake Beatles will start playing, after ten minutes, whatever, the audience will realise they've been duped and all hell will break loose. It's anybody's guess as what would happen next. Even Delaware wouldn't have a clue. The police will be pulling their hair out. The poor guys in the other band will have no idea what's going on, and meanwhile the Beatles are supposed to be at the commune undergoing conversion therapy.'

CHAPTER 46

A ROCKING GOOD NIGHT

Savannah tugged at Spencer's sleeve.

'Hey look, up ahead that's the Mercedes Limo with Jenny and the Beatles on board. Gus, give 'em a toot.'

'Shit, don't, Gus, that's not Jenny, that's a different limo. That's the bogus Beatles. Heads down, Savannah, don't let them see you.'

'You have to admire Delaware's attention to detail. I mean, another Mercedes, same model, same everything. Wow.' Savannah emitted a low whistle.

'Gus, put your bloody foot down. If we can get there before them, we can nip this thing in the bud. I'm not sure but I think that might have been that idiot Delgado driving. How does this sound? We position ourselves and wait until they all climb out of the limo, then it's simply a case of—"FBI, Ronny Delgado you're under arrest." We point our weapons at him…'

'He shits his pants.' Savannah cackled.

'Maybe, but he might do anything. I must admit it's looking good. And the main thing is surely we'll have everything we need to take Delaware down. The district attorney, everyone will have to get on board. Hell, this will be the story of the century.' Spencer's grin was as wide as the Golden Gate Bridge.

✳✳✳

The entrance to Candlestick Park was a river of people, everyone pushing, shoving in the same direction, a sea of joyful faces heading towards the stadium for the greatest rock act on earth. Gus edged the sedan along a narrow slip of tarmac leading to the rear stage door. Uniformed cops held the crowd back.

'Thank God, do you see what I see?' Savannah thumped the dash, grinning.

Gus edged their sedan away from the entrance and put the transmission into park. They had to force the car doors open as the throng of people pressed closer.

Two security guys unlatched steel barriers allowing the gleaming black Mercedes Pullman to glide to a stop next to the cavernous opening to the stage and dressings rooms. Trench-coated cameramen jostled for position, their flashes blazing like silent gunshots.

'Look at me, John. Hey, Paul, big smile for the camera.'

The Beatles all smiled and waved. Broad-shouldered bouncers shoved the press out of the way as they hustled the band inside. A smiling Jenny climbed out of the driver's seat. Gus and Savannah waved their badges, making their way to the Mercedes. Gus threw his arms around Jenny, exclaiming, 'What a girl!'

Jenny blushed but looked pleased. 'It was nothing really.'

'Listen up, guys, Delgado and the other band can only be minutes away. This could still get very messy,' Spencer warned.

Savannah nodded, pointing at a cop in a captain's uniform drinking coffee and chatting to a reporter, who was busy lining up the officer for a publicity photo.

'Now Stan, this better be on the front page of *The Chronicle*, you hear?' the captain barked. He looked impressive, big; he had that heavy demeanour that demanded respect. Savannah waved away the photographer.

'Not now, buddy. The captain's busy.'

'Hey, little lady, what in hell do you think you're doing? Beat it or you'll be spending the night in the drunk tank. Goddam female reporters.'

'It's not little lady, Captain. It's Special Agent Savannah Steele.' Savannah flashed her badge. 'Now drop everything and listen. We only have minutes if you want to avoid a bloodbath.'

The captain acknowledged the badge with a nod. 'OK, Ma'am. You have my attention,' he said quietly, throwing his coffee cup to the ground.

Spencer and Savannah explained the situation.

'Aha, I get it, I think. The other limo will be here shortly, eh? Jesus, I hope you know what you're doing.'

Four other SFPD officers milled around the stage door, the captain yelling, 'Ernie, Steve, you other guys come here, now!'

The captain quickly outlined the situation as he fired off orders to his men, who took up positions next to the portable steel entrance barriers. One ran off down the winding tarmac leading to the front of Candlestick Park. Savannah grabbed Jenny.

'You still have the keys to the Mercedes?'

Jenny nodded.

'Jump in and hide it behind that big semi. We want Delgado to turn up and not suspect anything. Let's hope he arrives, and the band gets out and he simply surrenders. What do you think, Spencer?'

'Nice thought.' Spencer rolled his eyes.

Spencer and Savannah turned their gaze to a sweating patrolman pushing through the crowd.

'Captain, Captain, the other limo is making its way in now. It's being slowed down by all these goddam teenagers. Apparently, the kids hanging around think it's the real Beatles; they're screaming and hollering like all get out.'

Its shiny black paintwork glistening, the majestic Mercedes nudged its way through the crowd, its three-pointed star leading the way through the unholy conglomeration of perfume, body odour and marijuana fumes. Tearful girls were being roughly pulled off its hood by brawny security guards. As the limo crawled through the last curve of the tarmac pathway and glided to a stop, the rear doors sprung open and the four Beatles lookalikes stumbled out. Seeing nothing amiss, Ronny Delgado climbed out wearing his crumpled maroon uniform like a temporary inconvenience. He gasped as he saw a grinning Savannah pointing her pistol straight at him.

'Nice to see you, Ronny.'

Guitarist Caspar chose that moment to shirtfront Delgado, with all the authority of a genuine rock and roll superstar.

'Hey, Delgado. Where exactly do we go, man?'

Ronny grabbed the unfortunate Caspar in a neck hold, thrusting a Colt 0.38 revolver into his neck.

'Any closer and the kid gets it!' Ronny screamed as he dragged white-faced Caspar to the driver's door.

'What the fuck's going on? Help me, please…someone.'

'Shut up,' Ronny yelled, jerking open the driver's door and using the boy as a shield before hustling him inside. A deathly silence fell over the onlookers. With a triumphant grin, Ronny clicked the lock shut, fired up the motor and reversed, the rear tires shuddered as they tried to gain traction. A girl screamed as the front fender hit her hard. She fell to the ground, her right leg bent at an impossible angle. A heavyset guy cried out as he was bounced onto the hood of the car. Poised for a moment like a crash test dummy, he was flung off and fell heavily, as the Mercedes swerved to avoid a group of people scattering in all directions. People screamed, trying desperately to avoid the heavy vehicle.

Savannah had both hands on her pistol. She waited a split second when Delgado looked behind. She fired. An easy shot. Centre mass through the windscreen. The magnum roared. The heavy round ricocheted off the glass, leaving a small nick on the surface.

'Jesus, I don't believe it. Bulletproof.'

The cops and the security guards stood like statues, stunned as the limo disappeared into the crowd.

CHAPTER 47

WHAT NOW?

His eyes like saucers, Caspar pushed himself to the far edge of the passenger seat. He gazed wildly around as the Mercedes roared away from Candlestick Park, his rock and roll future disappearing in the rear vision mirror.

'Mr Delgado, what's happening? I don't understand. I mean, I'm supposed to on stage. We're supposed to be playing. What…'

'Shut the fuck up. I'm trying to think.' Ronny grabbed the wheel with one hand, the other clutching his pistol, as he powered the big sedan through light traffic.

Silence reigned until Ronny turned onto South Van Ness Avenue.

'I guess I'm being kidnapped. At least you could tell me why? Stanford won't be too happy with you, will he?'

'You don't have any idea, do you, you little punk? It's over. You're not going onto the stage. You guys were just a fucking diversion.'

'What do you mean? Stanford had us lined up to make a television series. We're going to be famous.'

'Stanford was just using you. Don't you understand?'

'That's bullshit. Stanford loves me. We were going away on a holiday after the show, before the television series started shooting. Just him and me on his jet.'

'Yeah sure.' Ronny snarled.

'I know what this is all about.'

'You do, do you?'

'Yeah, I had you figured from day one. I saw the way you looked at me, at Stanford. You're jealous.'

'What the fuck are you talking about, you little queer?'

'Takes one to know one.'

A hush fell over the limo.

'Now you're moving into dangerous territory,' Ronny whispered.

'Nah, he told me all about you. He thought you were disgusting. Big Ronny BBQ Delgado, ex-star football player, but now just a fat pig. You think Stanford was using me? You idiot. He was using you.'

'I'm not a faggot!' Ronny screamed.

Caspar slid closer and placed his hand on Ronny's thigh. 'Are you sure?'

Delgado closed his eyes momentarily. He felt himself growing hard. He turned slowly and gazed at the boy's sleek auburn hair and his mesmerising deep blue eyes, they were almond-shaped and now seemed to be afire with passion. Ronny noticed the earthy scent that swirled around him. He gulped.

'No.' He shoved Caspar hard against the passenger door frame. The Colt sounded like a cannon in the confined space. Caspar slumped forward, a neat hole in the side of his head.

***

The wrinkled mountains were cocoon quiet when Ronny cautiously turned down a narrow track lined with knobcone pines. Leaning over, he opened the passenger door and shoved Caspar's still warm corpse onto the forest floor.

'Good riddance, faggot. Who's laughing now, eh?'

Reversing cautiously onto the blacktop and accelerating smoothly away, Ronny in fact wasn't laughing as he tried to figure out what he was going to tell Stanford when he saw a sign for the Diablo Mountain Inn. Still trying to come up with a convincing story, he drove slowly past the parked cars. Looking for what, he wasn't sure, police cruisers, or television production trucks?

Parking the car away from the other guests' vehicles he spotted a pay phone. With shaking hands, he dropped a dime into the slot.

'You've fucked up again, haven't you, Ronny?'

'Stanford, it wasn't my fault,' Delgado whined.

'It's on the news. They're saying you kidnapped someone.'

Ronny gasped. He hadn't counted on Stanford knowing this.

'Stanford, I had no choice. I almost didn't get away. They were waiting for us. I got no idea how…'

'So, who did you kidnap?'

'That guitar player, Caspar.'

'Is he with you now?'

'No, I couldn't help it, Stanford, honest…'

'Couldn't help what? What about Caspar?'

'The little prick went for my gun while we were driving. I nearly had an accident. Swear to God.'

'Let me guess. You killed him?'

'Look, Stanford…'

'Shut the fuck up, Ronny. We can talk about this later. This is too big to blow over. The Feds, the police, will be swarming over the commune any moment now.'

'But Stanford, you got protection. The Governor…'

'Not now you've fucked things up. It's gotten out of hand.'

'What do we do, Stanford?'

'I've always had a contingency plan, Ronny. Go straight to the that little airport near Clayton.'

'Why? What are we doing? Where are we going?'

'For Chrissake, Ronny, we're leaving, we'll talk about it later. The Lear Jet is fuelled up. We're leaving the country.'

'Me too? You want me to be with you, Stanford?'

'Jesus, I don't know why, but I'm not throwing you to the wolves.'

CHAPTER 48

A SHORT FLIGHT

Glimmering like faint fireflies, the runway status lights stretched along the length of the rarely used airstrip. The powerful Mercedes headlights illuminated the sleek lines of the Lear Jet 23, a small twin-engine, high-speed business jet. Its ability to access smaller airports had made it popular amongst wealthy individuals and executives. Parked next to the aircraft Ronny recognised Stanford's vehicle, a smart white Cadillac De Ville, his replacement for the stolen Rolls Royce. Next to the Caddy was an unfamiliar drab gray Chrysler Valiant.

A wave of hope, tinged with contentment washed over Ronny. It was sad that the US movement may have come to an ignominious end, but Stanford Delaware would power on. Ronny had total faith. Wherever they were bound Stanford would draw in converts like moths to a flame. Meanwhile he was tired, the stress of the day had taken its toll.

He pulled up next to the Cadillac. Imposing as ever, his bald head gleaming in the harsh Mercedes high beam, Stanford stood at the boarding steps, scowling at his watch. Delgado clambered out of the Mercedes.

'God dammit, Ronny, you took your time. Get on board, will you please?'

Ronny slammed the door shut on the Mercedes and pocketed the keys.

He followed Stanford into the small cabin. He was surprised to see three other men already seated, men he'd never seen before.

'Ronny, take a seat. Gentlemen, please introduce yourselves.'

The men nodded and spoke, one after another, 'Clive.'

'Anthony.'

'Walter.'

'You guys, you're all English, right?'

Ronny's long association with the criminal class meant his 'crook radar' was highly tuned. These guys were villains, no doubt about it. He recognised crude prison tattoos and the hard dead eyes. But why English thugs?

'Stanford, what's going on? Sorry, guys.' He nodded at the three passengers. 'I mean, I'm confused. I'm sure Clive, Anthony and, what was your name, pal?'

'Walter.' The heavy-set guy grunted.

'Yeah, OK. Walter. Terrible with names. So, Stanford, we have three English gentlemen I've never seen before and we're flying somewhere.'

The passenger door closed with a soft click. Then came a loud *poof* as the ventilation switched from the outside system. The lights flickered as they transitioned to the aircraft's system. The Lear Jet was airborne. There was silence until the seatbelt warning flashed off.

'Help yourself to drinks, gentlemen. Ronny, get me a beer. There's a good chap.'

'Sure.' Ronny made his way to the refrigerator. It was not his imagination; Stanford had adopted an English accent.

'I'll tell you what's happening, Ronny…'

'Hang on, don't you want me to tell you exactly what…' Ronny interrupted.

Stanford's eyes blazed.

'What's to know? Another Ronny Delgado stuff up.' He turned to the three passengers. 'Ronny aka BBQ Delgado. He's as sharp as a sackful of soup. I think he had too many knocks to the head. What do you reckon, Ronny, am I being a bit harsh?'

'Stanford, this wasn't my fault. When I got to the park…'

'Shut the fuck up. We have a long flight, and you're giving me a headache.'

'Where are we going, Stanford?'

'Didn't I say? As you have probably noted my associates are English, they're going to be my partners in merry England.'

Ronny gasped.

'England? Hell, I had no idea. How come I haven't met these guys before? I don't have a passport.'

'Don't worry about that. The shortened version of what's happening is this. I'm going to get the "Family" underway in England and Europe. As it happens, these gentlemen have been here for a week. I've been outlining my plans, but now things have just been accelerated. I tell you, Ronny, it's going to be bigger than ever…'

'And if you don't mind me asking, what are these guys for?'

'I need people with local knowledge, Ronny. Men who can help me overcome obstacles. As you know, we have to grease palms, sometimes use a little gentle persuasion. That sort of thing.'

'OK, I get the picture. Where do I fit in?'

'Sorry if I was a little hard on you, Ronny. I guess I was a bit upset that the wheels had fallen off so quickly. If we had managed to get the Beatles to the commune, I just know they would have embraced our ideals. I mean John Lennon, he would have just loved the whole thing. You must have heard his views on…'

'Yeah, yeah, I know, Stanford, and I'm just as unhappy as you are. Just so long as you and I are OK?'

'Of course we are. We go back a long way. You must be tired. Try and get some sleep.'

The airplane felt like home to Ronny; he'd flown in them so often. He could curl up and sleep as easily as dozing on his own bed. The engines roared, the winds buffeted, it was his sky born cradle, rocked by the winds far above the ground. His brain relaxed into dream time. There was a long way to go, and all he had to do was sleep and awake to new adventures.

Ronny stirred, as the aircraft lurched downwards. A buzzer shrieked. All of a sudden there was a whoosh, becoming a roar and then a powerful rush of air, followed by violent turbulence as if the aircraft was being ripped apart. Ronny screamed, two pair of muscular hands grabbed him, propelling him to the opening that had appeared where the door once was. He caught a glimpse of dark water. He was marched toward an exit, and his legs turned to jelly as the realization hit.

'Stanford, why? You said you wouldn't throw me to the wolves.'

'That's right, Ronny. I'm throwing you to the sharks.'

CHAPTER 49
IS IT ALL OVER?

Gazing forlornly through the window the next day, Spencer watched as the afternoon sunbathed the houses in its warm glow. Tiny specks of dust seemed to dance in the shaft of sunlight, slanting into the Palo Alto living room. Spencer wondered what would happen from here. Where was he going to fit in? Dale had all the updates, but he suspected, win, lose or draw, Stanford Delaware's Family was already yesterday's news.

Yet he hadn't woken up in back with Michiyo and Trilby.

He'd slowly come to the realization that this was the life he lived for. The adventure, the excitement and the satisfaction of destroying the bad guys. He loved his wife and daughter absolutely. Life in the next century was easy, but boring and predictable. Savannah could be annoying and unpredictable, but never dull. She really was the sister he'd never had. He realised with a jolt; he never wanted it to end.

'I've become an adrenaline junkie,' he muttered.

Savannah reclined in an easy chair watching baseball with the sound off. Jenny and Gus seemed happy enough sitting close on the two-seater. Spencer took his gaze away from the view and sat on the floor trying to choose a novel from the well-stocked bookcase. He glanced again at his Bulova

Accutron watch and wondered how and when he'd acquired it? He must ask Savannah. Car tires squelched on the driveway.

'It's one pm, everybody. Unless I'm wrong that sounds like Dale's car pulling in.'

Spencer grinned as he opened the door. 'One thing I will say, Dale, you are never late. I hope you're the bearer of glad tidings.'

'Not really, darn it. But it could be worse. Any chance of a coffee?'

'Leave it to me. Come in, everyone's waiting impatiently in the living room.'

Seated at the coffee table, mug in hand and a plate of biscotti in front of him, Dale took a gulp of coffee and bit into a cookie. His blue polyester suit looked like he'd slept in it.

'Ahem, first of all, I'd like to compliment you on a job well done. My apologies, Spencer, for not listening to you earlier when you suggested Delaware was planning something with the Beatles. It just seemed so farfetched. I do have a lot of news. The Governor, Tim Benson, realised he had been conned by Delaware and he actually mobilised the National Guard.'

'No kidding?' Savannah glanced away from the television.

'No, Agent Steele. Not kidding. These, converts, disciples, whatever you want to call them, didn't put up a fight. But it's a mess, on so many levels. Where to begin? Warrants have been issued for Delaware and Delgado, and a host of others.'

'Any clues on where our two star players are?' Spencer asked.

'Sort of. We found one of Delaware's cars, a Cadillac, at a disused airstrip at Concorde Airport, seven miles out of Clayton.'

'Was there a flight plan logged?' Savannah asked.

'Heavens to Betsy, we can't even establish what aircraft took off. And get this, there was another vehicle parked next to it, a crummy Chrysler Valiant and a big Mercedes limo. My guess is Delaware left with passengers. Including Delgado. But who, and where in tarnation did they go?'

'Dale, what plans do you have for all of us at the moment?' Gus held Jenny's hand.

'You're all on leave until further notice. Spencer and Savannah, if you don't mind staying on here in Palo Alto for the foreseeable future. You'll have to be available for an extensive debrief at our headquarters in Willshire Boulevarde, Los Angeles. Oh, and any suggestion that you, Savannah and Spencer, are going to be charged in relation any of the unfortunate deaths of Stanford's cronies have been officially dropped.'

Spencer hadn't been giving a lot of thought to the rising body count.

'That's a relief, Dale.'

'I thought we might have received a goddam thank you from the Beatles. Hell, we saved their ass.' Savannah rolled her eyes.

'Must you cuss all the time, Agent Steele? '

'Golly gosh, and heavens to goddam Betsy, I'll try really, really hard, Dale. Promise.'

'Dale, this is still big news, surely?' Spencer asked. 'The Beatles? The other band? The sheer audacity of the plot? I haven't seen anything on the news other than some people at Candlestick Park being hurt when Delgado took off in the Mercedes. And what about the kidnapping of the guitar player? It was a kidnapping, wasn't it?'

Dale held his head in his hands.

'Oh my gosh. It's actually kidnapping and murder.'

Jenny held a hand to her face.

'That poor kid. What happened, Dale?'

'We found a body not that long ago. Two hikers found him near the Diablo Mountain Inn. It's not been officially confirmed but it'll be the guitar player. Shot in the head.'

'Ronny Delgado has a lot to answer,' Spencer said, grim faced.

'It'll be the gas chamber, if we get him,' Dale said.

'What do you mean if, Dale? Spencer and I will track him down, and Delgado for that matter.'

'Really, Special Agent Steele? Really? And then, surprise, surprise, they both wind up dead with very big holes from that blasted cannon you carry. You two have finished with this case. Don't get me wrong, everybody from J Edgar down is very appreciative. But we do have a bit of a clue, well, not really a clue, just an avenue of enquiry. We found some papers in that Valiant sedan I mentioned.'

'I'm all ears, Dale,' Spencer said.

'No, you don't. I'm not about to tell you anything else. The only clue I'll give you is we think they've gone to another country.'

'Great, Spencer and I are happy to travel. Aren't we, Spencer?'

'You don't seem to listen, Steele. If we're correct, law enforcement in that country will arrest them. We extradite them, and that's that. Neat, tidy, no mess and no 0.357 Magnum. Got it.'

'If I shot them it would be in self-defence. For God's sake, Dale, Spencer and I know these two. We would be the best people to track them. By all means, call in local law enforcement wherever they happen to be, but we can be very useful, can't we, Spencer?'

'Um, yeah Dale, Savannah's right.'

'Where do you think they are, Dale? Mexico, South America, Europe?'

'Enough! Just drop it. Savannah, Spencer, read my lips: you're done.'

An awkward silence followed; Spencer could just hear the ticking of the mantle clock. Glancing at the television, an interview with a black ballplayer filled the screen. He thought it was Hank Aaron. Deprived of watching cricket, Spencer had finally embraced the American game and had gazed in awe at this power hitter. He took his eyes off the screen.

'Dale, there are a few loose ends.'

'What do you mean?'

'What about John, Paul, George and Ringo?'

'Who?'

'Honestly, Dale, I hate that crap they call music, but even I know their names,' a sulky Savannah said.

'I knew that. They're on their way back to England as we speak. Any more of those Italian cookies?'

'That's great, Dale, that they've gone, but what happened when they realised what a close call they had?' Gus let go of Jenny's hand.

'Actually, I was going to talk about that. It never happened, understand. We don't talk about it. No leaks to the press. Not to be mentioned.'

Spencer's jaw dropped. 'You've gotta be kidding, Dale. What about the Hilton? They sure as hell know what happened.'

'Spencer's right, Dale, and what about the three guys in the Beatle lookalike band? Surely they're going to exploit this whole thing to get some publicity,' Savannah added.

'Whoa, first things first. The Hilton people are very embarrassed. This incident reflects badly on them. They've sworn their staff to silence. The real Beatles have no idea whatsoever that they were very nearly kidnapped. The only thing they saw was that they had a new driver taking them to the show.'

'And those poor band guys, one of them murdered, don't tell me they won't sell their story?' Gus snorted.

'I can guarantee they won't be saying or doing anything.'

Savannah frowned. 'You look smug, Dale.'

'I guess you're right. I probably do. They've been told that they have come very close to being charged with conspiracy to kidnap and now with the discovery of their dead comrade, conspiracy to murder.'

'C'mon, Dale, that stinks. Those guys were victims. They had no idea they were being used. That would never stick.'

'Spencer. Let me tell you, the DA didn't see it that way. I had to use all of my influence to stop him from having them charged. Look at it from his point of view. Who in their right mind would understand what really happened? Golly, even I was swayed, momentarily, of course, and so were you and Savannah. Stanford and his happy juice were a powerful combination. Of course, I believe those unfortunate musicians were just pawns; they believed what they wanted to believe, but you surely must see it looks like they were complicit. Anyway, they've been told to shut their mouths and skedaddle.'

Spencer jumped to his feet.

'I've just had a thought, Dale.'

'And what would that be?'

'We don't know exactly how big Delaware's organisation is, or was. How do we know that he won't try and kidnap the Beatles again? I mean he's a very resourceful guy.'

'Don't worry about that. The English MI5 are on high alert, as are their regular police.'

'Did you say the MI5, not MI6?' Savannah queried.

'I was told MI5. What's the difference?'

'Well Dale, I remember from the course we studied at the FBI Academy about foreign law enforcement. As I'm sure you're aware, the 5 in MI5 represents the fifth letter in the alphabet, the letter E. The 5 represents threats to England, and with the MI6 the 6 represents the sixth letter in the alphabet, which is F, that F is for foreign. You say MI5 has been alerted? Stanford Delaware has gone to England, hasn't he, Dale?'

CHAPTER 50
A FAMILY HOLIDAY

LONDON 2015

Spencer stirred; he heard a clunk, followed by a whirring sound, then a voice, disconnected, not talking to him. Instructions, information.

'Ladies and gentlemen, welcome to London. Thank you for flying Singapore Airlines. The local time is 7.04 am. The weather is sunny, and the temperature is twenty-two degrees Celsius. For your safety and the safety of those around you, please remain seated with your seatbelt fastened and keep the aisle clear until the captain has turned off the seatbelt light. We wish you a pleasant stay in London and we hope to see you again.'

'Daddy, Daddy look, I can see The Tower of London, the Thames. It's so exciting.' Trilby's eyes were glued to the window of the aircraft as it made its descent.

Michiyo nudged him. 'Darling, I would say you have just set a new world record for sleeping on a plane. I swear you've been in the land of nod since we left Singapore.'

The skybridge hosted a river of people all headed in the same direction, the Heathrow terminal, gateway to London. As they strode along the passageway, Spencer once again felt the surge of optimism. Maybe this time he was here to stay.

In a daze but delighted to be back, Spencer gazed fondly at his beautiful wife and his long-legged daughter, who bounded ahead like a pup at a playground. At that moment he now realised his time travel experiences had to come to an end. His family were too precious. But how…?

'Must be in a brain fog after that sleep. Just refresh my memory. What's the plan, my darling? By the way, have I told you lately how much I love you?'

Michiyo clasped his hand, frowning.

'Have you been away again, Spencer? You couldn't possibly have forgotten. We've been planning this holiday for months. Trilby had a farewell sleepover at home two nights ago with her karate friends. She's so excited about getting her junior black belt. And remember you've been sitting up with her and explaining the monarchy, the history of Britain. Is this ever going to stop? I've pleaded with you to see a psychiatrist.'

'I'm sorry, Michiyo. It's just a memory lapse, honest.'

The clamour of voices, the rhythmic hum of the suitcase carousel and the excited chatter of their daughter ended the discussion.

∗∗∗

'Where to, Guv?' the elderly dark-skinned Cockney asked as he expertly peeled off into the maelstrom of traffic leaving Heathrow.

'Would you like to tell the gentleman?' Michiyo enquired tartly.

'Perhaps, you might…?'

243

'I think that might be best. The Pembroke Court Hotel, Notting Hill, please, driver.'

'That's a popular hotel. Close to Portobello Road. Lots of great restaurants. Trendy shops for the young lady.' He turned quickly, winking at Trilby.

Spencer's brows knitted. 'We haven't ever met before, have we?'

'Well sir, it's possible. I'm just about the oldest London Cabbie. I've been doing this since 1965. If you've been to London in the last 50 years…' The driver shrugged.

'Oh Spencer, just look, it's just like yours, hanging off the mirror.'

Spencer's jaw dropped; his heart raced. Dangling, glittering, twirling was a silver cornicello.

'What's your name, driver?' Spencer croaked.

'Sam. Everyone knows Sam the cabbie.'

'Sam, I have an ornament exactly the same as yours.'

'Oh yes, the cornicello. Pretty, isn't it?'

'If you don't mind me asking, where did you get it?'

Sam laughed.

'Honestly sir, if I told you how long ago I acquired it, you probably wouldn't believe me. Here we are, the Pembroke.'

Spencer gasped. What did all this mean?

'Please tell me. I really want to know.'

Sam smiled and held a finger to his lips.

Michiyo and Trilby strolled up to the white Victorian stucco entrance while Sam placed their luggage on the footpath.

'That's forty quid please, Guv.'

Spencer handed over two twenties and a ten.

'Keep the change. I really need to have a chat. Is there anywhere any time…?'

Sam smiled. He stuffed the notes into his pocket. He placed a hand on Spencer's arm.

'No, sorry chum, that's not possible. However, you should know, you're not the only one. One day it'll end and you'll have to decide.'

'Decide what, Sam?'

'You'll know when the time comes.'

In a swift movement belying his age, Sam jumped into the vehicle. The diesel motor clattered noisily as the cab disappeared into the bustling Notting Hill traffic. Spencer wanted to tear after it. What did it all mean?

***

'I can't believe it's still daylight. I expected it to be dark by now. The English summer is so different from Australia. That cab driver was a nice man. Did you give him a good tip?'

Now late in the day, Michiyo had begun unpacking her suitcase and was looking for hangers in the tiny wardrobe.

'I'll tell you what is different, no bloody air-conditioning. What? Did I give him a tip? Of course. Ten quid.'

Spencer's head was still spinning.

'A small price to pay, Spencer darling. And what a surprise, the cornicello, eh? Looked just like yours. Trilby thinks she's such a big girl now she has her own room. She'll be texting her friends back home as we speak. And the hotel is small but quite charming. I wonder if we have the room the murder was committed in?'

'Murder? Hell, when was that?'

'When you booked the hotel months ago. Honestly, you're a worry. Don't you remember you read out to me about a serial killer, Neville Heath, who murdered a lady in this very establishment.'

'Oh yeah, good old Nev, how could I have forgotten?'

'You don't remember, Spencer, I know. Anyway, they caught the bastard and hanged him in Pentonville gaol in 1946.'

'Of course I remember. But serial killers aside, let's drag our daughter away from her smartphone and wander into Notting Hill for some nosh and we can discuss our itinerary.'

***

A good holiday, good food, a good laugh, good company, so simple. The next week passed in a blaze of sightseeing, the Tower, the changing of the guard at "Buck House", Madame Tussaud's, shopping in Portobello Road and Harrods. Spencer revelled in spending time with his family and hoped he would awake each day next to his wife in London and not back in California. But he knew the puppet master pulled the strings. Sam the cabby had turned his world upside down. Were there really others? Was Sam one? He said it would end one day. What did that mean?

'Well, Michiyo, Trilby, our last night in London, tomorrow we catch the train to Brighton.'

'What's in Brighton, Dad?'

'It's a lovely beach city with great shopping, Trilby, they have an area called the Lanes, which is full of the cutest shops.' Michiyo beamed.

'Oh, and don't forget the Brighton Pavilion,' Spencer added.

'A pavilion? How interesting could that be?' Trilby turned her nose up.

'It's a bit misleading, Trilby; it's actually a palace. I think, from memory, it was the home of King George IV and for a while, Queen Victoria. It's been having some renovations and has just reopened. You'll love it.'

Spencer started to relax as they dined at the Osteria Napoletana restaurant in bustling Kensington Park Road. He felt as if he'd entered a dreamland—the happy chatter, the fragrances the easy charm and natural colours, but something wasn't right.

'Spencer, are you OK? The food is great. You seem preoccupied.'

'It's just that some of the colours are a bit sharp. The lights seemed to have got a bit bright, even the waiters' shirts, know what I mean?'

Michiyo frowned. 'No, I don't. But I remember. This has happened before.'

'Oh, Mum, I like Italian, and my linguine marinara is awesome.' Trilby twirled pasta on to her fork. She loved her new peasant-style blouse and bright blue pants bought from a market stall in Portobello Road.

'That's great, darling, leave some room for the Gelato Badiani.' Michiyo turned to him and placed a hand on his arm.

'Spencer, I think we should go back to the hotel. An early night, eh?'

Spencer nodded as he gazed at his wife and his daughter. A tear welled. He knew what was going to happen. He would be going back.

CHAPTER 51
DITCHLING

1966

The tavern stood on the High Street, its weathered stone walls bathed in the warm glow of lantern light. A rusty sign hung above the entrance, creaking with every gust of wind, its faded lettering promising cold ale and hot meals. The tavern's thick wooden door was scarred with countless scratches and marks, a testament to years of rowdy customers. The bar's front window was fogged with condensation. The smell of roast meat waffled through the front door mingling with the scent of wet earth from the recent rain. The crackle of the hearth fire was barely audible over the din of patrons shouting to be heard.

Squashed uncomfortably in one of the booths four men were engaged in earnest conversation. The men were quiet as the cheerful waitress placed steaming plates of roast beef and Yorkshire Pudding in front of them.

'Well, gentlemen, this is the Bull, in Ditchling.' The speaker was Captain Charles Beauchamp, formerly of the Queen's Guards, aka Stanford Delaware. His plummy public-school accent wavered occasionally, betraying his Californian birthplace.

The three men were aware of Delaware's deception but couldn't fathom whether or not Captain Beauchamp actually believed the fantasy he'd created. They decided it was safer to humour him. The murders had already begun.

'It sure ain't London,' Clive grunted as he swilled the last of his pint of Harvey's Best Bitter. He stared like a cobra seeking its prey, wide eyes black as inky pools. His hardened features and immobile face made him look like the psychopath he was.

'Would you sooner be back in Wormwood Scrubs?' Walter the pimp grinned, a slim dapper criminal known for extreme violence against the prostitutes who handed him their hard earned.

'Stanford, I mean, Charles, we're all grateful, aren't we, boys?' Anthony spoke, glaring at his comrades. A compact man in a gray suit, with a bland forgettable face, but a record of vicious crimes going back decades.

'I do hope you aren't going to be difficult, Clive. I need total loyalty and commitment. When I was in the Guards, loyalty was everything. Do you understand? Now, Clive, I asked you to deal with that annoying reporter, Dexter Dankworth. He's been asking too many of the wrong questions. Is it taken care of?'

Clive remembered Ronny Delagado's harrowing scream as he disappeared into the night sky. He knew to humour Captain Beauchamp.

'No, no, I'm cool, Charles. Dexter Dankworth is being eaten by pigs on a little farm near Hassocks Station as we speak. No, it's just that I'm a city boy. There's nuffink about the fookin' countryside I like.'

'Get used to it,' Charles said sharply. 'Tomorrow we're going to see Peter Morris at his 200-acre farm *Crossgoats*. We're going to make him a cash offer. It's perfect for The Congregation. I'm anxious to start recruiting as soon as possible.'

Anthony spoke. 'Hang on, Guv, the estate agent said it was sold subject to contract. He said this bloke Morris wouldn't go back on his word.'

'That's true. But I just love English law. Have you men heard of "gazumping?"'

The three men shook their heads.

'Here's how it works. Simple really. Until contracts are exchanged the seller is free to accept another offer.'

'Yeah sure, boss, but the estate agent said…'

'Clive, I hate negativity. This is where you, Anthony and Walter come in.'

Crossgoats was a beautifully presented seven-bedroom family home sitting centrally within landscaped gardens and grounds and farmlands of approximately 200 acres. The cities of Hove and Brighton were a mere nine miles away. Captain Charles Beauchamp had salivated as he inspected the wealth of character features, its exposed beams, large open fireplaces and cast-iron wood burners. The bespoke handmade kitchen leading seamlessly into the South facing dining room with its vaulted ceiling and minstrels' gallery had left him speechless. The grounds were impeccably kept with views towards the South Downs.

****

The elderly widower had eventually agreed on Captain Beauchamp's generous offer but declined to accept a ride to the Royal Sussex County Hospital in Brighton. Although his left humerus bone was broken he was able to drive his automatic Rover Sedan to the accident and emergency, where a bored nurse perfunctorily quizzed him about his injury.

'Silly really, I just fell over walking down the hallway.'

CHAPTER 52

NOT TAKING NO FOR AN ANSWER

Savannah came from the kitchen pink in the face, her hair pasted to her forehead with either steam or sweat,

'My God, Spencer, it's 7.04 in the evening and you've fallen asleep watching Cronkite.'

Spencer vaguely remembered hearing that American planes were bombing Hanoi.

'Hey, sleepyhead. Are you listening? I've been slaving over a hot stove all goddam afternoon.'

Spencer yawned. 'Sorry, I was a million miles away.' *And fifty years.* 'So, intrepid FBI Agent and sometimes chef, Savannah Steele, what's cookin?'

'It's a bit of a surprise. Come to the dining room.'

'Mmm, smells good. You've been a busy lady. Looks like roast beef, dauphine potatoes, green beans, roasted carrots and what might this be?' Spencer prodded with his fork. 'A light, fluffy, golden brown, and slightly crispy baked batter. It looks like—Yorkshire Pudding. Surely not. Americans don't have that. It's English. Why am I suspicious?'

'Don't be silly. And just for you we have an Australian wine, a Penfolds Grange Hermitage. Cost a goddam fortune. Personally, I'd sooner have a Bud.'

Spencer gazed in awe at this legendary Australian Shiraz Cabernet Sauvignon, a thousand perfect grapes, the gift of the rich brown earth and a generous Australian sun. He savoured the red wine.

'Awesome. That is so good. And I know how much it costs. I know you; you're manipulative. What's going on?' Spencer couldn't help himself. He burst into laughter.

'What's the joke? I went to a lot of expense and effort on your behalf.'

'Savannah, I just thought of something funny.' He didn't want to say, but he thought, as he had so often thought before, that Savannah was so honest and transparent that her efforts to manipulate were as obvious as a brick wall.

'So, what's going on?' Spencer repeated.

'Nothing is going on. I was just feeling creative. I actually enjoy cooking.'

'Just like you enjoy women's magazines and going clothes shopping. Not. C'mon Savannah. Out with it?'

'Have you tried the Yorkshire Pudding? I've never made it before. Is it OK?'

'Perfect. Now talk!'

'I just sort of wanted to, you know, get you in the mood, so to speak.'

'In the mood for what exactly?'

'England.'

'You're kidding!' Spencer spluttered.

'No, just listen. I've spoken to Dale; he's given us a month off. I've told him you and I are going to spend it at home in Marina Del Rey.'

'This is just like when you and I went to Miami and I thought Dale had sanctioned our mission. And how many dead were there?'

'For God's sake, Spencer, that's irrelevant. This time it's different.'

'Exactly how is it different?'

'Well, for a start, this time you'll know Dale hasn't approved.'

'Silly me.' Spencer rolled his eyes.

'I have a sort of plan. Sort of.'

'Hell, Savannah. I can't go to the UK.'

'Why not? You have a US passport, courtesy of Dale and the FBI.'

'Savannah, be reasonable. We don't know for sure Delaware is in England. Even if he was there, it'd be the needle in the bloody haystack. Where would you start?'

'I'll tell you, if you'd like to listen.'

'And what about a weapon? There's no way the Brits are going to allow you to bring that cannon of yours into the country.'

'Let me worry about that. Let me tell you what I've worked out about tracking down Delaware.'

'This wine is very good.' Spencer studied the wine bottle. 'Wow, the 51 vintage. I'm impressed.'

'Then it's settled?'

'What? Hang on. What's the connection between roast beef, Yorkshire Pud, a great bottle of wine and a trip to bloody England?'

'Haven't you ever heard that old saying: *there's no such thing as a free lunch?*' Savannah smiled triumphantly.

'Let's hear it.'

'I knew you'd come round. Now, you want some more beef?'

Spencer shook his head.

'Listen up. Where did we first see Stanford?'

'At that rock concert in San Francisco.'

'Yes, and remember after that, purely by chance we went to the Winterland Ballroom and that woman who I had to drag you away from, gave you a pamphlet about the "Family"?'

'I get you.'

'Also, I was chatting to Maria, she and her late husband also first met Stanford at a rock concert in LA. She was saying how that Señora Gorda had a beautiful voice.'

'Señora Gorda?'

'It sort of means a rather large lady in Spanish. The group was the Mamas and the Papas.'

'Oh right, Mama Cass. Yeah, she is a little plump, I guess.' Spencer grinned.

'Here's what I think, Spencer. England is currently the centre of the universe as far as that goddam so-called music is concerned. I'll bet you another bottle of Grange that good ole Delaware will be promoting concerts in Britain. He'll have his trailer…'

'Caravan.'

'What?'

'In England they call a trailer a caravan.'

'Important point. For Chrissake. Anyway, that's what I think he'll be doing.'

'It's a bit attention seeking, don't you think? Stanford Delaware, the "Family". It's bound to get the attention of the FBI, the CIA, and anyone else that's on the lookout for him.'

'Agreed. But at the moment there are so many peace movements, anti- capitalist movements, save the whale, and so forth, he will be just another one. All he would have to do is create a new identity. He's no doubt been manufacturing gallons of his happy juice and remember the movement, is "Stanford". He can change his name, his appearance, whatever but the same charismatic son of a bitch will still be able to sell his message. I'll bet he's probably got something up and running as we speak.'

***

Leaving a house is easy. Leaving a home is hard. Spencer had become attached to the Palo Alto bungalow. He loaded his meagre possessions into the new sparkling white Chevrolet Impala and turned for one last look, and wondered would things ever be different? *You can only play with the cards you've been dealt.*

Savannah twisted the key and the engine roared to life.

'Don't you just love it? Sounds great, don't you think?'

'It sounds like a motor. What am I missing?'

'That, my dear, is the sound of a 275- horsepower-327 cubic inch Turbo Fire V-8.'

'Wow. I think. What time do we get to LA?'

'I have never known a man to be so disinterested in automobiles. Late afternoon, I guess. I phoned Inez and she'll have dinner waiting. And just for you, she's making, sushi, tempura and yakitori. I can't tell you how much I've missed her.'

'Great, Inez does wonderful Japanese food. Did you tell her we were going to be off again so soon?'

'I thought I'd wait until we were on our second margarita.'

***

The sun sat like a ball of copper in the driver's side window as they turned right onto North Grand Avenue. It burned the sky red and orange in the same bright colours as lobsters and prison jump suits, Spencer thought with a grin.

It was a deception. Sunsets in Los Angeles did that. He knew it was the appalling smog that made their colours so brilliant. The car radio blared. The Rolling Stones were singing *The Last Time* as they pulled into the driveway at Marina Del Rey.

CHAPTER 53

TIME TO ROCK AND ROLL

Lustrous as onyx stones, the thick fashionably long hair transformed Stanford Delaware into Captain Charles Beauchamp. His new wig and his bushy moustache made him look like the rock and roll impresario he now was. Gazing with satisfaction at the log cabins being built by teams of carpenters, plumbers, electricians and myriad other trades people he could see it all coming together. Fire engine red Bedford cement trucks poured foundations, an endless convoy of trucks delivered lumber and building supplies. It wouldn't take long. He could feel it in his bones. Time had passed, it was now spring, 1967. The messiah had arrived.

***

Beauchamp smiled contentedly at the progress also powering ahead at the historic concert hall, known as the Brighton Dome a part of the Brighton Pavilion, the former palace of King George IV. The whole massive complex contained the Corn Exchange and the Studio Theatre. All three venues were linked to the Royal Pavilion Estate by a tunnel to the Royal Pavilion in the Pavilion Gardens and through shared corridors to the Brighton Museum. Captain Charles Beauchamp had convinced a rapt collection of councillors and politicians that he would, at his own expense, completely renovate and refurbish these crumbling national monuments, but in the meantime, he had total control.

Tonight was going to be on a scale England had never seen before, along with strobe lights and banks of floodlights, follow spots, Fresnel lights, emitting a concentrated beam of coloured lights. Stunning new inventions, the fog haze machine and lasers were going to create the most dramatic and visually engaging stage effects ever. Headlining direct from Australia was supergroup Velvet Concord.

'Ladies and gentlemen, you are witnessing the start of a new world order.'

Charles paused. Packed like sardines, the enthusiastic crowd in the Studio Theatre cheered, mesmerised by this man's charisma and helped along by liberal quantities of a particularly invigorating orange-colored fruit drink. By any measure the first Charles Beauchamp concert was a huge success. On the screen a silent black and white movie of happy people toiling in fields, singing around campfires and swaying to a rock band played constantly. The movie depicted a land of Nirvana, Utopia. The "Congregation" would change the world. The movie was a three hour collage of life at the Diablo Mountain commune. It had something for everyone. Happy couples strolling through the woods, mothers nursing contented babies, long-haired teachers in a classroom instructing the children. It was a masterpiece of propaganda; Goebbels and Stalin would have been impressed.

'The first cottages at Crossgoats, near the beautiful village of Ditchling, are being completed as we speak. Who will join me?' Beauchamp bellowed. The crowd cheered.

Clive, Anthony and Walter patrolled the theatre, ladling drinks into paper cups and keeping an eagle eye open for troublemakers. There were none. Putting a cup to his lips, but not drinking, a slim young black guy watched the proceedings with interest. He'd driven his London cab the fifty miles to Brighton.

CHAPTER 54

SAM

Atlantic Ocean 1788

The man opened his eyes slowly, every tiny muscle working to prise open the eyelids that felt like they'd been glued together. As his state of consciousness gradually returned, he tried to move but was overcome by a ferocious pain that tore through his whole being. Almost afraid to look, he willed himself to cast a furtive glance over his body; his arms and torso were bloodied and bruised. Iron shackles bit cruelly into his ankles. He slumped forward, feeling the bile rise in his throat. He vomited.

Little by little he became aware of his surroundings, making no sense of anything. Around him were others, wretched, shacked like him, moaning, wailing or seemingly unconscious, maybe dead. The stench was sickening and the bile rose in his throat once again. He was pressed up against another man, a man like him, a black man.

'Where are we?' he croaked, his throat so parched he could barely whisper.

'We going to a place they call Jamaica. We slaves now.' The other man's voice broke with despair.

London 1960

Sammy Campbell woke with a start. Stumbling out of bed, he realised he was drenched in sweat, his cotton pyjama top clinging to him.

'Thank God, or Baron Samedi,' he said as relief surged through him, falling back in a chair, he let out a huge breath. He was back. The horror of the slave ship he knew would be embedded in his mind forever. *What sort of people could do this to their fellow man?*

Wrenching open the refrigerator door, he grabbed the carton of orange juice and drank straight from the tear at the top. Still shaking, he plopped down on a kitchen chair. The early dawn light sluiced through the half open timber shutters of the kitchen of his comfortable flat in fashionable St John's Wood, London.

Sammy's parents had immigrated from Jamaica three decades ago. Sammy had been named after the voodoo God, Baron Samedi, believed by his followers to be the master of the dead as well as a giver of life. His paternal grandmother, Amina, a devotee of voodoo, had told him he was one of the chosen. At the age of thirteen she'd given him the silver cornicello, now hanging around his neck.

'Treasure this, Sammy. It must follow you everywhere. Do you understand?'

'Yes, Granmadda,' he'd said. And he only remembered this commandment some years later when he'd suddenly woken up a slave.

Sammy had been a whiz at school, a keen sportsman and talented boxer, useful to defend himself when the racial taunts had become violent. His parents mortgaged their two-up two-down in Ealing to pay for his higher education. Sammy had a photographic memory and also the ability to grasp complex mathematical concepts. He sailed through his studies without breaking a sweat. He'd also been awarded an Oxford Blue in boxing. His last three matches had ended in knockouts. After gaining an MBA in business at Oxford University he'd joined venerable stockbroking firm, Rowe and Patman, in the early 60s. He discovered he had a flair for the baffling new world of options trading. Calls and puts enabled clients to leverage their way into ever-expanding portfolios. Bonusses and a huge salary made him feel invincible. Riding high, he drove a white MG sports car and owned a trendy two-bedroom apartment in a very white upmarket suburb. He'd even toyed with the idea of changing his name.

***

'Sammy… Is that really your name? You gotta be kidding. Bit of a cliché.' She'd giggled.

The Chris Barber Band had just performed their latest hit *Petite Fleur* at the Marquee Club in Wardour Street, Soho. Good-looking Sammy had been chatting up a beautiful dolly bird wearing a stunning floral Cristobal Balenciaga cocktail dress. Her disdainful upper-class accent had intrigued him when he bought her several flutes of overpriced champagne, but it was clear his exotic appearance and Cockney accent meant he had no chance. Disheartened, Sammy swilled the last of his bubbly and slunk out of the club, deciding in future he'd be known as Sam. He consoled himself with the thought that his life allowed little room for romantic entanglements.

Sam Campbell had a secret. Sam Campbell was a time traveller. Heightened colours of everyday objects, cars, bright clothes, even traffic lights, were the only warnings that would trigger a journey back in time. It was always the same. He'd go to sleep and wake up fifty or even a hundred years in the past. It had begun quite by accident. The cornicello had been thrown carelessly into his sock drawer after the passing of his grandmother.

He remembered the first time when his hand fell upon the intricate silver ornament as he searched for an odd sock. A jolt had run through his body like an electric shock.

'Holy hell, what was that?'

That was when it all began.

And now he knew it was happening again. Powerless to stop the inevitable, he braced, spinning helplessly as his body was jettisoned through the blackness of time and space. As the arpeggios of Chris Barber's trombone and Monty Sunshine's clarinet gradually faded, the sensations of freezing air and the earthy smell of horse dung enveloped him.

CHAPTER 55
A SERVANT'S LIFE

London 1888

He awoke, groaning. *No no, I don't want to be here.*

He shuddered. The smelly straw-filled mattress rustled as he moved. He was back. Sam remembered a quote about London that haunted him.

There's a hole in the world like a great black pit,

and the vermin of the world inhabit it

and its morals aren't worth what a pig would spit.

Immediately, he knew who he was and where he was. His other life. His other home. Closing his eyes, he hoped against hope it was a dream.

'Get up, you lazy beggar.' A rough hand shook him awake. Sam shivered and cursed. His life, for he knew not how long, was manservant, driver and general dogsbody for prominent barrister and teacher, Montague John Druitt, whose educated and sophisticated veneer disguised a sadistic monster. Sam had controlled himself when Druitt mercilessly whipped hungry street urchins, who were only begging for pennies.

'Sorry, Mr Druitt.'

'Have the brougham ready at the front door in half an hour.'

'Yes sir. Please sir, what time is it?'

'What? What does that matter? Let me see, it's approaching midnight. Now get moving or you'll feel the back of my hand.'

Sam splashed water on to his face from a bowl next to his bed. Dressing in his crisp white shirt, plain dark-coloured waistcoat, black frock coat and necktie he sat back down on the bed and laced on his boots. He could feel the cornicello around his neck, on its leather thong. Stumbling down the stairs he made his way to the rear of the house and into the mews entrance where the stables housed the smart brougham carriage and Bessie the mare. He scooped up a woollen scarf sitting on the elevated wooden seat and wound it around his neck.

'Hello girl.' Sam stroked Bessie's head. She whinnied in pleasure.

If Bessie was surprised at being hitched into the carriage in the middle of the night, she didn't show it. In a practised motion he fitted the harness, collar and leather traces. Sam felt as if every bit of joy had been sucked out of him, replaced by a feeling of dread. The music and gaiety of the Marquee Club was a distant memory. His hands shook as he held the reins and the brougham clattered over the ancient mews cobblestones.

'Why does the miserable bastard go out in the middle of the night like this?' He mumbled to himself as he pulled up outside of the fashionable three-storey house in Belgravia. The cold night was tucked under a woollen dove-gray sky; Sam's feet crunched on the ice as he made his way up the steps and rang the bell. He stood stamping his feet against the cold. His breath appeared as a visible cloud.

Wearing a black double-breasted frock coat, stout boots, a top hat and grasping a black cane with an ornate silver crook handle, Druitt seemed happy, excited even.

'Are you familiar with Whitechapel, Sammy?'

'Yes sir.'

'Good, good. I knew I could rely on you. We want Buck's Row. You know it?'

'Yes sir, Mr Druitt.'

Buck's Row. Whitechapel. I don't understand.

London looked slightly more down at heel as the brougham made its way through Blackfriars and Southwark. Sam felt sorry for the pinched faces of the harlots as they smiled and waved. *What a way to make a living.* As the carriage turned into Buck's Row, immediately parallel to the Whitechapel Road, a snow flurry made the mean streets look a little cleaner.

Sam started as the cane handle rapped hard on the glass partition. Sam jerked the reins, Bessie plodded to a stop.

'Wait here. I shan't be too long.'

Mystified, Sam wrapped his scarf tightly around his neck, watching as Druitt disappeared into a swirling mass of snow that obscured all but a few yards ahead of him. The frigid wind beat upon his exposed flesh as the chill slowly seeped into his bones.

He thought about leaving his driver's seat and climbing into the relative warmth of the carriage's cabin, but thought better of it. It had seemed like hours, but in reality it had probably been about twenty minutes. He could just make out Druitt's top hat and leonine features as he strode towards the brougham. Druitt stopped and peered into the gloom.

Obviously satisfied no one was watching, he yanked a rag out of his coat pocket. Holding his cane at arm's length with one hand he pulled the silver handle, a menacing steel blade appeared. Carefully wiping the dagger, he then threw the cloth carelessly into the gutter. Either Druitt hadn't realised Sam was watching or perhaps he just didn't care. Either way he slid the dagger back into its innocuous sheath and made his way back to the carriage.

'Thank you for waiting, Sammy, m'lad. Belgravia, if you please,' he said with forced congeniality.

CHAPTER 56

MURDER MOST FOUL

Sam had just loaded the brougham with Mr Druitt's wine and spirits supply from Berry Bros and Rudd at 3 St James's Street, London. Good German wines, and those from Rheingau and Franken seemed to be Druitt's quaffing choices, along with some Portuguese Hock. His next stop was Hatchards Book Shop in Piccadilly to pick up a handsome leather-bound tome, Gray's Anatomy.

As he accepted the book and requested it be added to Mr Druitt's account, he noticed a Times newspaper poster fastened to the counter.

WHITECHAPEL'S BLACK RECORD. ANOTHER HORRIBLE MURDER.

He picked up a copy of the Times, brazenly saying to the assistant, 'Just put the tuppence onto Mr Druitt's account.' Sam was convinced Druitt wouldn't notice and two pennies would buy a bar of Cadbury chocolate. He climbed onto the driver's seat, grabbing an apple he'd filched from Mr Druitt's kitchen and began reading, crunching on the juicy fruit as he pored over the lurid details of the crime.

Mary Ann Nichols, known as Polly Nichols, was found murdered and mutilated in the Whitechapel district of London.

Sam wondered with curiosity what business Mr Druitt may have had in Whitechapel in the middle of the night and at exactly the same time poor Polly's miserable life had been so gruesomely terminated. But as unpleasant as Mr Druitt was, Sam couldn't believe he was the perpetrator of such a horrible crime. Sam had never met a real murderer, so far as he knew, and couldn't bring himself to consider that he was working for one.

Still, the thoughts and questions kept on haunting him. Why would he do such a thing? Surely Mr Druitt wouldn't have as assignation with a street prostitute. The threat of disease alone would be a deterrent.

As far as Sam could see, Druitt appeared to have no interest in the fairer sex. Sam knew there were exclusive men's clubs where men paid exorbitant sums for discreet encounters, but if Druitt went to those establishments, he certainly wasn't taken by Sam. The vision of the knife kept flashing before him. There must be another explanation. Perhaps he'd been attacked by a footpad, a local hoodlum may have tried to rob him and he'd used his blade. After all, Whitechapel was a rough area. If so, then why was Mr Druitt there late at night in the first place?

Days passed. Sam's days were a nonstop routine of boot cleaning, plate polishing, waiting at table, even helping Ada the cook make bread.

'Ere luv, did you 'ear there was another 'orrible murder?' Elsie Lewis, the pert young scullery maid, told Sam at breakfast. She brushed against him as she placed the pickled herring, bread and a cup of tea in front of him. Sam's ears pricked up.

'When was this, Elsie?'

'Two nights ago. I'm glad we have a strong fella like you, Sammy, to look after us.' She batted her eyes at him.

'It's not Sammy. It's Sam,' he said firmly.

Well, that's not Mr Druitt, he didn't go out two nights ago. Well, if he did he certainly didn't have me drive him. Relief flooded through Sammy.

'We got some nice pigs' trotters for supper.' Elsie started clearing the breakfast things away. 'Well, I better get to work. I have to wash Mr Druitt's shirt and waistcoat. Lumme, what a mess.'

'Really, how on earth would a gentleman have dirty clothes. It's not as if he does any work. Well, real work, I mean,' Sammy added hastily.

'He told me he got a bad nosebleed last night while he was at the Reform Club. You wouldn't think so much blood could pour out of somebody's nose.'

So, Mr Druitt doesn't always want me to drive him.

A cold pit began gnawing at the bottom of Sam's guts.

***

Months passed. Elsie and Sammy were officially walking out. The hints of marriage were becoming more insistent. Elsie didn't seem to mind Sam's non-English heritage, ignoring the mutterings from the other servants. The attraction between them had become a tangible thread in the air without words being spoken. Sammy wanted to put Elsie out of his mind, but her bubbly and infectious nature were proving to be irresistible. How long would he be here? Would it be forever? But then everything changed.

Ada's round face normally beamed with warmth; she had a sturdy build that radiated strength. 'Ere lad, 'ave a butcher's at this if you 'ave the time. I 'ope they catch the sod. 'anging would be too good for 'im. If 'e comes near me, I'll show him what for.'

She threw a copy of the Daily Telegraph in front of Sammy, the headlines shrieking: *GHASTLY MURDER IN THE EAST END. DREADFUL MUTILATION OF A WOMAN.* Mary Jane Kelly had been found in her rented room in Miller's Court, Spitalfields.

The day had been long, driving the brougham through busy London streets. Sam had finally completed the long list of errands. Arriving back in Belgravia in time for supper, he removed the harness and bridle, and did the usual checks for any signs of injuries. Bessie nuzzled him as he groomed her, removing the sweat, dirt and debris.

'You're a good girl, Bessie.' Giving her a final pat before closing the stable doors and trotting up the servants' entrance, into the kitchen.

'Ere 'e is. Sit down, lad, I'll get you a nice cup of tea.'

'Thanks, Ada. Where's Elsie?'

'Er sister in Shoreditch is poorly. Poor thing. I think she 'as the cancer. Elsie 'as gone to help 'er out. Do some shopping or summat,' Ada grunted in her northern accent.

'Is Mr Druitt home tonight?'

'No luv, he went out. Said 'e would be 'ome late.'

Sam could feel his heart hammering against his ribcage. *This is crazy.*

'Where does the sister live, Ada?'

'Charlotte? Let me think. She lives in lodgings in Old Street. Not far from the corner of Kingsland Road. It's number 122, room 30. Just near the Shoreditch Station.'

Sam stirred sugar into his tea and took a tentative sip. *This is plain silly. Mr Druitt couldn't be the killer. Elsie's a sensible girl. There's nothing to worry about.* Placing the still full mug on the table, he jumped to his feet.

'Sorry, Ada, no supper, I have to go out.'

Ada's mouth moved noiselessly, her eyes wide. She eventually found her voice, yelling, 'What do I tell Mr Druitt if he returns?'

But Sam was already out the door.

Bessie stamped her foot as Sam placed the harness on her. Clearly, she thought her working day was over. Sam palmed a sugar cube. He knew there'd be hell to pay if Druitt discovered he'd taken the horse and carriage without permission. It could mean getting sacked, or even criminal charges. He knew if he didn't have a job, he'd be joining the down and outs sleeping rough.

***

The fog was spook-gray, lifeless and motherless; this deathly vapor was the infamous London pea souper. Its ghostly scarves wrapped the city in a mist, bringing death to the old, the infirm and the very young. Sam applied a match to the carriage lights hanging on either side of the brougham. The whale oil burned, emitting a pallid glow.

Nervously, Bessie picked her way through the quiet streets. Sam couldn't help feeling the cold hand of dread. The only sound seemed to be the clattering of steel shod hooves on the cobblestones.

Jumping down from the carriage, Sam struck a match. Set within the wall a chipped plaster sign declared *This is the corner of Kingsland Road and Old Street. 1796.*

He was beginning to regret his impetuous night foray. It didn't really make sense. If word got back to Druitt? But then he thought about sweet Elsie. *Find the sister's lodgings, make sure everything is OK.* Maybe Elsie would be ready to come back to Belgravia. The thought of them sitting close on the driver's seat on the return journey was appealing. On the other hand, she might want to sit in the cabin, like a lady. He could imagine her saying 'ooh, this is ever so posh.'

As he was about to set out to find the lodgings, he could see a dim shop light further up Old Street. Sam knew the two businesses you could count on being open in heavy fog were the taverns and the fish and chip shops.

Sam surveyed the rundown street, trying to work out where number 122 would be. He shivered, not only from the cold. As he glanced again in the direction of the shop, he could make out the figure of a person, man or woman, he wasn't sure. He glanced again at the sign and guessed that number 122 must surely run in the direction that person was heading. Was it Elsie? Sam gasped as he saw a tall figure melt out of the shadows. This was a man. The outline of a top hat illuminated briefly in the shop window. How many top-hatted men would be walking the streets of Spitalfields in a pea soup fog?

Bessie seemed to be asleep. Sam strode off in the direction of the top-hatted man, now disappeared into the mist. He could hear his own heavy breathing. His welted sole boots sounded like gunshots as they thudded on the brick footpath. The tantalising aroma of fish and chips washed over him as he passed the shop. He could barely see an arm's length in front of him. Had the gentleman entered one of the tenements?

The next few minutes unfolded like a choreographed scene in a West End crime play. As the fog lifted a little, Sam could just make out the back of the man, his heavy cloak obscuring his body. Sam fought to stifle a gasp as the man raised a long dagger intently above his head. Only then could Sam see the figure of a woman, slightly built and no match for an assailant, backed up against the wall of a tenement house. The man lunged at the woman, clenching his hand around her throat. Her eyes bulged. Now pressed hard against the brick wall, hands flailing impotently at her attacker, she was helpless to fight back. All Sam could hear were strangled gasps from the woman and the banging of her heels on the wall behind her. Fish and chips lay scattered across the pavement.

Sam grabbed the man by his collar, hurling him backwards. Letting go of the woman, the man swung around, the knife a foot away from Sam's chest.

Sam gasped. 'Druitt.' For some reason he was surprised, but the yawning chasm in his guts had known. It was frozen hard down there, in his stomach.

'Sammy, what the hell are you doing here?' Druitt's eyes widened, his mouth open.

There was a momentary pause. *Christ, it is Elsie.* Now released, Elsie screamed long and loud.

Sam almost laughed when Druitt said, pleadingly, 'I can explain.'

Knocking the knife to one side, Sam hit Druitt hard in the solar plexus. As Druitt doubled up in pain, Sam hit him three times, short hard blows to the head. Not killer blows, they bounced off his ear and forehead. Recovering quickly Druitt faced Sam, knife in hand. He jabbed twice. Sam dodged. Druitt grinned, then a vicious thrust and the knife slashed Sam's arm. Fortunately, the heavy coat absorbed a lot of the damage, but Sam felt the sting and then the sensation of blood running down his arm onto the pavement. Druitt slammed Sam against the wall, left hand on his throat. The knife now poised on his jugular. Sam had visions of the slave ship. *Would I have been better off?*

'Listen, Sammy, I said you didn't understand. This trollop, this slut gave me the pox. There's no cure. I'll go mad, just like Lord Churchill. You would've been next.'

'Sam, don't listen to him. He forced himself on me. Anyway, I'm cured. I had a bit of a problem, then it went away.'

Sam's head spun. He couldn't believe what he was hearing.

'She's lying, Sammy, there's no…'

The brick came crashing down on Druitt's head. As he collapsed, Elsie fell on him, crying as she pounded with all her might. The brick raised and fell three times. Druitt's skull split open.

The shrill sound of the policeman's whistle rang out loud and clear followed by the sound of large leather-clad feet banging on the cobblestones. Sam leaned against the wall as needle sharp bolts of pain shot through his shoulder. His teeth clenched so hard his jaw ached. His body trembled and in spite of the cold, sweat dripped down his forehead.

'Thank God you came so quickly, constable. This man was attempting to murder a lady. I stepped in…'

'Which lady would that be?'

Sam's head spun around.

'She must have gone.'

'Turn around. Hands behind your back.'

***

The prison cell was barely six feet by four. The walls were the same thick gray stone as the dwellings in the area. But instead of a wide window there was a small opening with thick iron bars. The Commercial Street Police Station in Shoreditch was a cheerless establishment.

Sam looked up hopefully at the sound of footsteps. A tired man wearing a frock coat and high waisted trousers with black dominating the colour palette turned the key in the lock. Still handcuffed, Sam sat on the bunk, leaning against the wall. Nobody had been interested in his wound.

'I'm Detective Constable Riley.'

Riley pushed his bowler hat back and started to work a toothpick on his rear molars.

'Why am I still handcuffed, Detective Constable? I have written a statement outlining the facts.'

Riley guffawed, taking a dirty handkerchief and wiping the thick lens of his wire framed spectacles.

'I must admit, young fellow me lad, a nigger who can read and write, well, now I've seen everything.'

Sam swallowed hard. Riley wasn't a saviour.

'So, what happens now, Detective Constable?'

'Well, boyo, I give you top marks for creativity. I read your statement. You must think we're stupid. We've been busy since your arrest. We know your name is Sammy Campbell. The man you murdered was your employer, highly respected Barrister, Montague John Druitt. We found his carriage in Old Street. It's obvious you brought Mr Druitt there by carriage. He decided to stretch his legs, go and purchase some fish and chips. You followed. Using the fog as cover you attacked him, either to rob him or because you had a grievance. Mr Druitt bravely defended himself, but you hit him repeatedly over the head, killing him.'

'This isn't what happened. Druitt was attacking Elsie Lewis, a scullery maid in his employ.'

'You're going to hang, Sammy Campbell. Like I said before, you must think we're stupid. You're a good-looking darkie, I'll say that for you. Let me guess, you've been leading this poor Elsie Lewis on, and I'm sure she'll say anything, so you won't swing. If you think I'm going to allow a nice English girl to perjure herself for the likes of you, you have another think coming.'

'I want a solicitor.'

'A solicitor, eh? Who do you think you are? A solicitor? And who would pay for that? No, Sammy Campbell, you have been charged with murder in the first degree and you shall hang.'

CHAPTER 57

TIME TO GO

S am stood on his bunk, hoisting himself up to the window, wincing at a shaft of pain in his arm. Few carriages were passing. Sam knew tomorrow the whole roadway would be crowded, the pavement lined with stalls and costermongers' barrows. He wondered how long before his trial at the Old Bailey and then the execution? Without a barrister he knew he was doomed.

I can't very well ask Mr Druitt to represent me.

Would Elsie visit? Or would she distance herself because she'd delivered the killing blows? He stretched out on the hard bunk. He'd always held the English Police in high regard but the attitude of Detective Constable Riley was beneath contempt. Why didn't this officer at least query why Druitt would go to dangerous Spitalfields in the middle of a heavy fog, just to buy fish and chips?

Sam pondered whether Mr Druitt was the man the press had dubbed *Jack the Ripper*. His natural optimism battled to make headway but deep down he thought justice would be done. The light from the end of the long corridor seemed to be very bright. Sam pulled up the worn blanket, rested his head on the horsehair pillow and turned his face to the wall.

A vision of Druitt laughing but with a shattered head appeared in his mind. Elsie screaming. Then a million sounds of a century of life compressed into seconds bombarded him as he spun and turned, end over end. It seemed to go on forever. Then, peace came; warm fingers of sunshine streamed through his window and played gently on his face. He glanced at his watch. It was 7.04 in the morning.

Bloody hell, I'm going to be late. My first appointment is at 9.00.

***

London 1960

'Good morning, Brenda.' Sam said breezily to the pretty switchboard lady as he entered the reception of Rowe and Patman.

'I'm not sure it is, Sam. Mr Patman wants you in his office. He's not happy.'

As Sam crossed the trading room, he could see the activity was intense. Brokers were screaming into phones. It looked like chaos. *What the hell is going on?* He cautiously entered Patman's office.

Red faced and sweating, Neil Patman clenched a phone in his white knuckled fist.

'Yeah well, do your fucking worst. It's not our fault!' he screamed, slammed the phone down and put his head in his hands. Sam had never heard Neil swear. Patman looked up.

'Sit down, Sam. No, you might as well stand, this won't take long.'

'Neil, what the …'

'I'll tell you what the hell is happening, hotshot. The Dow dropped over 2000 points. Our market is going to do the same. You and your bloody options. I should never have let you talk me into them.'

Sam remembered Neil's excitement when he'd explained the concept. He shuddered. He knew what was happening.

'Our wealthiest clients are going to lose millions. The aristocracy doesn't like losing money. All of those put options will be exercised. It's going to be a bloodbath.'

'Neil, if they just…'

'You're fired, Sam. Don't bother looking for another job in the industry. You're finished. Collect your stuff. Security will escort you out.'

***

Sam watched the news on his PYE black and white television, coffee in hand. He thought about Elsie, sadly realising he simply had to move on. Another victim of Dickensian London.

Neil Patman's prediction was correct. Sam cautiously evaluated his situation. He owned his car and his home. His extensive share portfolio was being decimated, but Sam was convinced it was only temporary and most of his stocks were defensive. He'd be OK. But what was he going to do with himself?

Whatever happens, it's better than being a manservant for Mr Druitt, or being hanged at Newgate.

Tired of feeling sorry for himself, Sam decided to seek out the bright lights. Needing company, he phoned his journalist friend, Dexter Dankworth.

'Hey, Dexter, how about joining me tonight? A few drinks and a show.'

Dexter and cockney Sam were an odd match. If Sam were to use one word to describe Dexter, it would be elegant. He had the kind of face that stopped women in their tracks. His upper-class accent, tasteful dress sense coupled with genuine empathy made his interviewees tell all. No wonder Dexter was the star reporter for the Daily Mirror.

Good seats were still available to see the hit *Oliver* at The New Theatre in St Martin's Lane. Sam and Dexter loved it, laughing uproariously at the sanitised depiction of Victorian London. After a beer at the Salisbury Pub in St Martin's Lane, Sam decided to walk home. Dexter hailed a cab.

'Great night, Sam. I gotta go. I'm off to Brighton tomorrow.'

Still laughing to himself at one of Dexter's jokes, Sam passed the Duke of Wellington in Wardour Street when he heard screams coming from a dimly lit alley.

'Fucking pansy. Hand over your wallet.'

'Hey, let him go.' Sam strode over to the pair. A young guy wearing a black drape jacket with a velvet collar and high-waisted drainpipe trousers had a slightly built middle-aged man pressed hard against the brick wall. His fist bunched ready to punch again. Blood spurted from the older guy's nose; he cowered, pleading with his attacker. Sam recognised the kid as one of the local teddy boys, renowned for violence.

'Piss off or you'll be next.' He glanced quickly at Sam, not seeing a threat.

Sam grabbed the burgundy velvet collar; it ripped as the kid staggered backwards. '

'You fookin' bastard. Look wha you done.'

Swinging wildly, his face crimson, he launched himself at Sam, who easily deflected the roundhouse punches. Sam drove a fist hard into the stomach, following through with a classic uppercut. The teddy boy collapsed, rising briefly to all fours, vomiting what looked like several pints of bitter. He sat up leaning against the wall, groaning. Sam knew the fight had gone out of the lout. He knelt next to the victim.

'Say pal, are you OK?'

'Oh yes. Thank you, dear. Let me find my glasses.' He scrabbled around on the rough pavers. 'Here they are. What's that around your neck?'

CHAPTER 58
REVELATION

The Admiral Duncan pub in Old Compton Street, Soho, clearly catered for a certain clientele: friendly, colourful and noisy. Everyone seemed happy. Sam pushed his way through the crowd, balancing a beer and a gin and tonic.

'Over there.' Sam pointed to a newly vacated booth and the two men took a seat. Sam's shirt had opened in the scuffle and the cornicello was now clearly visible. He held out a hand.

'Sam Campbell. I say fella, is your nose OK? It looks sore.'

'Bert Weadley. Nah, it doesn't hurt too much. I hope I'm still beautiful. So, Sam Campbell, tell me about that.' Bert pointed.

'It's…it's a cornicello. A sort of heirloom.' Sam noticed Bert's accent. Not English.

Sam placed the gin and tonic in front of Bert, who took a delicate sip.

'Yes, I know. First of all, I'd like to thank you saving me from that brute. He was awful. He seemed so nice when I bought him a drink earlier.'

Sam wasn't sure what to say. 'I guess, you…I mean he was…'

'Don't be embarrassed, Sam, love. I'm a fairy. Queer as a three-pound note. It's not the first time this has happened. Tell me about that,' he asked again.

'What's to say? It's an heirloom. Like I said. Why are you interested, Bert?'

'You're a traveller, aren't you?'

All of a sudden, the noise of the crowd seemed to fade. Sam's stomach twisted.

'What?'

'You're a traveller,' Bert repeated.

'What do you know? Who the hell are you?'

'Where to start? Did you really think you were the only one?'

'I hadn't really thought about it. But who are you? Some sort of queer fortune teller? Sorry, Bert, that was a bit unkind. It's just, you've given me a shock.'

'That's OK, love. I used to be a traveller myself.'

Sam spluttered into his beer.

'You're kidding? You used to be? I didn't think it was something that was optional. I thought it just happened. I mean, it's not like I have any control. It just…I just find myself spinning out of control and when I come to that's it; I'm in another century. So how do I get out of it?'

'Do you really want to, Sam Campbell?'

'What do you mean?'

'Haven't you learnt so much? You have lived in real time in other centuries. You have seen injustice, man's inhumanity to man, as well as the beauty and the growth of the human race. I wouldn't have missed my experiences for the world. But I simply got fed up with the uncertainty, so I retired.'

'You retired? How does that work?'

'Do you want to hear my story?'

'You know bloody well I do. Let me get some more drinks.'

'My buy. Same again?' Bert jumped up and headed for the bar.

Sam's eyes followed his every move. He half expected Bert to disappear into thin air, whisked away to another century. Threading his way back through the crowd, Bert returned, placing the drinks down, and a packet of crisps.

'Busy, isn't it? How's your night been?'

Sam took a long swallow of his beer. 'For God's sake, Bert…'

'Sorry love. Where to start? As you can probably tell, I'm Australian. It was about twenty years ago. I was a private in the Australian Army. It was horrible. A ghastly butch uniform. Of course it was the war. Why they thought I'd be any use to them… Anyway, a dreadful bully named Tiny, big and brainless, picked on me, saying really nasty things. Then I was saved. There was this lovely fellow. Ever so handsome. He rescued me. No one picked on me again.'

'Nice story. But I don't…'

'Shhh, I'm getting there. He was a strange one. Said he had amnesia. It was odd. No one knew who he was, or where he came from. The more I talked to him I realised he wasn't like everybody else. Subtle things, he had an innate wisdom, like he knew stuff but wasn't going to let on. He was curious. It was if he wanted to absorb everything he could about the world around him. He was secretive about things. His amnesia story just didn't make sense. I realised he just had to be a traveller.'

'Did he have a cornicello?'

'No, he didn't. But there are some travellers who don't seem to have our connection. They just are. So, I decided he was the one.'

'What do you mean, Bert?'

'You can choose to pass it on.'

'You're kidding.'

'No, Sammy.'

'It's Sam.'

'Of course. Sam. Now, where did you get your cornicello?'

'From my grandmother. Hang on, are you saying…'

'Yes Sam. That's exactly what I'm saying. Your grandmother was a traveller.'

'So you just handed yours over to this chap, what was his name?'

'His name? His name is Spencer Marlowe.'

CHAPTER 59
WHAT TO DO?

S am idly picked at the crisps. He had a million questions and didn't know where to start. He realised once you delved beneath the façade of Bert's outrageous personality, he was a very shrewd and intelligent man. Sam was stunned when Bert explained all he knew about the cornicello and how he'd been able to choose to move on.

'Where did your cornicello come from, Bert? '

'Well, to tell the truth, it's shrouded in mystery. My ancestors had a shameful past, so I was told by my father.'

'This is amazing, Bert, tell me the gory details please?'

'If it's true, it's awful. My great great grandfather was a sea captain, a slaver, taking unfortunates to Jamaica.'

'Christ, Bert. A slaver?'

'Sadly.'

'You wouldn't believe it, Bert; I was one of those slaves. I don't remember much. I remember being chained into the hold; it was hell on Earth. Fortunately, I don't remember much more.'

'Do you know the name of the ship you were on?' Bert asked.

'Good question. Let me think, I think it was the Clotilda.'

'It gets curiouser and curiouser. Great great grandfather was the captain of the Clotilda. Anyway, he settled in Jamaica and he apparently had a child to one of these slaves. The mother gave him a cornicello. That's where it becomes confusing. He apparently got out of the slave business and became some sort of missionary. But there was more than one.'

'More than one what, Bert?'

'Cornicello, love. A few Englishmen were either given them, or they stole them from the slaves. But here's where you can see the power for good the cornicello represents, because it wasn't long after that the slave trade ended. Whether or not the cornicello contributed to that, we will never know.'

Sam paused with a crisp at his lips. He'd been so enthralled that he hadn't been able to eat a single one. 'Jesus Christ, Bert, I had no idea. So, the travellers, you don't know how many? No, but wherever they go, they are good people. They do good things.'

'Did you do good things, Sam?'

Sam remembered Druitt and his part in his death.

'Yes, Bert. I guess you could say I did.'

'Let's change the subject. Later on, we can tell of our experiences. So, my lovely, what do you do to earn a crust?' Bert asked.

'I am, that is I was, a stockbroker.'

'Was?'

Sam explained his unfortunate situation.

'The long and the short of it, is I have no idea what I'd like to do now. Did you tell Marlowe about the cornicello when you gave it to him, Bert? I would love to have a word with him.

'Hmm, of course you would. He could turn up anywhere at any time. To answer your question, no, it wasn't the time or the place. He was in the brig for beating up this awful bloke, Tiny. But I just knew he was right for the cornicello. Getting back to your situation… it's a big world, the time factor shortens the odds. Eventually you're bound to run into him. Who knows in which century or which country. Why don't you choose a career where you meet lots of people from all over the globe?'

'Nice thought, Bert, but what sort of job would that be?'

'Why not, no pun intended, become a London black cab driver?'

***

Sam discovered it wasn't easy to become a London cabbie.

'Three to four years. Are you serious?' Sam said to The City of London Transport Authority Officer.

The "knowledge" involved memorising hundreds of routes through London, before you could become one of the iconic London black cab drivers. Sam purchased a second-hand Vespa scooter, and with a London A to Z directory he set about committing to memory every one of the circuitous itineraries laid out by the examiners. His photographic memory enabled him to sit the exam in an unprecedented six months.

Unbelievably, he took to his new career like a duck to water. Not much stress, a good wage, nothing like his previous earnings, but it provided a comfortable lifestyle. He always had a wide circle of friends. His closest buddy, Dexter, regularly confided the latest scandal or controversy. Sam would tell Dexter about the villains he picked up, where they went and who they were meeting. Three gangsters who seemed to lead a charmed life; Clive Drager, Anthony Voss and Walter Mortemyer were regular customers. They were reputed to be taking over the Kray brothers' crime empire.

Every morning before getting behind the wheel, he'd hang the cornicello from the rear vision mirror.

Years passed. Bert had gone back to Australia, promising to write.

That day, in the spring of 1967, started like any other. Sam checked his watch.

'Damn.'

Grabbing his coin holder and stuffing the cornicello into his pocket, he ran to his garage. He'd slept in and feared he'd missed the early football crowd. For the very first time he forgot to hang the cornicello on the rear vision mirror.

CHAPTER 60
WHAT'S REAL?

Brighton 2015

The train ride to Brighton was a sweet meditation as the English countryside passed by. A masterpiece of art. Spencer drifted in and out of sleep. Michiyo poked him in the ribs.

'Honestly, Spencer, you've been like an old man lately. You keep falling asleep. We're coming into Brighton.'

'Sorry, Michiyo.'

Spencer turned to his daughter, and asked, 'How are you enjoying the holiday, Trilby?'

'What? Oh, sorry, Dad. It's been awesome.' She went back to the game on her iPad. Spencer knew the kids of the day loved their electronic devices; he just didn't get it, although he did remember a fleeting interest in Pacman when he was younger.

'Enjoy your game, darling. But remember we're surrounded by history.'

Trilby smiled, rolling her eyes as she kept playing. 'Thanks, Dad.'

***

Spencer knew he'd been going back, but this time his memory was playing tricks. He remembered leaving the house in Palo Alto. He remembered being with Inez and Savannah at their charming home in Marina Del Rey. He knew they flew to England, but there his memory stopped. He saw flashes, the most prominent among them a young chatty cab driver.

'So, my love. What's on the agenda?' Spencer yawned.

'Catch a cab to the hotel. I'd like to go to the Lanes. I've read so much about them. They're very historic.'

***

Spencer paid the taxi and stared at the gleaming white façade of the Grand Hotel, Brighton. The Regency-style building with its pale stuccoed exterior and its classical-style mouldings and bay windows were exactly as he remembered. But he'd never been here before, had he?

'Dad, hurry up. Mum's waiting for you at reception. We want to get unpacked and go shopping. I want a new pair of jeans.'

'Sure, darling.' Spencer stared at his beautiful daughter, the image of her mother, with her long black hair and Asian features.

***

'I think we've done the shopping thing.' Michiyo grinned.

'And I got my new jeans.' Trilby proudly held up a paper bag from Profile Fashion.

294

Michiyo spoke. 'I'm ready for a coffee. This looks nice. Very cute. That Little Tea Shop. Let's try that.'

Spencer opened the front door. 'Yep, they do great carrot cake.'

'How would you know that?' Michiyo queried.

'Oh, um, I guess I must have read it somewhere.'

Spencer was starting to feel uncomfortable. Colours were too bright; the bubbly wait person's vivid purple dress hurt his eyes.

'How about we have an early night, then we check out the Royal Pavilion tomorrow?' Spencer yawned.

'Spencer, you can't be tired already, surely?'

CHAPTER 61

LONDON CALLING

London 1967

Savannah handed Spencer a book, 'I know you like reading. It's a long flight. I thought you might like this.'

'That's very nice of you, Savannah.' Spencer accepted the gift. 'Hell, I've heard of weighty novels, this weighs a ton.'

'It's the History of The English-Speaking People by Winston Churchill. It's not a light read. I know you like that kind of stuff.'

Spencer placed it into his hand luggage. They settled into the eleven hour flight to London in the comfortable Boeing 707. Savannah ordered a beer; Spencer opted for a Jack Daniels and soda. Spencer stood and reached into the overhead locker.

'What are you doing, Spencer?'

'I thought I'd start on that book you gave me.'

'Actually, I'd rather we had a chat, you know, about how we're going to track down Delaware.'

'I thought we'd sorted that out. We're going to check out music festivals. Make enquires with the Metropolitan Police about any cults that have sprung up.'

'Sit down. Talk to me.'

'What about, Savannah?'

'Hey, do you remember when we were on that flight to Tokyo? The meals arrived and I said the lady sitting opposite had frog's legs and you said, "Yes, and her friend's aren't much better". I wasn't used to your Aussie sense of humour.'

'I remember. I also remember how you just about started World War three with the Yakuza. One thing that does concern me is if we do find Delaware we're going to have a few problems.'

'Whinge, whinge. Like what?'

'Dale doesn't know we're here. We're going to have to get the English Police involved if we're going to get Delaware arrested, then start the extradition process. All of this and we're not carrying any accreditation. Or was it your plan to locate him, then we tell Dale what we've done and he or his superiors start whatever the process is?'

'Details! For God's sake, Spencer, let's just focus on finding the son of a bitch. We don't know for sure he's even in Britain. Even if he is, he might be retired and living by the sea, maintaining a low profile.'

'If he's not, and if he's up to his old tricks and we get close to him, you can guarantee he'll have that thug BBQ Delgado with him and some other villains. Delgado and Stanford know us. They'll be armed; that's for sure. You can't rely on your trusty cannon. This is England, there's no way you'll be able to get a weapon.'

As the conversation went back and forth, they ate and drank and discussed English history, and politics. Savannah was a little to the right of Atilla the Hun.

'Doesn't time fly? Look, Spencer, we're coming in to land. What's the name of the hotel you booked? You never did tell me why you chose that one.'

***

'There's the taxi stand.' Suitcases piled high on the luggage cart, Savannah and Spencer waited in the long line of tired people all waiting to be transported all over London.

'Let me grab those bags for you, sir, madam.' The friendly cabbie grabbed the bags and stowed them inside the cab.

'Where to?'

The London cab was very different from the large American taxis. Compact and designed for purpose. The little diesel rattled into life.

'The Pembroke Garden Hotel in Notting Hill, please, driver,' Spencer said. Why had he chosen that hotel? There was something hazy in his memory, but for the life of him he couldn't remember.

The chatty driver chatted breezily about England and London, with lots of useful tips about the Underground and what shows were on in the West End.

'The Pembroke Gardens Hotel is very popular. It's well located near restaurants and a tube station. People have probably forgotten there was a horrible murder there about twenty years ago.'

'Really?' Savannah's ears pricked up. 'Did they catch him?'

'Oh yeah. His name was Neville Heath. Serial killer. They hanged him.'

'A good ending.' Savannah smiled.

Spencer frowned. *I knew that.*

'Here we are. The Pembroke.' The driver easily slotted the nimble cab into a small parking space.

'Spencer, would you mind paying the driver? I'll go and see about checking us in.'

Spencer had been very impressed with the likeable cabbie. Intelligent and well informed.

'How much is that, Sam?' Spencer glanced at his name tag.

'That's seven quid, please.'

Spencer handed him a ten pound note.

'Keep the change. Savannah and I are going to be in London for a while and we'd appreciate someone like you who knows what's going on. Are you available?'

Sam shook his head.

'Actually, you've caught me at a bad time. I'm off to Brighton for a few days.'

'That's a shame. Well, when you get back we'll probably still be here. My name's…'

'Hey Superman!' Savannah yelled, 'Stop gas bagging. We need our passports.'

'I got it. Superman. Right?'

'No, it's Spencer Marlowe.'

But Sam had already peeled off into busy Pembroke Gardens.

***

Spencer rapped angrily on Savannah's door.

'Spencer, how nice. I was just unpacking, can it wait?'

Spencer stormed into the room holding a book, 'I was wondering why the bloody thing was so heavy.'

Splayed open, Winston Churchill's epic had been hollowed out. Spencer grabbed the hidden metal pieces.

'This would be—the magazine, the handguard and a few other assorted bits—at a guess, the components of a 0.357 Magnum revolver. Correct?'

'I was going to tell you, honest.'

'Oh, and I see a towel on your bed, with some lumpy bits under it.'

Spencer whipped it off.

'What do you know? Looks like boxes of bullets and the remaining pieces of the puzzle. Savannah, how could you? If we'd been caught the consequences would have been horrendous.'

'I'm sorry. Truly I am.'

'Bullshit. You're sorry you got caught. You must have known I'd open that bloody book.'

'Hell, I thought you were going to open it on the aircraft.' Savannah grinned. 'It was pretty neat how I deflected you, don't you reckon?'

'Savannah this could have been jail time. You would have lost your job. And what about me?'

'For Chrissake, Spencer, they were never going to look. And just remember all of that gear I smuggled into Mexico: grenades, assault rifles, pistols and they saved your ass. Remember when I brought down that chopper?'

'Yeah, I admit that was awesome, but…'

Savannah placed a hand over his.

'Honestly, Spencer, I am sorry. I hate deceiving you. But we need every asset we can muster up. Your karate skills are, to use your terminology, "awesome" but if we find Delaware and his gang, they will have firepower. And would you believe the goddam English Police don't even carry guns. What sort of Mickey Mouse country is it where cops don't carry?'

****

'I'm beginning to think we've been wasting our goddam time. How many more of these blasted events can there be? The National Jazz and Blues at Uxbridge, would you believe, the International Love-in, at Alexandra Palace, the Blenheim Palace Festival, The Burton Constable Hall All Nighter's Festival of Color. Don't these people work? Are you listening, Spencer?'

'Yeah, but we have heard Cream, Hendrix, Pink Floyd. How good was that?'

'My ears still hurt.'

'Maybe Stanford has simply given up. After all, his gods, the Beatles, have stopped performing. It's probably a coincidence but the performance at Candlestick Park was actually their last live show. I wonder if they found out how close they were to being kidnapped?'

'Is there anything interesting in the New Musical Express?' Savannah asked as Spencer leafed through the authoritative music paper.

'Wow, yes!' Spencer exclaimed.

'Tell me?'

'Elvis and Priscilla are getting married.'

301

'Spencer!' Savannah shrieked.

Spencer gave her an impish grin. 'Sorry, you're not a romantic, are you?' He couldn't resist a chance at a jab, after the Magnum debacle.

'Is that it? I'm just about ready to go home.'

'There is one thing.' Spencer studied the paper.

'Really? OK, let's hear it.'

'There's a new rock and roll impresario, an ex-British military guy, he's running a music festival in Brighton. That's about fifty miles from London.'

'That's certainly not Delaware. He's not English. Sounds like another waste of time.'

'You're probably right but the New Musical Express has a photo of him. Look.'

Savannah grabbed the paper and studied it.

'C'mon Spencer. Delaware's bald. This dude has magnificent long black hair. I'd love hair like that. You're clutching at straws.'

'I'm not so sure. Look again. Imagine that guy without the moustache and the hair.'

CHAPTER 62

BRIGHTON

Wishing he hadn't opted to drive, Spencer felt more comfortable now he was in top gear. The little red Mini weaved through the heavy traffic, the tires making their monotonous hiss over the rain-washed motorway.

'All it does is rain in this goddam country. I'm glad you're not changing gears now that we're on the highway. I reckon you crunched every time. Why didn't you hire an automatic?' Savannah perused some Brighton tourist brochures.

'They're not popular in England apparently. And it's motorway, not highway.'

'Thanks for sharing.'

***

No matter how much one has enjoyed the variation and scenes of the journey the sight of the hotel lobby is always a welcome relief. Their rooms at the Grand Brighton had stunning views of the famous Brighton Pier and beach.

After checking in, they decided to take a stroll through the enchanting Lanes of Brighton. On every storefront were posters advertising a succession of music events run by *The Congregation* and presided over by Captain Charles Beauchamp. That Little Teashop in the historic Lanes was certainly cuteness overload, but coffee wasn't high on their agenda. Spencer pored over the New Musical Express, getting all the details of the upcoming music event at the historic concert hall, a part of the Brighton Pavilion.

'Jesus, Spencer, I hate tea.'

'This is England. And they make lousy coffee. But you gotta try the carrot cake.' Spencer swallowed the last morsel.

'There's a concert tomorrow. The headline band is Mayfair, they have a fabulous girl piano player. She has a great voice.'

***

It became clear immediately that they were in the right place. This operation had Stanford Delaware written all over it.

'Can you believe it? San Francisco all over again. The same trailer, I mean caravan. Rock and roll and gullible people. And look there's some thuggish looking guys handing out paper cups of that blasted fruit drink.' Savannah shivered.

Spencer cast his eye around as well. 'And look at just how many security guys there are. Stanford's obviously already made a lot of converts. It looks like just another music event, but I'll bet they'd do whatever the prophet tells them to do.'

There was an easy grace to the parkland surrounding the Royal Pavilion now thronged with eager music lovers. Spencer and Savannah stood in the line waiting to buy tickets at the canopied ticket office. Buskers, playing a variety of instruments, competed with one another. Vendors selling fish and chips and burgers did a roaring trade. A bearded dishevelled man holding a sign advising that the end of the world was nigh, screamed as a black shirted security guy hustled him out of the park. The predictable pervasive smell of marijuana hung in the air.

'Hey look, Savannah, would you believe it? Just ahead in the queue isn't that the taxi driver, Sam, who picked us up at Heathrow?'

'You're right. He said he was going to Brighton.'

'We'll have a bit of a wait before we go into the theatre. I'm going to say hello; he was a nice bloke.'

Tickets in hand, Spencer and Savannah approached Sam leaning against an ancient oak.

'Hi, Sam. Remember us?'

Sam tilted his head quizzically.

'Not sure. You both look familiar. Hang on, I remember. Heathrow to Notting Hill. The Pembroke. You're Superman, right?'

Spencer grinned. 'Is it a bird? Is it a plane? Savannah calls me that.'

'Hi, Sam. Nice to see you again. Music lover, huh?' Savannah held out a hand.

'Sort of, I guess.'

Spencer got the impression Sam wasn't keen to prolong the conversation.

CHAPTER 63

TROUBLE

1967

Captain Charles Beauchamp cursed. He stared hard through the one-way window of his caravan.

'Walter, have a look over there.'

'Yeah, boss, at what?'

'Over there, the tall guy standing next to that woman wearing a red anorak. They're chatting to that black chap.'

Walter stared hard, smoothing his immaculate hair into place.

'I don't know those two, but here's a coincidence, I know the other guy, the geezer they're talking to.'

'Go and get Clive and Anthony. Something's not right.'

'Give me a clue, Captain. What's up?'

'Just fucking get them. Those two are FBI, there's only one reason they could be here.'

Beauchamp paced angrily up and down the caravan, not taking his eyes off the trio. He was tempted to have a glass of cordial but he knew he had to have his wits about him. The minutes seemed like hours.

What's keeping Clive and Anthony? He glanced again at his watch. Finally, the door swung open. The two men entered. Clive looked annoyed.

'What's the problem, Charles?' Clive never referred to Beauchamp as Captain Beauchamp pointed.

'You took your blasted time. Look, that tall guy over there is Spencer Marlowe. I don't know exactly who he is but he's an Aussie and he's trouble. The broad next to him is Savannah Steele, she's FBI. That other turkey walking away, I don't know, but Walter said he knew him.'

Anthony stared.

'What the fuck? The black's name is Sam something. He's a London cabbie; he's picked us all up many times.'

'I don't care about him. It's the other two who are the problem,' Charles snarled.

'Yeah, well you should care, Captain. The cabby was a mate of the journalist who wound up as pig food.' Clive sneered.

Walter strolled over to the fridge and grabbed a beer. 'What do you want us to do, boss?'

'I think you know the answer to that, Walter,' Charles answered, poker faced.

'For fuck's sake, Charles, dream on. There must be about a thousand people out there. What do we do, just walk out and shoot them?' Clive exploded.

'Calm down, Clive. Nothing worthwhile is without risk. When I was in the Guards…'

'Cut the fucking crap, Charles. You were never in the fucking Guards. Save the bullshit for the punters. Now, do you have any reasonable ideas?'

Beauchamp eyed Clive coolly. He'd decided that when things were sorted, insolent Clive would be dead Clive. For now though he swallowed his pride.

'Sorry, Clive, if I've been a bit out of sorts lately. This is what I want. Simple but effective. You're all armed, right?'

The three men nodded.

'Open your coats, show them your pistols. Tell them everything is OK, any bullshit you want. Tell them I just want to talk to them. Make it clear you'll blow their fucking heads off if they don't cooperate.'

'Great, and then what? For fuck's sake, boss…' Anthony frowned.

'Escort them into the theatre. Take them into the tunnel, into my quarters.'

Clive nodded. 'That should work.'

'Get them into the tunnel. I'll join you there. I want to find out just what exactly they're up to and just what we're up against.'

CHAPTER 64

THINGS THAT GO BANG

Brighton 1967

Sam threaded his way through the crowd and headed off in the direction of the theatre. There was no plan. He had no idea just what he was looking for. Dexter Dankworth had come here looking for something and he hadn't returned. But now he knew he was losing his grip, his focus. He tried to fight it. He felt unnerved. The sun was like a pool of golden snakes, glistening in the sky, slithering in circles. Dazzling colours made him wince. A little girl in a bright yellow dress ran past laughing as she bounced a vivid red ball. Sam groaned, holding a hand over his eyes. *Not now. Please.*

'Well, if it isn't Sam, the fookin' taxi driver.'

Sam shuddered. The moment of confusion passed, as if a veil had been lifted. He wasn't going anywhere. He stared into Clive's dead black eyes. At the same time he felt something hard thrust into his ribs.

'Clive! What the fuck's your problem?'

'No problem, laddie, you're going to come with me, nice and quiet. Nothing's gonna happen, so long as you behave. There's someone who wants to have a nice little chat.'

Sam quickly made a decision. Clive Drager had a fearsome reputation. Sam had no doubt he would pull the trigger at the slightest provocation.

'Sure thing, Clive.'

***

'How about a quick ale before we go inside the theatre?' Spencer eyed the beer tent.

'I don't think so, pal.'

Spencer jumped as he felt the muzzle of the pistol pressed into him. His head spun around to see a well-built guy, nattily dressed with a cream high-necked double-breasted jacket, flared burgundy trousers and a black automatic. He glanced at Savannah; a big guy invaded her personal space. Spencer figured he had a gun as well.

'You two are coming with us. There's somebody who wants to talk to you. Any fucking move and we shoot.' The guy with the neat hair snarled.

'We'd better do what the gentlemen want, Spencer.' Savannah glanced at him and winked. 'Hey, love the outfit,' she spoke to the man next to Spencer.

Spencer shook his head. He knew how Savannah's mind worked. Her boundless confidence verged on the suicidal. They were going to see Stanford Delaware, that was obvious.

***

Banks of speakers on either side of the stage, and rows of lighting cans dominated the Studio Theatre. The dozen stage hands and roadies must have just finished the setting up. Laughing and chatting, they strolled off towards the entrance. Savannah, Spencer and Sam were marched along the aisles.

310

Spencer glanced around. *What the hell can possibly happen here? And where was Delaware?* He turned to Savannah, who shrugged. *Perhaps Delaware really only wants to have a chat. Scare us off maybe? But what the hell could they possibly want with a taxi driver?* He glanced at Sam, who gazed ahead, stony faced.

'Down 'ere.' The dead-eyed Clive pointed to a narrow space leading to the back of the stage.

Behind the hastily erected stage Spencer could see an ancient stone fireplace, tall enough for a man to stand with room to spare. Anthony, while still pointing his automatic, stepped into the fireplace. Reaching into the dark recess, his left hand groped. They heard a clunk, then a whirr as the rear wall slid to one side, exposing a dark passageway. All of a sudden Spencer wasn't so confident Delaware only wanted a chat. They stepped into the clammy passageway.

Spencer's mind whirled. It was obvious the tunnel would have been there since the Royal Pavilion, the old Corn Exchange and the Studio Theatres were built in the 1780s. Sure, it was a secret tunnel, but how much of a secret?

Spencer reasoned there would be no shortage of history buffs, town planners and countless other entities who would know of its existence, but that didn't help them. He had a mental picture of the layout of the Royal Pavilion complex and figured the tunnel either led to the Corn Exchange or the Pavilion or both.

The way was lit by weak electric globes. They were marched single file. Spencer looked for any opportunity to strike but knew the three gunmen had all the advantages. As they turned a corner, the tunnel expanded dramatically. Spencer's jaw dropped at the sight of a huge dormitory. They blinked at the bright lights. At least fifty fit young guys lolled on bunks, chatting, reading novels or playing board games.

'Jesus, Savannah, can you believe this?'

Floor to ceiling racks contained hundreds of long guns and assault rifles.

'Hell, he could start a goddam war,' Savannah grunted.

'Shut the fuck up,' Fashion Plate snarled.

They passed a row of modern bathrooms before entering another tunnel and then, a modern businesslike steel door. One hand on his pistol, Anthony half turned as he inserted the key and opened the door, the pistol pointed unwaveringly. A wedge of bright light appeared as an antechamber opened up before them, adorned with rich tapestries, a modern double bed, a small television and a Baldwin upright piano. The room was cluttered with some impressive paintings, some of which Spencer recognised; a Monet, a Renoir and another he couldn't put a name, though it still had the look of a hideaway, something temporary. A Rolling Stones ballad, *As Tears Go By*, played softly on a gramophone. He wondered if Stanford had plans for the Stones. He quickly discarded that idea.

Spencer figured Stanford's new home must originally have been some sort of a retreat for a long dead monarch. Maybe he had liaisons there that Mrs Monarch didn't know about. Stacked in a corner, foldup chairs and assorted building materials, cans of paint, ladders made it look like work in progress. Seated behind an ostentatious, small, round rococo table was the man himself. Three of the chairs were placed in front of the table. The lustrous black wig and bushy moustache did little to disguise Stanford Delaware. The same magnetic eyes and powerful presence dominated the room.

He's a nutcase, but an impressive nutcase.

'So, Spencer Marlowe and of course, Special Agent Savannah Steele. Sit down. And what's this prick's name again?' Stanford pointed at Sam, who was staring open-mouthed at Spencer.

Spencer, Savannah and Sam obediently perched on the chairs.

'This prick's name is Sam Campbell, and I want to know what happened to Dexter Dankworth,' Sam replied.

'Do you now? Give him a smack, Clive. Cheeky little blighter.'

The sound of Clive's vicious backhander reverberated across the room. His garish gold an onyx ring sliced across Sam's cheek. Sam cried out as the strike drew blood.

'You bastard!' Sam launched himself at Clive.

Anthony swung into action, clubbing Sam viciously on the back of his head with his pistol. Sam collapsed on the floor, groaning. Savannah helped him to his seat. He sat, dazed but conscious.

'Let's get down to business, shall we?" Stanford Delaware said, in thickly accented English.

CHAPTER 65

SURPRISE SURPRISE

Brighton 1967

Sam's mind reeled. *His name's Spencer Marlowe. Had Bert Weadley known our paths would cross?* So many questions flashed through his mind. His head hurt, but he knew he wasn't befuddled. Deciding the best option was to pretend he was semi-conscious, he lay back in his chair, groaning.

What's Spencer Marlowe's interest in Captain Charles Beauchamp? Is Marlowe FBI? He's Australian, that doesn't add up. Is Savannah Steele a traveller also? He remembered Bert saying you would live forever unless you didn't. Like, unless one of Beauchamp's goons puts a bullet in the back of your head.

He was beginning to understand why Weadley had opted out of being a traveller. He'd said he wanted to grow old disgracefully. Right at the moment, all Sam wanted was to be back in his cab, working, enjoying life. He thought back on his travelling experiences; they certainly hadn't been fun. He shuddered at the brief moment he could remember of the slave ship, grateful that his memory was so incomplete. Victorian London had just been a gruelling unpleasant chapter that could have seen him dangling at the end of a rope.

But this was now. It was Sam Campbell in 1967 AD. *Could he be rescued or was this going to be the end?* He desperately wanted to talk to Marlowe, but this wasn't the time or the place.

CHAPTER 66
THE MONOLOGUE

Brighton 1967

Charles carefully removed his wig and placed it on a mannequin head stand.

'It does itch,' he said cheerfully. 'Now, Marlowe, Steele, you will tell me everything I need to know.'

'You've got Buckley's mate,' Spencer growled.

'Buckley's?' Stanford raised an eyebrow.

Savannah piped up. 'Even I have trouble keeping up with Spencer's Australianisms. But I'm pretty sure it means go to hell.' Glancing sideway at Savannah, Spencer's brow furrowed. She didn't seem concerned. *Does she have something in mind?*

'Tell me, Stanford…' Spencer was cut short.

'Captain Beauchamp, if you please,' Charles barked.

'Of course. I was just wondering what happened to the lovable but accident-prone Ronny Delgado?'

'Not that it's any of your business, but I guess you could say he went for a swim and didn't return. Right, boys?'

Clive, Anthony and Walter grinned.

'However, back to the problem at hand. I really need to know exactly who is involved. Is Dale Fletcher in England? Is he liaising with MI5 or 6? You will tell me. Clive, in particular, is very creative when it comes to extracting answers. Aren't you Clive?'

Clive licked his lips.

'Oh yeah and I'd like to have some quality time with Savannah, know what I mean?'

Clive's next words sent shivers up Spencer's spine.

'Yeah, I don't think any man would want her after I've finished.'

'Enough. We're not animals,' Charles barked.

'Oh yeah, of course. I forgot that wasn't your thing, Charles.' Clive sniggered.

Beauchamp opened a drawer and produced a small automatic. 'You're forgetting yourself, Clive.'

'Two can play at that game.' Clive raised his hand, showing his pistol. The two men glared at each other.

Spencer watched the interaction, bemused, half expecting the two adversaries to shoot each other. It was obvious Stanford didn't have the same level of control and hero worship he had back in San Francisco.

'Can we please concentrate on these three, and stop this bullshit?' Walter had been quiet up until now. 'I sure as hell want to know whether the bloody FBI or the Old Bill are onto us. My gut feeling is these two are acting on their own, or we would have had company by now. But to be on the safe side, I reckon, get Clive to do his stuff. I don't give a fuck what he has to do to get them to talk. I would suggest start with the tart first and let this Marlowe bloke and the taxi driver watch. And by the way, I'm happy to have a nice time with the lassie.' Placing his hands on his genitals, he thrust them forward. 'Sorry if you don't like it, Captain, but boys will be boys.'

Anthony leered at Savannah.

'Enough! We have questions and we will get answers,' Beauchamp grunted. 'Tell me who you've been dealing with in MI5? Was it William Wyman or that idiot Brian Jones?'

'Before I answer that, I have to ask, just where did you get the arsenal we saw in the dormitory? All those long guns and assault rifles?'

'Weapons are never difficult if you have the money and the contacts. In this case it was those morons, the IRA. Anything that's used to foment revolution in England has their backing. And that revolution is coming. Barry McGuire said it all. Who could forget *The Eve of Destruction*? Surely you were moved… Enough about that. Let's focus on the main game!' Beauchamp thundered. 'Tell me who you've been dealing with in MI5,' he demanded again.

Spencer glanced sideways at Savannah. 'I'm impressed. How did you know the name of the operatives, Jones and Wyman, Stanford? Or should I say, Charles?' Savannah replied. Spencer was trying, and failing, to get her attention but also not let on. It was a needle he wasn't able to thread.

'Was that other guy, Peter Townshend, involved also?'

Savannah sighed dramatically. 'Your information is spot on, Captain.'

Charles threw his head back and laughed.

'Brian Jones and Bill Wyman are members the Rolling Stones and Townshend is a guitarist in the Who. You're here on your own. I doubt anyone in the US has any idea. Boys, I think we can simply eliminate them. Even though I don't really approve of that sort thing, if you want to have your fun with the woman, go ahead. Make sure Marlowe and the cab driver watch, then shoot them.'

Spencer's head swivelled. Gun in hand, on his left, Clive sat like a coiled spring. It seemed to Spencer he was awaiting the captain's command, then it would be game over. Beauchamp's pistol lay on a blotter, within easy reach. Anthony, in his ultra-skinny burgundy suit with its narrow lapels and short jacket, leaned nonchalantly against a wall looking bored, smoking a cigarette, the butt of a German Luger just visible in a shoulder holster.

Walter yawned, slouched on a chair on the left of Sam. His 0.38 dangled in his hand. Sam's head slumped on his chest. His breathing sounded laboured.

It seemed to Spencer as if nobody wanted to make the first move. He had no doubt they would be killed. Walter and Anthony clearly had designs on Savannah, but how would that work? Spencer knew brutal rape wouldn't present any morality issues. It was obvious there was tension and little trust between the four. They would have to deal with Savannah who was unlikely to cooperate, even with the threat of death. She knew they were planning to kill her anyway. Finally, Anthony threw his butt to the ground. 'Well, I guess I'm first. On to the bed, bitch, get your fucking clothes off.'

Savannah climbed to her feet.

'I'm sorry, darling.' She turned, her expression gave nothing away.

Spencer tensed, he knew something was going to happen.

Savannah slowly unzipped her bulky anorak.

'There is one thing I'd like to say, Stanford. Stanford the Prophet Delaware.' She sneered.

'Oh really? Your insolence may make you wish for a quick death. Speak your mind. Choose your words carefully.'

'I will. Stanford Delaware, you have lived too long.'

Spencer sprang into action; he drove his right fist into the side of Clive's head hitting the pterion, the region where four bones of the skull meet; the head's weakest point. A fist that could smash house bricks met little resistance. Spencer felt his knuckles sink into brain matter.

Savannah's hand grabbed the Magnum as it jumped from the spring-loaded holster. She fired. Before Walter or Anthony could so much as blink the bullet had done its business. Stanford The Prophet's face became a red pulpy mess, the round exiting in a gory splatter on the wall behind. The slug sounded like an artillery shell in the confined space.

Spencer realised that in Britain guns were hard to come by, clearly. It hadn't occurred to Stanford's minions to check for weapons. The lack of communication between the villains had been a fatal error.

Sam flew out of his chair and hurled himself at Anthony. Spencer watched helplessly as Anthony fired, blood gushing from the side of Sam's head. Sam grabbed Anthony's gun hand and landed a superb uppercut. The jawbone crunched. Anthony slumped to the floor. Walter jumped to his feet but before he could fire, the Magnum roared twice. His head shattered and his chest opened up with blood pumping out like a burst water main.

'Sam!' Savannah yelled.

'Sam, are you OK?' Spencer felt like an idiot asking.

Sam plonked down on a chair. 'I think I'm gonna live.' He managed a weak smile.

Spencer ran to one of the bathrooms and grabbed towels. Sitting next to Sam, he carefully dabbed the side of his head.

'How about that? The bullet travelled along your skull just above your ear. Christ, it's bleeding like hell.'

'The natives are becoming restless.' Savannah tapped Spencer on the shoulder. They heard fists banging on the steel door; harsh voices demanding answers.

'Sam, are you OK to walk?' Savannah asked.

'Walk? I can run. But where to?'

'There's only one way. The tunnel will finish somewhere in the Pavilion. I'd imagine it would be in a bedchamber or drawing room perhaps. Let's just hope wherever it goes we aren't locked in.'

All the colours in Spencer's world exploded.

CHAPTER 67

WHAT YEAR IS IT?

Brighton 2015

Michiyo held Spencer's hand as he jerked awake.

'Darling, are you OK?'

'I'm fine, really.' But he wasn't OK. He had just fallen asleep on his feet. They'd spent the afternoon exploring the Royal Pavilion and it was almost closing time. Through the huge windows of the north drawing room, they could see the sepia tint to the silver black sky as if it already knew the wind and the rain would wreak havoc. Then the lightning, a dazzling dance in the sky, a crackling burst of thunder and the heavens opened up.

The room was exactly as it was in the days of King George IV. The King, a renowned gastronome, had built tunnels connecting the Pavilion, the theatre and the corn exchange so he could walk between them without curious onlookers laughing at his ever-widening girth.

'Dad, Mum, read this.' Trilby read from a brochure retelling how the monarch had berated his French chef about his expanding waistline. The haughty chef had responded *your Highness, my job is to tempt your appetite, not to control it.*

Michiyo, Trilby and Spencer had spent the afternoon marvelling at the Regency splendour of the stunning palace. Its unique Indo-Islamic exterior was heavily influenced by both Chinese and Indian fashion with Mughal and Islamic architectural elements.

Spencer had been dazzled by the lightning. He knew something was wrong. Images of gunfire, screaming and panic. He was running down a long passage, Savannah had a gun in her hand. A young guy, bleeding from a head wound, panted beside them. The image would disappear.

'Spencer, you don't look well.'

'I'm going to the bathroom. I'll be OK. You and Trilby keep exploring. I'll be with you in a few minutes.'

Spencer walked into the bathroom and everything went black.

CHAPTER 68
THE GETAWAY

Brighton 1967

Spencer stopped running and leant against the wall of the tunnel.

'For Chrissake, don't stop now. We're coming to the end. Look, there's a door!' Savannah yelled.

Behind them they could hear angry voices. The sound of soft-soled shoes echoed off the walls of the tunnel. They stopped running as they were confronted by a wide oaken door. On the adjacent wall they could see a rusty cast iron wheel covered in dust. Sam grabbed the thick metal, grunting as he tried to turn it.

'It's not budging.'

Spencer felt as if he were spinning. Sound and light were building to a crescendo. Shaking his head, he tried to concentrate. Savannah and Spencer grabbed the old metal and slowly the door groaned open. The tunnel flooded with light as they all leapt into a vast room.

'Bloody hell, we made it. Are you OK, Sam? Sam?'

CHAPTER 69
THE MOMENT OF TRUTH

London 2015

Still shaking and confused, Spencer stared at Sam. He saw an old black guy with grizzled gray hair.

'I told you that one day you could decide.' Sam grinned.

Michiyo grabbed Spencer's arm, her brow furrowed as she stared at Sam. 'I remember you. You're the taxi driver.'

Trilby gaped. 'Dad, what's going on? Are you OK?'

'I'm fine, sweetheart.'

Spencer's mind was as clear as a bell.

'Michiyo, you're not going to believe this. First of all, I'd like you to meet Savannah Steele.'

Spencer turned and scanned the room.

Michiyo frowned. 'There's no one else here.'

'Savannah's not a traveller, Spencer.' Sam placed a hand on Spencer's shoulder.

'Oh my God. Is she OK? What became of her? She's in trouble.'

'What became of her? I can't help you. This is decision time. Do you want to remain a traveller?'

Spencer stared at Sam; his mind in a whirl. Savannah… wasn't here. It was all jumbled in his mind. What was now and what was then, none of that was clear.

This was his chance. A normal life beckoned enticingly, but Savannah was in deep trouble.

THE END

If you enjoyed *The San Francisco Affair,* a review or kind word on Amazon or Goodreads would not only be appreciated but would guarantee more Spencer and Savannah stories.

ACKNOWLEDGMENTS

Many thanks to Brent Meske for his professional editing services and his great cover.

A special thanks for the input from my beautiful wife Jenny for her sage and incisive suggestions and guidance.

I am also grateful to Liz Read, from the Armadale Writing Group, who added another layer of editing and subtle refinement.

KELVIN WHITE AUTHOR

I'm a West Australian author, having been born in Perth and living in WA for most of my life.

As with so many authors, my background is awash with many careers; taxi driver, musician, roof tiler, shoe salesman and a plethora of others.

Given that I have always been an avid reader, it was probably inevitable I would eventually put pen to paper. My first publication was the time travel adventure *The Singapore Saga*, featuring central character Spencer Marlowe. I was delighted when positive reviews appeared on Amazon and Goodreads. I was hooked. The first "Spencer" novel was followed by the next instalment *The Hawaiian Intervention* and then *The Manhattan Sting*, introducing Special Agent Savannah Steele, who appeared in the next two instalments, *LA Confrontation*, *The Chicago Story* and now *The San Francisco Affair*.

Amidst churning out the "Spencer" series I have also published, along with co-author Allan Butler, our rock and roll memoir *Oh How We Rocked*. This memoir, complete with photos of the bands and musicians we worked with, is a fun look at the music scene in Perth in the 1960s 70s and 80s.

Having enjoyed writing my rock and roll life, my next project was the crime novel *Birthright*, this time in collaboration with acclaimed Perth author Bruce L Russell.

Bruce added a whole new dimension to the writing experience. Having won the prestigious TAG Hungerford Award for literature and also holding a doctorate in creative writing, Bruce's writing skills are evident in *Birthright*.

Bruce and I released a subsequent crime novel, published by Vivid Press. *The King of San Francisco* is a crime novel involving South American warlords and drug traffickers. Set in the United States and Guatemala in the 1970's, it's a thrilling read.

I have found the collaborative writing experience to be very rewarding and an extraordinary learning platform, as a consequence I have also collaborated with American author Tali Sandbridge on the crime novels *Undercover Heat* and the sequel *The Dogcatcher*. Both are police procedural story's alternating between New York, Perth, Sydney and then finally Bali. Raunchy, sexy and gritty, they are fast moving thrillers with a great cast of characters. Tali and I have already begun another psychological thriller, *The Killer Below*. Once again with central characters, NYPD detectives Kimberly Biche and Gage Madden.

And now a look at the next Spencer Marlowe story, *The Bali Connection*.

A PREVIEW

OF THE FORTHCOMING SPENCER MARLOWE ADVENTURE

THE BALI CONNECTION

CHAPTER 1

WHAT'S HAPPENING?

The old man shivered. 'Why is it so cold, damned cold?'

Was the fire out? Sprawled on a lounge chair, a blanket draped over bony shoulders, he stared blankly at the offending fireplace, vaguely remembering it glowing with a radiant orange flame and how it always brought a dancing glow to the heart of the home. Where was everyone? Mary? Where was she? One of the servants had been ill. That's right, Mary had cook make chicken soup. He frowned as he glanced at his stained dressing gown.

'It's the damned war of course. I'll be joining the regiment soon enough. Have to get myself cleaned up. Need a shave.' He ran a hand over his bristly chin. His head slumped to his chest, he awoke with a start, 'Burton, where are you man? See to that fire at once. And lay my dress uniform out.' In total darkness, the big house in Oxfordshire near Blenheim Palace stank of mould and the decaying corpse of a Jack Russel terrier lying by an empty food bowl in the expansive kitchen. A black and white television flickered noiselessly. Total silence reigned apart from the sound of skittering rodents. He vaguely remembered a man, American, trying to enter the house. Wanting to talk. Why hadn't Janet, the maid, answered the door?

Nothing about bland Leconfield House in Curzon Street, London gave any indication of its function. Built for Lord Leconfield who had died in 1901, it was now the home of MI5, the United Kingdom's domestic security service. It's responsible for counterintelligence and security within the UK, focussing on protecting national security from threats originating within the UK.

Special Agent Dale Fletcher of the FBI addressed the smoke-filled room of incredulous intelligence officers who listened, casting bemused glances. Thirty men and noticeably no women. Dale didn't approve of the long hair and the colourful mod dress of some of the agents.

A tall, lean officer dressed in a velvet jacket and paisley trousers held up his hand.

'Yes, and you are?' Dale asked. We'd never allow this flower power rubbish with our officers back home.

'Jonathon Vaughan- Winters,' the officer replied. Dale tried not to roll his eyes. He recognised a condescending aristocratic drawl.

'I have a couple of issues with what you're telling us, Special Agent Fletcher.'

'I see. And what would those issues be, Mr Winters?'

'Vaughan-Winters, actually, sir. Yes, you're saying two of your agents that you initially had no idea were in this country, have uncovered a plot in Brighton threatening national security and these said agents are now in mortal danger, and need rescuing, is that the case…sir?'

'That's exactly the case, Mr Vaughan-Winters.'

'And I'm given to understand the head of this…movement…for want of a better word is Captain Charles Beauchamp, ex the Guards?'

'That is so.'

'Hmm, where I have a problem sir, is the fact Captain Beauchamp is a gentleman of impeachable honour from a highly respected family, and frankly sir, I for one can't imagine Beauchamp being involved in such a business.'

'Quite so, Mr Vaughan-Winters. I have been to see Captain Beauchamp. As you say, a distinguished career indeed. Let me see.' Dale referred to a manila folder. 'Service in France in the First World War and the Middle East in the Second. The recipient of both the George Cross and the Distinguished Service Order. As I have said, I have been to see Captain Beauchamp, and although our discussion was brief it was immediately apparent that the gentlemen in question had advanced dementia. Not surprising as he is in his late 80's. I have notified the authorities and I believe he's been looked after. Frankly I was a bit surprised such a worthy gentleman could have been allowed to get into such a state without intervention. But far be it from me to criticise how your country looks after its elderly.' How do you like those apple,s chum?

Dale noticed the angry glances and murmuring from the officers.

'It's obvious to me that an American, wanted by our FBI, has assumed the identity of Captain Beauchamp.' Dale stared hard at the officer.

'And what's his name, Special Agent Fletcher?' an officer who gave his names as Richard Smart, asked.

'His name is Stanford Delaware.'

'Just how big of a threat can this…this megalomaniac be, Special Agent Fletcher?' Sir Roger Coleman, a sparse haired older man, the head of MI5 asked. Wearing a Saville Row tweed suit and smoking a pipe, Sir Roger looked to Dale like a character out of central casting, more suited to playing a cop in an Ealing comedy movie.

'Good question, Sir Roger. Delaware, aka Beauchamp, had a huge organisation in the States, with a commune of over 1000 people. But what was more frightening was the apparent infiltration of the police and judiciary. Fortunately, as far as we know he simply hasn't had the time to set up here in Britain on the same scale, but underestimate him at your peril. We have recently been able to foil a plot by his so called "Family". A plot so audacious it could have been a movie script. As a consequence, before we could execute a warrant for his arrest he fled the country, we believe in his private jet. There is no doubt he would have access to literally millions of dollars.'

As Dale waited for more questions it dawned on him that neither Sir Roger or the other officers were convinced. At that moment one of the double oak doors sprung open and a woman with steel gray hair and a business-like blue suit ran to Sir Roger's side, whispering in his ear as she handed him a folder. Dale could just see "Top Secret "in bold black print.

'Thank you, Doris, that will be all.' With a curt smile she scurried out of the meeting room. Sir Roger waited until the door shut. 'My apologies but just relax while I have a look at what apparently is an unfolding situation. Special Agent Fletcher, would you mind taking a seat? This is something of an emergency. My apologies of course.'

Sir Roger strode out of the room, folder in hand.

Dale glanced around before sitting on a bentwood chair next to a short muscly guy in a pinstripe suit, floral shirt and a loud purple tie. Officers chatted amongst themselves. Dale kept glancing at his watch, feeling like an unwanted relative at a family picnic. Twenty long minutes passed; Dale glanced again at his watch, wondering whether he'd been forgotten. Finally, Sir Roger burst into the room. Dale sensed a change.

'Gentlemen, it seems we have a development. Sorry Special Agent Fletcher, can we hold it right there for just a moment, it looks like your information is correct. Damn and blast. Gentlemen I'm scanning this information as we speak. My God. It appears at first glance the IRA are involved and have supplied this Beauchamp, Delaware blighter, with ordnance.'

A buzz of chatter spread around the room. Dale took a second glance at the assembled agents and quickly realised they weren't necessarily upper-class toffs. As hands were raised, questions and answers rattled like gunshots. These men were being galvanised into action. He'd forgotten Britain had stood up to the Nazis and some of these older men had very probably been in the thick of it.

***

THE ROYAL PAVILLION

Spencer sighed with relief when the heavy door clunked into place. Grabbing a priceless Regency chair, he smashed it against the wall and wrenched off one of the ornate legs, jamming it into the iron wheel of the opening mechanism. 'That should slow the bastards down.'

'I still, have trouble getting my head around the extent of Stanford's organisation? How many guys were living in that tunnel do you think, Spencer?' Savannah asked.

'Don't know, at a guess I'd say fifty. And the size of those barracks. All underground. And the weapon? My God, handguns, long guns…'

'Yeah, and sub machine guns. He really is serious about starting a God damn war,' Savannah scowled.

'They'll be breaking through that door any time now. We only have minutes before they figure how to open the bloody thing.' Sam winced.

'You Ok Sam? Hell, you're still bleeding,' Savannah inspected the nasty gash just above one ear, where he'd been grazed by a bullet.

'Never better,' Sam flashed a tight smile and leant unsteadily against a wall, leaving a red smudge on the teak panelling.

'Where the hell are we Spencer? Inside the Pavilion, somewhere, I guess? 'Savannah stared, open mouthed.

They turned their gaze onto the magnificent floor-to-ceiling gilded mirrors, and the stunning view of the city of Brighton. The room looked like a movie set with its Regency chairs, chaise lounge, harpsichord and a subtle muted carpet.

'This is the north drawing room,' Spencer said confidently.

Spencer was sure that in the future he'd visited Brighton with his wife Michiyo and daughter Trilby. Snatches of their holiday in Britain kept flashing in his mind, then disappearing. Madame Tussauds, the Tower, Harrods. Trilby laughing as a stray dog barked at one of the Queens Guards, resplendent in his scarlet uniform and bearskin hat. It worried him that memory seemed to become elusive, haphazard, so that he didn't know what was a dream and what was reality. Did he come to England in the future or was he simply losing his mind? He shuddered.

'How the hell would you know that?' Savannah asked.

'What? I'm not sure. I must have seen it in a brochure I guess.'

Spencer's mind whirled. Trilby and Michiyo standing here. Trilby tinkling the harpsichord keys, Michiyo saying she mustn't do that. The picture in his mind so vivid it hurt. He had been there! If only he could put the pieces together. He fingered the cornicello hoping it would help. Was it a dream?

The banging on the tunnel door and the muffled yells of angry men grew louder. Spencer realised that they were not out of danger. They jumped at a sudden crack of thunder. A quick glance at the windows showed great networking forks of lightning lighting up the graphite sky as the heavens opened up.

'We really gotta go. Sam, we have to move it.' Spencer heard a thump.

'Sam, Sam.' Savannah screamed.

Sam collapsed on the floor moaning.

'Sam, mate, we have to get going,' Spencer pleaded. But it was obvious Sam was down for the count.